The Secret ORPHANAGE

BOOKS BY BARBARA JOSSELSOHN

LAKE SUMMERS SERIES
The Lilac House
The Bluebell Girls
The Lily Garden
The Cranberry Inn

SISTERS OF WAR SERIES
Secrets of the Italian Island
The Lost Gift to the Italian Island
The Forgotten Italian Restaurant

BARBARA JOSSELSOHN

The Secret ORPHANAGE

bookouture

Published by Bookouture in 2025

An imprint of Storyfire Ltd.
Carmelite House
50 Victoria Embankment
London EC4Y 0DZ

www.bookouture.com

The authorised representative in the EEA is Hachette Ireland
8 Castlecourt Centre
Dublin 15 D15 XTP3
Ireland
(email: info@hbgi.ie)

Copyright © Barbara Josselsohn, 2025

Barbara Josselsohn has asserted her right to be identified as the author of this work.

All rights reserved. No part of this publication may be reproduced, stored in any retrieval system, or transmitted, in any form or by any means, electronic, mechanical, photocopying, recording or otherwise, without the prior written permission of the publishers.

ISBN: 978-1-83618-613-7
eBook ISBN: 978-1-83618-615-1

This book is a work of fiction. Names, characters, businesses, organizations, places and events other than those clearly in the public domain, are either the product of the author's imagination or are used fictitiously. Any resemblance to actual persons, living or dead, events or locales is entirely coincidental.

To David, Rachel, and Alyssa
And all the children to come
And to those who don't stay silent

ONE
NOVEMBER 1942

Celina grasped the handle above the car window as her brother fought to straighten the steering wheel. To her right, a low wooden fence mere inches away seemed a sorry barrier against the deep gorge beyond it and the rushing stream far below. Max loved his black Citroën, but right now his shaky breath and widened eyes, which she could see from the side, did not convey much confidence in his prized machine. Silently she started to count backward from ten, hoping the road would even out before she reached one. But then a fresh bump sent the rear of the car fishtailing, creating a storm of gravel and soil that shot up from the ground and bounced off the metal exterior.

"Jeez," Max said, beads of sweat now forming along his hairline, which she noticed had receded since she'd last seen him. He had aged in the last three years. War could do that, she thought. Another winding curve appeared, and she felt her body lean toward him, their shoulders colliding.

"This is ridiculous," he growled as he worked again to bring the car under control. "We shouldn't even be here. We could have found an attorney in Lyon instead of making an appointment with the one here. We could have been on our way home already."

"Yes, but I wanted to come here," she murmured. "You know that." It didn't help for Max to complain about this again, how they didn't have to make this trip, how they should have been crossing the ocean on their way back home to Maryland by now. As she'd explained, she had to see this one town, this one house. There was a good chance she'd never be back in France again.

"We've been over this a thousand times," she said once the road straightened and the car steadied. "We'll see the house and then find the law office. It's early. Even if we squeeze in a quick lunch before our appointment, we can still be back in Lyon before dark. Please try to understand."

He exhaled. "I do understand. I don't mean to make you feel bad. It's just... Shoot!" he exclaimed as they swung around another sharp bend, this time nearly colliding with a huge cedar tree on the driver's side. Max pounded on the brake, which caused yet another fishtail. Celina reached for the dashboard.

With the wheels aligned, Max brought the car to a full stop. He closed his eyes and breathed in, the sound audible from the back of his throat. Celina looked over, feeling guilty even though he'd said he didn't want her to. But she'd put him in a difficult position. He'd come from Switzerland to fetch her so they could return home together, and she'd refused to leave France unless they came here first. Her husband, Emile, had spoken so fondly of Paillettes au Sommet, this beautiful mountain village where his grandfather had grown up. He'd always intended to bring her here and show her why the town had this name, the way the water below shimmered and glittered when seen from the nearby summit on a sunny day. He'd wanted to show her the house his grandfather had left to him, the home he'd hoped they'd move into when they were ready to leave city life for good. It now seemed the least she could do for him. To see the house before she sold it. It was hers now.

Paillettes au Sommet. The glitter at the summit. Such a beautiful name for a village. She'd always thought she would write a children's book with that title. And Emile would illustrate it. Oh, they'd had so many ideas for books! They'd imagined the pages of each one at night, the words and the pictures, when she'd curl up next to him in the small living room of their Paris apartment, the single light from the lamp low because they could barely afford the rent let alone the electricity. When he'd shared beautiful memories about this remote village, it had taken their minds off what was happening around them in Paris, the daytime patrols of angry German soldiers, the nighttime raids, the danger Emile was putting himself in with those secret meetings. Paillettes was like a dream they could imagine together. It pained her that her first glimpse of this village would be without him.

She watched Max put the car back in gear, his breath still loud. "I appreciate you doing this," she said.

Max paused, then grinned and tugged on a strand of her honey-blonde hair. "Anything for the princess," he teased, using Dad's nickname for her.

Celina nudged his hand away and readjusted her navy-blue felt hat. The baby in a family with three older brothers, she'd always had a special place in their father's heart. She knew her parents would be so glad to finally have her and Max back. With mail disrupted due to the war, she had no idea if they'd gotten any of her letters. They had to be worried about her. They probably didn't know any of what she'd been through.

"So where is this house, anyway?" Max asked. The road was straight and level now. She expected he'd soon reach for a cigarette.

"I'm not exactly sure," she answered. "Emile told me it was up a final hill to the left once you can see the village center."

"Another hill? Why am I not surprised?" Max grumbled.

She ignored his comment and looked at her hands on her lap, clad in her best gloves. She didn't own many fine clothes, the way she had back in Maryland, but she'd worn her pleated skirt and her blue belted coat today, the nicest items she had. She knew Max would expect her to look well-dressed when they met with the lawyer. She was glad her coat was warm; she'd expected the mountains to be cold in November, but she could tell through the thin car windows that the temperature was even lower than she'd anticipated.

Suddenly Max gasped. "Dear God!" he said. She looked forward. Ahead of them was a steep hill that seemed to rise to the clouds.

She pressed her lips together. "I think this is the worst of it," she said, hoping that would calm him. "That's how Emile described it. A final steep hill, then a little dip, and suddenly the town would appear. Like magic," she added, and the memory made her voice crack.

"I wish you'd met him," she said.

Max patted her hands, then grasped the steering wheel firmly and pressed on the gas pedal. Suddenly, the car lurched forward, gathering a dangerous level of speed. Max pulled the steering wheel to the right, the left, and the right again, but the tires didn't respond. Before Celina knew it, they were tumbling sideways over and over as the car plummeted down a hill.

It took her a moment to figure out what had happened, to understand that the car was now upside down with them inside, their heads touching the top of the interior. Through the windshield, she could see a small street, the streetlamps hanging from their posts and the stores all seeming to rest with their roofs pointing toward the ground and their doors floating in midair.

"Are you okay?" Max asked.

"I... I think so." She looked at her gloved hands, then ran her fingers along her chin, her neck, down to her legs. "You?"

"Yeah, I'm okay," he said. "Did we actually flip over? I can't believe it, I— Hey," he added, looking at her. "You're bleeding. Your head."

"I am?" She reached up and touched her forehead. Her hat had fallen off as they'd tumbled, and when she took her fingers away, there was a smear of blood on her glove. "I guess. I don't think it's too bad."

At that moment she heard a commotion beyond the windshield and saw a handful of farmers in overalls running their way. She cranked her window open and two men reached inside to grab her under her arms and pull her out. Once her body had cleared the opening, they helped her stand, holding her by her elbows. She looked around. Her coat was mud-stained and she felt a little dazed, but except for the sting of the cut on her forehead, she didn't feel any pain.

"*Tout va bien?*" one of the men asked.

She nodded. At least, she thought she was okay. As the farmer went to rescue Max, she tested out her legs, taking a few steps toward a nearby thicket of trees.

That's when she saw something pink near the tree trunks. And heard a small whimper. She walked a few steps closer. There, in the underbrush, was a bundle wrapped in a pink blanket. Two dark eyes looking out from beneath long, dark lashes. Two tiny legs kicking beneath the pink covering. A set of little red lips, parted. The beginning of a smile.

Celina knelt, and as her fingertips touched the blanket, she felt the outline of a safety pin. She turned over the blanket's edge and saw a small note handwritten on a scrap of lined paper attached to the fabric:

> *S'il vous plaît, prenez soin de ma petite fille jusqu'à ce que nous puissons être à nouveau ensemble.*

Elle s'appelle Brielle Aimée.

She pressed her hand to her lips as she translated the note in her head:

Please care for my baby girl until we are together again.

Her name is Brielle Aimée.

TWO
OCTOBER 2018

Rachel left work at four o'clock as usual and drove the short distance to The Bremson. Parking her white Civic in a visitor spot, she grabbed the strap of her shoulder bag and climbed out of the car. The bag was heavier than usual, and she smiled to herself in anticipation of how the surprise inside would be received. Walking along the tree-bordered pathway, she reached the three-story brick building and stepped through the glass doors. The shiny marble-tiled atrium was decked out for fall, with festive orange and yellow hardy mums and a few ceramic turkeys on the round center table. Still, she thought, the air seemed heavy. Stagnant. As it always seemed to, no matter how colorful and vibrant the seasonal decorations.

Signing in at the front desk, she gave a wave to the uniformed security guard and headed down the hallway. Passing the resident dining room, game room, and library, she proceeded to the closed door on the left with the small sign that read MEMORY CARE. She rang the buzzer, and a moment later the lock released. A middle-aged woman wearing a floral tunic and white pants opened it. The sound of a blaring TV tuned to a game show was coming from the multipurpose room across the floor.

"Rachel, come in!" The woman tossed her thick gray braid behind her shoulder and motioned her to enter the small foyer.

"Hey, Kate. How's my grandfather?" Rachel took off her jacket and straightened the hem of her white short-sleeved sweater over her black pants.

"He's having a good day," Kate answered. "We've been lucky this fall. The warm weather agrees with him. They just finished a game of bingo, and he's outside enjoying some fresh air before dinner. Did you bring something? Another keepsake?"

Rachel patted her bag. She'd read in an article on dementia recently that it was beneficial to share cherished items to spur conversation and warm memories. So last week she'd brought a picture of her and her grandfather at her sixth grade moving-up ceremony at school. She couldn't believe how much he'd remembered and how wide his smile had been, as he recalled what it felt like to see her on the stage from his seat in the auditorium. Two days ago, she'd brought the set of pens he'd used in his office at the publishing company. He'd held each one in his hand, pantomiming the action of translating a French manuscript into English.

Today's item, she knew, was the one he'd cherish the most.

"Terrific," Kate said. "I think it really helps him. Go ahead, you know the way."

Nodding, Rachel walked through the dining room to the sliding doors that opened on to a narrow, brick-walled terrace. She stepped outside and looked around, the soft breeze calming as it rustled her long, light brown hair. There was a group of elderly men and women sitting at a round table stringing beads, and another group painting landscapes, dipping slender brushes every so often into small paper cups of water and swishing them on the ovals of their watercolor kits. Two women in wheelchairs sat at one end of the terrace, listening to show tunes playing from a tabletop speaker. At the other end was a lone man sitting motionless at a card table.

Her grandfather.

She hated that he was here. It seemed a cruel conclusion to a life that was never happy to begin with. Her grandfather had been sullen and often unpleasant to the people who once passed through his life every day—the mail carrier, the drivers who delivered groceries or medicine or packages, the guy who read the gas meter on the side of the house. Growing up, Rachel had heard him yelling at kids whose dogs peed on their lawn: "Get your dog onto the street, you hear? It kills the grass!" And he'd never cared much for the lawncare guy either: "It's too early in the morning to make all that racket! Come back later!"

But to Rachel, her grandfather had always been her tender, devoted protector. She'd moved into his house when she was five, right after her mother died. Her father had left home when she was a baby, and when the court couldn't locate him, her grandfather was appointed her legal guardian. She hadn't known before then that she even had a grandfather. She met him for the first time when he showed up at the neighbor's apartment to get her, an imposing, stiff-backed man with silvery hair. But she soon grew to love him, and she knew he loved her, too. She knew it from the way he'd walk her to school every morning when she was little, staying with the adults on the sidewalk as she and the other kids scampered down the path to the schoolhouse door. He never waved or gathered her in a bear hug or called out, "Have a great day!" the way the moms, dads, and babysitters surrounding him did. But through her classroom window, she saw that he was always the last to leave. He'd wait until she had been safely inside for several minutes before turning back toward home.

And he was always there on the blacktop six hours later when she emerged from the school building, an umbrella or a heavier coat or even a pair of boots in his hands for her to quickly change into if the weather had turned during the day.

Though they had a housekeeper who did most of the cooking and cleaning, and helped her tame her thick, unruly curls, it was her grandfather who made the cream cheese and jelly sandwiches for her lunchbox, and arranged baby carrots and raisins and apple slices into smiley faces for her school snack, the apples somehow never turning brown. She remembered how he'd bring a bowl of chicken noodle soup and crackers to her bed when she was sick, the soup always the perfect temperature, hot but not so much that it would burn her tongue if she took a big mouthful.

And she remembered how she'd crawl into his lap on the rocker in the tiny, enclosed sunroom after dinner, while Mrs. May finished the dishes in the kitchen and then left for the night. The sound of water running in the sink and cabinets closing was a comforting backdrop to the quiet interlude. Her grandfather loved the sunroom because of the rock garden beyond the wide bay window. He said it reminded him of France, where he'd grown up. When it was bedtime, he'd tuck her under the covers and sit next to her on her mattress. She'd loved how his pale cheeks shone from the light of the pink-shaded lamp on her night table. That's when he'd read aloud their favorite book, *The Little Lost Fish*, usually once but on some nights, for a treat, a second time. She never tired of the words or the pictures, or of his quiet voice sweeping over the gentle, satisfying rhymes.

Making her way across the nursing home terrace, she reached his chair by the card table. "Hi, Papy," she said as she bent down to kiss his cheek. He was so thin and withered, and it never failed to jar her. Even as an older man, even as recently as eight or ten years ago when he was well into his eighties, he'd been dashing, with his silver hair parted on the side, the strands glittery and delicate like tinsel. With his straight nose and square jaw and slight cleft in his chin. He'd been a big presence when she was growing up, tall with a good physique—strong shoulders, a raised chin, an impossibly straight posture. There were times when she thought he must have spent time in the military—surely no one stood that erect without being drilled. But she never learned if he had. She knew very little about him, other than that he came from France to New York as a young man after World War Two and worked as a translator for a small publisher until he retired. And that he was the only family she had.

Rachel looked into his eyes now, searching for a glint of recognition. Sometimes he didn't seem to know her at all. On those days, she'd sit next to him and stay quiet, hoping that his absent stare meant he was visiting someplace pleasant deep within his memory. But today, his eyebrows rose and his thin lips widened into a smile within a few short moments of receiving her kiss.

"Rachelle. My Rachelle," he said. Even though he'd lost most of his accent, he still pronounced her name the French way. "You've come back to pay me a visit. Hey, hey," he called, pointing his finger at one of the attendants walking by, a young man with a thick black beard named Marcelo. "You see? My granddaughter came to visit me. A lucky grandfather I am."

"You are a lucky man, indeed," the man said warmly with a nod. Rachel smiled. The staff all knew her. She'd been told she visited way more than any of the other residents' families.

"Ah, Rachelle," her grandfather said when the attendant had walked on. "Tell me how you are. How is your job? How is the library?" These days her grandfather couldn't say what he'd had for breakfast or sometimes even where he was, but he never forgot her choice of career. He'd been so proud when she'd earned her master's degree in library and information science and began working as a librarian at a private research library in Locust Cove. He loved literature, and he loved research. He asked her the same questions every time she came, never remembering the details she'd covered the last time. Still, she was always relieved when he asked. It meant she hadn't completely lost him to dementia. Not yet.

"It's good," she said. "I'm working hard. I just developed a series of online programs on research methods and tools. My boss, Brian, is very happy with how it's going. And we have a new curator of rare books. He's very smart. You'd like him a lot."

"And the rest of your life?" her grandfather asked. "Are you in love yet, my darling?"

She smiled at the question, another one that she answered at every visit. But she knew he asked it because he cared about her. She found it touching, how much he wanted her to find love, considering that he'd had so little in his own life and that the only one he'd ever seemed to truly love was her. She hated that his memory was failing, but she also thought that if he had to grow old and forgetful, at least there was this upside. At least he no longer remembered his loneliness and failed relationships, including those with his wife and his only child, Rachel's mother. At least he looked happy now when he asked about romance.

"That's slow going," she said with a little chuckle and felt her cheeks redden.

"So... there's something to tell?" her grandfather said, his eyebrows raised. "And what is the young man's name?"

"No, no, it's nothing," she said, looking down to hide her smile. It didn't make sense to elaborate. Yes, she'd finally met a guy she liked, a guy with the delightful name of Griffin, but at this point what they had was the furthest thing from a relationship. They hadn't even met in person yet. They'd only exchanged phone calls and a few videochats since their paths crossed when she was recruiting experts for her online series. It was just a crush, she'd repeatedly told herself. And that was fine for now. She loved the way she felt, that tickle in her stomach or shiver along her shoulder blades, when she pictured him or saw his number show up on her phone. It was delicious to think he could be the one, and to imagine the romantic ways their chance meeting could progress. Too often in her dating life, reality had been a let-down. Infatuation was fun compared to discovering that someone was not nearly as perfect as she'd first believed.

"Let's not bother about that, Papy," she said. "I have something better to talk about. Something to show you." She reached into her shoulder bag and pulled out a large envelope, then placed it on the card table in front of them. Inside was their original copy of *The Little Lost Fish,* the one he'd read to her every night so long ago. She'd found it yesterday when she'd gone through the boxes in the hall closet of her apartment, looking for the winter clothes she'd packed away last spring.

She slid out the book, which still struck her as beautiful, despite how old and worn it was. The spine was cracked and the cover illustration of a purple fish with silver scales was faded, the once-vibrant hues now pale or even brown in spots. Her grandfather had told her he'd heard about the book when he was in France and found a copy in a bookstore after he'd settled in New York. It had been the oldest book on her bookshelf when she was little, and she remembered how carefully she'd turned its yellowing pages. Now, they were even more discolored, and a few were sticky, possibly from dampness or traces of strawberry jelly or melted chocolate that had been on her fingers as she'd stroked the pictures long ago and her grandfather read the words.

"Ahh," her grandfather said, a sigh of affection and familiarity. Rachel loved how he instantly recognized the storybook. "*The Little Lost Fish*. And what a fine edition. So old. So handsome."

"It's the copy we had at the house, remember? We read it every night when I was little."

"Yes, I remember. I wish my eyes were good. Read a page to me, won't you?"

"Read a page? How about the first page—"

"No, the page I love. You know the page. Please, my darling."

"Um... okay. Of course, Papy," she said and opened to the page he was referring to, with the picture of the little fish swimming in a choppy gray sea, the sky above overcast. She wished he hadn't asked for that one. She didn't know why this had always been his favorite, with its ominous illustration and words that conveyed a subtle suggestion of surrender, even death. But she couldn't refuse him. She had brought the book specifically hoping he'd remember it. She found the page, near the middle, and began to read:

The baby fish searches with open eyes
I'm going home, home now, his song
To the place where my heart lies
To the home where I belong...

She paused and looked up, and saw that her grandfather's eyes had become glassy. Oh, no, she thought. Tears were often the prelude to a retreat into his private world, and she wanted him to stay with her for at least a little longer.

"No, Papy, no," she said, handing him a tissue from her bag. "Please don't cry. This is a happy book, the fish is saved, remember? Look at all the things we used to love about it. Like the picture at the beginning, the big one with the baby fish and his mom, remember?"

She flipped to the front, but the first few pages were stuck together along their top edges. Placing the book on the table, she slid two fingers underneath the top page to pry it loose, speaking all the while to distract her grandfather from the words that had made him sad.

"See? Here's the very beginning, the title page—C. Tailleur, the name of the author."

Her grandfather nodded. "C... Yes, C... Cee... Cece..."

"C. Tailleur, yes. And let me just loosen these next two pages so you'll see that picture—"

"Cece!" he repeated. "Her name is Cece."

"Right. That's her initial. We never knew what it stood for. I think she kept her actual name private—"

"No, it was her name! They called her that. I heard them!"

Rachel caught her breath. She knew she wasn't supposed to contradict him. That's what made him agitated, Kate and the other attendants would say. It was best to humor him when he said something odd. But still, this seemed too strange a statement to ignore. He didn't know this author. He'd found the book in a bookstore. Was he losing his grip even on this book that they'd loved? *No!* she thought. He couldn't forget what they'd shared every night. If he forgot those bedtime readings, then what would she have left of him?

"Papy, stop," she said firmly. "Try to stay with me. We only knew the book. We didn't know her—"

"I did know her! Of course I did! Because of the crash. But she didn't stay long. It was Switzerland—"

"Papy, come on. You were never in Switzerland," she said, continuing to loosen the pages. "Let me just find that illustration we both loved, you'll remember... yes, here we go..."

She finally worked the pages free and began to gently turn them, hunting for the special illustration. But then she noticed something that made her stop short. In front of her was a page she didn't recognize, a page she didn't think her grandfather had ever shown her. There were two lines of type, a short dedication: *For Brielle Aimée.*

Brielle Aimée. Her mother's name.

She stared at the words until they started to blur. It wasn't a typical name. She'd always been charmed at how unusual it sounded to her ears. Could there have simply been another Brielle Aimée in the world back then? Or had this book been dedicated… to her mother?

"They called her that!" her grandfather was saying. "The children!"

"Wait, what?" Rachel asked.

"They called her that. Please, you must listen! They called her Cece. Even the children!"

"The children? What children? Wait, Papy—did you really know this author?"

"You're not listening!" he shouted. "She had no home! She didn't belong. She didn't come back. She didn't come back!"

"Who?" she asked. He'd never said anything like this before. "Who are you talking about? Is this about my mother? Papy, was this book dedicated to her?"

"I told you!" he shouted. "I tried! I tried!" He pressed his hands on the arms of his chair and started twisting his shoulders, attempting to stand. Suddenly, Kate and Marcelo were at their table. Kate closed the book and pushed it aside, then knelt next to her grandfather.

"It's okay, Henry," she murmured. "You're safe. It's okay. Take a breath."

Rachel took the book and slipped it back into the envelope. Her grandfather grew quiet, although he looked stunned, his eyes fixed straight ahead.

"I think he's hungry and probably tired, too," Kate told her, stroking his shoulder. "Maybe it's a good time for you to head home. Don't worry, we'll give him some dinner and get him ready for the evening. I'm sure he'll be fine."

"But, I—" Rachel started, then nodded and put the envelope in her bag. She hated that she'd upset him. Maybe she shouldn't have read that page about death. Maybe in that case he'd be okay now. She longed to ask him again about the dedication.

But she worried that at this point, even the mention of that name, Brielle Aimée, could set him off again.

She nodded to Kate and Marcelo, and headed through the living room. An attendant unlocked the unit's door, and she made her way out of the building and to the parking lot. She wished she knew what had triggered her grandfather's words, what was behind his mention of Switzerland and a crash and children and someone who didn't come back. What if her grandfather had sought out this book to read every night because he really did know the author? What if there had been something he'd tried to stop—but couldn't? What if there was a connection with her mother?

And what if that had set the stage for all that happened after? For his loneliness and isolation? For the fact that she'd never even known she had a grandfather until her mother died and there was no one else to care for her?

She had to find out the story behind the dedication.

THREE
NOVEMBER 1942

The baby was so perfect, she could easily have been mistaken for a doll. Her creamy cheeks were chubby and round, and her eyebrows formed perfect crescents below her feathery dark hair. Her eyelashes were long, and when she blinked, they rested delicately atop the thin skin just above her cheekbones. She was still except for her gentle kicking and the small breaths that made her chest move beneath the pink blanket. When her dark eyes met Celina's, they opened wide and her eyebrows rose, as though she was eager to be picked up.

"Hello, sweetheart," Celina whispered. "How did you get here? Where's your mama?"

The baby's mouth spread into a grin, and she wriggled her body. Then she opened and closed her mouth a few times, as though she was imagining her mama's breast and could practically taste the milk that would fill her empty belly. Celina felt a pang in her chest, as if milk in her own breasts was being let down, as if her body was still preparing to nourish another. Even though that never was to happen.

She touched her chest reflexively as she smiled at the baby.

How old was she? Two months? Three? Celina had never learned all there was to know about babies, how they grew, what they ate. She'd never gotten that far. What was clear was that this little girl had been well cared for and well-fed. Surely no mother would willingly give up such an angel.

The baby was calm for now, but watching her lips move, Celina worried that she was hungry and would soon start to fuss. She didn't know what she should do. Had this child been left here for someone specific to find her? Would that person be coming soon? Or had she simply been abandoned? Celina knew one thing—that she couldn't leave her out in the cold. She had to bring her somewhere warm and then worry about where she belonged.

"Hey, baby girl," Celina whispered. "Don't be afraid, okay?" On her knees, she slid her hands and forearms beneath the small bundle and slowly lifted her. The baby was more solid than Celina would have expected. Not heavy but dense. Such a delightful combination of fragile and sturdy. Close up, her skin looked fresh and delicate, almost translucent. Celina could see some faint blue veins above her ear.

In her arms, the baby yawned and turned onto its side, rooting into Celina's coat. For a moment, Celina imagined how Emile would have smiled at the sight of her cradling a baby. They had both been sure theirs was a girl.

She heard the sound of someone approaching. "Cel?" Max said. "You okay?"

She jolted at the sound of his voice, and a branch smacked against her temple. Great, she thought. Another blow to her poor head. Her movement jostled the baby, who squinched up her face as though about to let out a fearful wail. Celina pulled her in closer. And that's when she noticed there was additional writing on the note pinned to the blanket. One small word at the very bottom. *Cachée*. She gasped. It was the word, a kind of code, Emile had taught her when they lived under Nazi occupation in Paris. It referred to someone who was in danger. Or had to be concealed. Or needed a new identity.

Someone Jewish.

"Cel?" Max called again. "You okay?"

"What?" she said, barely registering Max's words. "I mean, yes. I'm okay..."

"Look, they got the car upright, but it doesn't seem to be starting," Max said, his voice drawing closer. "Thank God a policeman just showed up, and thank God he speaks English. I can't understand a thing those farmers are saying. But it seems there's a mechanic nearby, and I think someone went to get him. I swear, I should have put my foot down, we never should have come or— What are you doing, anyway?"

Celina slowly rose, pressing one hand on the soft ground for leverage, still holding the baby to her chest. On her feet, she turned to face her brother.

"What the hell..." he murmured.

She raised her shoulders. "She was just lying here."

"Whose is it?"

"I have no idea."

"But where's the mother?"

"I don't know."

"You found her in the bushes? Who leaves a baby under a bush? This whole trip has been a nightmare. Let's get the car moving and get out of here."

"But..." Celina lifted the baby, as though Max needed reminding of what she was holding.

"We'll hand her to someone in charge. I mean, there's a cop right there by the car. Maybe she was kidnapped. Someone's got to know who she is."

"Max," Celina said. "Please. She wasn't kidnapped. You know what this is..."

But he was already returning to the car. Celina looked down, and the little girl turned her face upward. When their eyes met, the baby cooed. It felt so good to have a baby in her arms.

She followed Max. To her left, she could see what was no doubt the policeman's vehicle parked alongside the field. The policeman, whom she now saw had freckles and fiery red hair, approached them. "These gentlemen are telling me that the mechanic is out on a job, monsieur," he said to Max, speaking in English and gesturing toward the two farmers who still remained near the crash site. "I don't think you have much choice but to wait, unless you think you can get it started yourself."

Celina listened as Max asked how long the mechanic might be, since they wanted to head back to Lyon soon, and the policeman answered it would be about an hour. That was when she felt the farmers' eyes on her. They seemed agitated in a way they hadn't been before. And the only thing that had changed was the presence of the baby. She saw one of the farmers make a rocking motion with his arms. Then his eyes darted toward the policeman and back again. He looked hard at Celina and shook his head.

"We're expected at the law office a little past noon," Max was saying to the policeman. "Can we walk there? Is it okay to leave the car unattended?"

"Yes, the center of town is just past the... Oh, madame!" the officer exclaimed, looking at Celina. "Your baby! I didn't realize you had a baby in the car. Is she hurt?"

Celina glanced at the farmers. They both fixed their eyes on her again and then looked away. They clearly didn't want her to tell the truth about the child. She suspected she was in the middle of something very big. And this baby's life depended on her playing along. Maybe the farmers' lives as well.

"No, no," Max told the officer. "That's not our baby."

"Not yours? Then whose—"

"My sister..." Max started but Celina shifted the baby to one arm and grabbed his forearm with the other one.

"Max, you're confusing him," she said, then turned to the officer. "I'm sorry, what he meant to say was that this isn't *his* baby. She's mine. You see, this is my brother. My husband—he wasn't able to make the trip with us. And the... my baby... she's fine. Look, she's fallen back to sleep already."

The officer nodded. "*Très bien*. If you'd like, I can give you a ride into town." He pointed toward his vehicle.

"No, no, thank you," Celina said before Max could put in a word. She didn't want to spend any more time with this man than was necessary. "It's not too cold, fortunately. The fresh air will be good for... for my little girl."

"Okay, then. I'll leave you here."

"Yes, thank you," Celina said with a big smile. "Thank you very much for your help."

They all watched the man cross the field. When he had started to drive off, Max turned to Celina.

"Why did you say all that?" he demanded. "What the hell is going on?"

She gestured toward the farmers. "They wanted me to."

"They *wanted* you to?"

"They were signaling to me, so I knew I had to..." She sighed. "Max, I think this baby is Jewish. And I think she'd be in danger if we gave her to the police. If this policeman realizes why this baby is here..." She paused and shook her head.

"So what do you propose we do?" Max asked. "I mean, you don't want to keep her, do you?" He looked at her, then rolled his eyes. "Oh my God, you think you can keep her, don't you?"

"No. No, I know I can't," Celina said. Even though that was exactly what she wanted to do. She'd wanted a baby for so long. She'd come so close to having one. "I only want to save

her," she added. "I want to make sure she'll be safe before we
go."

"Do you even realize what you did?" Max asked. "You lied. To the police! You lied about who *this* is." He pointed toward the blanket.

"She's not a *this,* she's an innocent child—"

"And now you're the furthest thing in the world from innocent. You want to get yourself arrested? You don't even know how she got here. Maybe she was just…"

"Just what? Just accidentally wrapped up and tucked away under the bushes? She was hidden here by her mother. Or someone her mother gave her to."

"You don't know that. You don't know she's Jewish."

"No, I do. Look." She flipped the edge of the blanket over so he could see the note. "I know what this means. *Cachée.* Emile uses that word all the time. It means she needs to be hidden."

Max took a few steps away from her and looked across the park toward the gorge, running his fingers along his jawline. Then he walked back.

"Gel, these are dangerous times," he said. "You don't go running to the police. Certainly not about *this.* Look, I know you miss Emile, I know you think you loved him—"

"I *did* love him—"

"But this isn't some spy game. We're booked to go back to the States in two days. Do you know how hard it's become to get out of this country with the war going on? It's only going to get worse if the Germans take over this part of France as well. And the government here in the free zone, they're basically a puppet of the Nazis anyway. You get yourself involved in this mess, and you may never be able to go home. It's a terrible world, but that's the way it is. Let's wait for the mechanic, get the car to start, and then find the policeman and hand the baby over."

"But I already told him she's mine—"

"We can get around that. I'll say you were dazed from the

crash, that you didn't know what you were saying, that I need to get you to a hospital—"

"No—"

"And then we'll take off before they figure out what's really going on and track you down for lying in the first place. Maybe we don't even wait for the car, if it's going to be a big repair. Maybe we just leave the car with these guys"—he pointed to the farmers—"and take a train instead. Anything that will get us out of here. You don't even need to go to the lawyer, okay? We'll deal with the whole matter when we get back to the States. Dad has contacts everywhere. He'll work it out for you."

Celina let him finish, then shook her head. "I'm not giving this baby to the police."

"But—"

"Madame!" one of the farmers called out. She looked over, realizing from the desperate tone of his voice that he'd been trying to get her attention for a while.

"Yes? *Oui?*" she said.

He began to speak in French, pointing as he did to a large house that she could make out around a small curve and up at the crest of a nearby hill.

"What? What did he say?" Max asked. "I heard ofelinakray. What's ofelinakray?"

"*Un orphelinat secret,*" Celina told him. "It means a secret orphanage. That building over there. It seems they're expecting her. I don't understand it exactly, but these guys looked terrified when I was holding the baby there next to the policeman, and they were so relieved when they realized I wasn't handing her over. Let me just take her there, and then we can go and forget this whole thing ever happened, okay?"

"Why can't they take her?" He pointed to the farmers.

"I don't know… but how would it look if I gave them my baby right here and then left town? It's a scary time, you're right. People could be watching. The policeman could be watching." She had learned that from Emile, too. To never believe you were uninteresting. To never believe that someone didn't want to know what you were up to.

Max pressed his lips together and inhaled loudly, his hands on his waist. She knew he felt cornered. He wanted nothing to do with the war. And yet, she also knew he was a good man. As frightened as he was, he wouldn't want to be responsible for turning a baby over to the Nazis.

"Okay, but I'm coming with you, too," Max said. "I'm not letting you go— Oh damn!" he exclaimed as a bicyclist clad in overalls pulled to a stop along the road. "That's got to be the mechanic. Great, on a bicycle." He rolled his eyes.

"I'm sure he knows what he's doing," she said. "Why don't you stay here and talk to him? I'll take the baby up there, and I'll see if I can get a bandage for my head. If it's an orphanage, they surely have a first-aid kit. And we'll be on our way home before you know it."

Max groaned. "I hope the guy speaks English."

"He probably doesn't," Celina said. "Do your best. How hard is it to communicate that the car won't start and you'd like him to fix it?" Max scowled at her, and she shrugged. He'd been living in Europe on and off for years but had yet to perfect his grasp of any European language. He'd told her he hadn't needed to, that English was the universal language of the export business.

He held his breath, his cheeks puffed, and then blew it out. She knew he didn't enjoy taking directions from his little sister. He'd thought he had the whole day planned out, and he didn't like changes or surprises. But he clearly understood he had no other choice.

"Come back soon," he muttered and then he went toward the mechanic.

She waved at the farmers, hugged the sleeping baby closer to her, and started for the large building on the hill. She knew she was doing the right thing. That Emile would be proud of her.

And yet she also had the uncomfortable feeling that things wouldn't go as smoothly as she'd described to Max. She had lied to a policeman and was evidently smuggling a Jewish baby to a safe house.

She was in it now.

FOUR
OCTOBER 2018

That night, back in her apartment, Rachel changed into a pair of sweatpants and a tee shirt, warmed up some leftover chicken and vegetables with rice in her small galley kitchen, and sat down at the table in the living room to eat. In front of her was her grandfather's worn copy of *The Little Lost Fish* open to the dedication page. She rested her chin in her palm and studied the words. *For Brielle Aimée.* The name made her think again about her mother. Oh, how she'd loved her! Her beautiful mother, with that wavy, auburn hair and dangly gold earrings and pretty pale eyes, more gray than blue. And her singing voice, so pretty even when they were just sitting cross-legged on the rug and singing nursery rhymes—"The Itsy Bitsy Spider" and "Hickory Dickory Dock," and "If You're Happy and You Know It." Rachel remembered how she'd sing about half of each song but then stop so she could curl up in her mother's lap and listen to her finish the rest. And then there was their morning ritual, how her mother would wake her up with a kiss on the cheek and say, "I am the luckiest mommy in the world because I get a whole new day with you!"

And Rachel always responded, "No, I'm the luckiest one in the world! Because I have *you*!"

"I'm the luckiest."

"No, *I* am!"

"I love you the most!"

"No, I love *you* the most!"

They'd go back and forth like that until she felt filled to the brim and scurried out of bed to brush her teeth.

And then, out of nowhere, her mother was dead. It all happened so fast, and she was so young, it was mostly a blur. She didn't even remember who'd told her about the car crash, although she assumed it was the old lady next door with whom she stayed on the first few nights. The woman made it clear that Rachel was only there temporarily, so Rachel kept expecting her mother to somehow return. Then one day an elderly man showed up and said he was her grandfather and she'd be living with him from now on. Rachel didn't remember crying for her mother, although she was sure she must have. Mostly she remembered desperately wanting to be no trouble to her grandfather, because she never wanted to be left behind again.

And this was what made the fish book so important to her, at least when she was little. If the little fish could survive for so long in the ocean by himself, then surely she could manage on her own too, if she ever had to.

It hadn't occurred to her when she was little to ask her grandfather why she'd never met him before. She'd just been so glad he was there. But often since then, she'd thought how strange it was that her mother had never mentioned him. Why had he been a stranger that day he'd shown up to fetch her? And why had he never wanted to talk about the daughter he had lost, Rachel's mother? He also never mentioned Rachel's father—nor did he speak about his wife, Rachel's grandmother. Rachel had learned from her mother that her grandmother had in long ago, but her grandfather had no pictures of her and never shared any memories.

What had happened to isolate him so? Rachel had longed to find out, but she'd never dared to ask. Such questions were sure to hurt his feelings. And the last thing she ever wanted to do was hurt the grandfather who had shown up in the nick of time to rescue her and keep her safe.

Taking a forkful of rice, Rachel gently turned the pages, studying the pictures of the ocean and the waves and the glittery baby fish being tossed about, alarm in his eyes. Even now, she could remember breathing fast and clutching her grandfather's arm when they got to the parts where the fish was in danger of being captured or swept away. She'd never fought those emotions; the fear she'd felt only made the joy of the ending all the sweeter, when the baby fish finally found his mom and his home.

It filled her with nostalgia now, how familiar these pages looked to her. She was surprised that she still remembered all the intricacies of the drawings and the verses. She hadn't spent any time with the book since childhood, except for a short period during graduate school. She had inherited her grandfather's love of reading, and after finishing college and working at a clothing store for a couple of years to save money, she had decided to pursue a Ph.D. in literature and begin a career in academia. She'd proposed writing her doctoral thesis about the author of *The Little Lost Fish*, C. Tailleur, who was believed to have worked in the Resistance during World War Two. But she'd soon discovered that most of the information about C. Tailleur centered around her determination to avoid attention. It wasn't even clear if she'd been killed during the war or had survived. The research led Rachel down so many dead ends that she eventually lost the motivation to continue.

But more than that, she'd started feeling guilty. Her grandfather had made it so clear that he never wanted to talk about being in France during the war. So she'd felt it was wrong to delve into a field of research her grandfather couldn't stomach. She pulled out of the Ph.D. program and switched over to attain a master's degree and become a librarian. The last thing she'd done before withdrawing from the English department was to type up her notes about C. Tailleur and save them in a file housed on the department's network. Not that she imagined she'd return to them, but she wasn't the type to leave strings untied. It had never crossed her mind that one day when he was in a nursing home, her grandfather would suddenly start talking about C. Tailleur and claiming that he knew her. But even if she wanted to take a look at those notes, she had no idea if they'd been purged from the system...

She suddenly breathed in and sat up straighter. No, that was wrong—she hadn't saved that file to the school's network. In the end, she'd thought it made more sense to save it to her own computer. The file, she remembered, contained what was generally known about C. Tailleur—and if she still had it, there might be tidbits related to her mother's name, the book's dedication, and what her grandfather had been trying to tell her this afternoon. Of course, she no longer had that computer—she'd bought a new one three years ago. Had she been smart enough to transfer all the files over—even the ones she didn't think she'd ever have reason to open? If she had that file with her notes, she'd be in business.

She fetched her laptop from her nightstand and, sitting on her bed, turned it on and searched through the alphabetical listing of her old documents. And with a mixture of surprise and excitement, she found it: "C. Tailleur Research," the document she'd saved before abandoning her Ph.D. She opened it up and saw that it contained a list of bullet points that she'd written, drawing from information in the scarce group of articles and book chapters she'd found. According to the list, C. Tailleur was an American who lived in France during the Nazi occupation, in a small mountain village in France known as Paillettes au Sommet, which meant Glitter at the Summit. C. Tailleur, the research had shown, had stayed for a time in a building that purported to be a school but was secretly accepting and housing orphaned Jewish children. She was believed to be one of the people in charge of the operation.

And while she was living in the secret orphanage, the research further showed, she wrote *The Little Lost Fish*, a children's book that appeared to use the character of a fish as a metaphor for the Jewish children she was protecting. Some scholars had hypothesized that she'd included clues for Resistance fighters hidden within the book's verses, although this was never confirmed. The book was published in 1965 in the United States concurrently with French, Italian, and Dutch versions. But despite how successful the book was, with multiple printings in the U.S., the author remained a mystery, with no one knowing who she was or if she was even alive when the book was published.

Then Rachel read the last two bullet points in her document:

- *Many believe that C. Tailleur was killed while helping lead Jewish children to safety in Switzerland, but this has never been proven.*
- *C. Tailleur is a pen name. Her real name is unknown, although reports are that she went by the nickname Cece.*

Rachel shook her head in wonder. She hadn't remembered the information in these two bullet points at all, but now she saw how important they were. This afternoon her grandfather had called the author Cece and said something about how she'd been in Switzerland. If her grandfather knew this, then surely he had known her for real.

Could it be that her grandfather and Cece had been friends? Or even more than friends? Was it possible that the book was dedicated not just to someone with the same name as Rachel's mother—but *to* Rachel's mother? Could her mother have been related to Cece? Could her mother have been Cece's daughter, if Cece hadn't died during the war but had gone on to live for many more years?

And most important, was it possible that Cece was still alive today? And if so, was there a way to find her and ask her these questions?

Her phone rang, and Rachel went to the table in the living room where she'd left it. She looked at the number. It was Griffin, calling to videochat. She smiled and quickly smoothed her hair with her hands. Though she was preoccupied with all she'd just discovered, she was still excited that he was calling. She hadn't heard from him in more than a week.

"Hi," she said as she answered. He seemed to be in a restaurant, as there were tables and people behind him, and the sound of dishes and glasses clinking. He looked so handsome, with his short, light brown locks, tossed to the right in a tousled but decidedly tidy way, and the hint of a beard around his jaw. His blue eyes were wide-set, his bottom lip was deliciously plump, and the tip of his chin formed a sweet, gentle "v."

"Hey, Sherlock," he said, his tone warm and cheerful. "How's it going?"

She laughed. He called her that because of the way they'd met. She had been seeking novelists and journalists to be part of the library series she was developing, and her childhood friend Nancy, who worked at a small television station in D.C., had suggested Griffin. He'd been a reporter for a time with her station, and she'd said he was on track to be a network correspondent. Rachel ended up inviting him to be one of the speakers, and the night after his appearance before an online audience of library patrons, he'd called to thank her. That led to a conversation about her job in the library, which led to a conversation about his career aspirations, which led to a conversation about life and love and fate and all the topics that people talk about when they're getting to know one another. They'd stayed on the phone for nearly two hours.

"Oh, not too bad," she said.

"Not too bad? That's the best you can say?"

"Well, it's just…" she started, then paused. She was tempted to tell him what had happened with her grandfather, but decided to hold back. She loved that he could tell something was up with her, but it felt too soon to lay all her dirty laundry out on the table. Now was the romantic time, the time when they each were putting their best foot forward. Trying to come across as fun, smart, and supremely low-maintenance.

"It's nothing," she said. "Never mind. How's your work going? Where are you now?"

She watched him on her phone as he took a gulp of beer and put the wide-mouthed glass back on the table. She loved everything about him. Like the way he was dressed, in a white tee underneath a plaid button-down shirt. His clothing was always casual but also neat and tailored. And she loved his demeanor—how he came across as smart and sharp. He seemed naturally comfortable in his own skin, never needing to try that hard to achieve a certain flair. She loved the energy he gave off, engaged and attentive but not too intense. She didn't think he had ever had to rush to do anything—catch a train, make a meeting, meet a deadline. He seemed the type of person who existed in a world where things always worked out. The kind who didn't have that simmering, nebulous dread she always seemed to feel deep inside. He had found the key to living well. She wanted him to make her a copy.

"Just arrived in Geneva," he said.

"Still working on the fighter pilot piece?" It was the documentary assignment he'd discussed during his talk, about his search for a French fighter pilot whose plane went down somewhere in the Italian Alps during World War One.

"Yeah—it turns out there are geologic formations here that might have influenced the path my errant pilot took," he said. "The producer wants me to extend the trip now that we know what he might have been thinking as he flew over this region. We're pretty sure he headed toward Germany next."

"That's so cool," she said, feeling a touch of disappointment. He'd called into the online program from Paris, and she was sorry he was still so far away. She'd been hoping he'd return to the States soon so they could meet in person. If he were here, she might actually have felt comfortable enough to open up about her grandfather.

"You sound excited," she added.

"I am. And exhausted. I mean, I thought I was in pretty good shape, but my body isn't used to the kind of climbing we did last week. I arrived here around noon and I checked into the hotel and basically passed out. Woke up starving, so luckily Geneva's full of great places open late into the night."

"What is it there, midnight?"

"Almost one." He tilted his head and put on a sad expression, his lips in an exaggerated frown. "So now you look sad again," he said. "Come on, Rache. What's going on?"

"It's nothing—"

"I think it is."

"No, it's just..." She hesitated. She still thought it was too early to reveal all the drama in her life. She didn't want to bring him down when he was so excited about his story. But he seemed to care about her.

"I haven't told you about my grandfather, have I?" she said.

"Only that he took care of you after your mother died."

"Well, he's a complicated person." She went on to tell him about her visit and the strange mention of her mother's name in the book, of how upset her grandfather had become and how

...said things about the author that were there in her notes. It was terrible to see him like that," she said. "Wanting to tell me something but unable to do it. He's so old and sick. I don't even know how much time he has left."

"Oh, Rachel," Griffin said. "I'm sorry. My grandmother had dementia. I know how hard it can be."

"It feels like there's something that's been locked inside of him," she said. "He never wanted to talk about it before, but only he was finally trying to tell me. Like that nickname, Cece—how could he have known that unless he knew her? I think the author knew my grandfather, and maybe she knew my mother too."

"Can you find her? Is she still alive?"

"I don't know. There were all these reports that she died trying to save Jewish children from the Nazis. But it's never been confirmed. She may be alive. I don't even know how to begin to find out."

He shook his head, looking apologetic. "I should be able to help. I am an investigative journalist, after all. But this isn't my kind of research. I don't do the academic stuff. I'm the kind of reporter who goes to the place where I think the information is, and I dig in. That's the way I've always been."

She nodded. She remembered him saying that during the program. How he liked to have "boots on the ground," as he put it—how much more likely it was that he'd discover things if he brought himself to the source...

"Hey," he said. "What's up? You floated away for a second there. What are you thinking?"

"Nothing, nothing," she said. "It's... I mean, what you just said. Maybe... you know, maybe I should do that too. Maybe I should go to France—to that little town where this author lived when she was working with the Resistance. Maybe that's the key to figuring all this out." She couldn't believe what was coming out of her mouth. She'd never been to Europe. She'd lived a quiet life here in South Cove, the same town where her grandfather had raised her, the same town that housed the library where she worked. She'd never even been out of New York, aside from a few high school trips to Philadelphia and Washington, D.C., with her social studies classes.

"But I don't know," she said. "It's not possible. I can't just up and leave. I have my job."

"You can't take a few days off?"

"Of course I can. I do have vacation days. But... well, I can't leave my grandfather for that long," she added softly. "He expects me. I'm there two or three evenings a week. I think it would be hard for him if I didn't come. Although to be honest, maybe he wouldn't even realize. He doesn't have a great sense of time anymore." It was true, she thought. Whenever she showed up, she could tell he had no idea of whether she'd last been there three months or three days or three minutes ago. And perhaps if she went to France, she could find answers that would soothe him. He had been so upset. She needed to make it better.

"You have to do what feels right," Griffin said. "But I do know that's how I get my stories done. There's nothing like being there. You'll see things you'd never find in a book."

She nodded. She should go there, where C. Tailleur—Cece —stood and walked and ate and lived. Where she wrote the book that meant so much to her grandfather. The place that could hold the answer to why her mother's name was in that dedication.

"So where is this town?" Griffin asked.

"It's called Paillettes au Sommet. It's a little south of Lyon, from what I understand, and—"

"No kidding, Lyon? That's only about an hour's train ride from Geneva. Here's an idea. What's today, Wednesday? If you can get here by the weekend, maybe I can head over and meet you. I'm wrapping up my interviews here tomorrow and then

I'm waiting to hear where they want me to go next. I may have a few days to myself next week. And it's about time we meet face to face, don't you think? It's the perfect location, France. What a story we'll tell our kids one day."

She felt herself blush. He was kidding, but the truth was, she'd love to have that story to tell. It seemed like the greatest romance she could ever imagine—finally finding the truth about her past as the first step in building a wonderful new future. She'd never even considered doing something like this before—taking off and traveling to Europe to follow some hunch. If she hadn't met Griffin, she might not have thought about it at all.

But now that she had, and she'd said it out loud... it seemed like she had no other choice.

FIVE

NOVEMBER 1942

Clutching the baby to her chest, Celina turned from Max and the car and started up the road toward the house the farmers had pointed to. It was strange to have a sleeping baby in her arms, and yet it also felt natural, like something she'd been waiting for her whole life. She looked down at the little girl in the cozy blanket cradled in her arms, her eyes closed, her eyelids thin and translucent, her long black lashes resting lightly on her cheeks, which were round and reddened from the fresh autumn air. What would it be like if this child were truly hers? It was a game she sometimes played when she was alone, a silly, pretend game, an escape that comforted her. She'd see a mother pushing a carriage down the street and imagine how things would be if she were that mother. Would it soon be feeding time? Storytime? What did the nursery look like? What color the sheets, the curtains, the rug? What toys would be in the toy box, painted pink or blue and stenciled with moons and stars and yellow suns, their rays spreading outward?

It was a version of the game she and Emile played on Sunday mornings last fall. They would leave their flat and stop for coffee and pastries to bring to the park nearby. There, they'd find a bench where they could sit and watch children on the swings and seesaws and climbing bars. Her morning queasiness had usually disappeared by that hour, and she could enjoy the delicious treats they'd chosen—macarons or éclairs or pains au chocolat. She was always ravenous by then, even though she'd had a breakfast earlier of tea and crackers, trying to settle her stomach. The changes and shifts in her body were a constant source of amusement and surprise to both of them.

They'd smile at the babies who tumbled and then cried for their mamas, at those that were strong enough to pull themselves up on the climbing bars, at those who were shy around strangers and those who were bold. Every once in a while a particularly brave little boy or girl would come right up to them and ask for a taste, until their embarrassed parent would rush over and apologize and take them by the hand and entice them with what was planned for lunch in just a little while.

"Shy or outgoing—which?" Emile would say. The questions rarely varied. Nor did the answers. They just became more detailed, more descriptive, with every subsequent conversation. It was the same way Emile approached his illustrations. He'd start out with a light pencil touch, but then he'd go over the lines, making them thicker, adding color. The more he went over those first faint lines, the more the drawing would come alive, until it all but popped off the page.

"Shy," she'd start off. "Quiet and polite."

"But with a great sense of humor."

"Absolutely. Loves to laugh."

"Big eyes."

"Sandy curls."

"Sticky little fingers from all the treats her papa gives her."

"You can't give her too many! She has to eat a good lunch!"

And the words would flow and flow, more and more of them

with each passing week, as they painted a picture of their still unknowable baby.

Funny, she thought now as she continued up the hill with Brielle in her arms. She and Emile had always expected they'd have a girl. Of course, they never found out if they were right. Celina could only wonder now. Just like she could only wonder what would have happened if they had heeded all the recommendations to leave Paris sooner. But they delayed. They loved Paris. They were foolish, naïve. She'd known it was inevitable that they would one day have to go. She just hadn't realized how urgent it was.

The house was now visible, set back from the others on the road. It was the color of milky coffee, two stories surrounded by dense pine trees. There weren't many windows, just a few scattered ones along the front-facing wall. They were small—so different from the homes she'd known. Her family's house in Madison Falls, a country-like suburb north of Bethesda, had two large windows in each of the four upstairs bedrooms, a huge picture window in the living room, and multiple glass doors along the back wall of the kitchen. She supposed the reduced number and size of the windows here was intentional, a way of protecting those inside from the harsh winter winds. And the same was probably true of the narrow doorway.

She imagined that Emile's grandparents had probably lived in a similar house to the one she was now approaching. Since Max was set on leaving Paillettes as soon as they could, and the crash had delayed them so much, she knew she'd probably never get to see it. She was sorry for that. Emile had told her such wonderful stories about it. He'd said that his grandfather had lived through some of the most brutal winters imaginable when he was a young boy. Grandpère's family, he'd explained, would store up food like squirrels in anticipation of multiple days in a row, or even a whole week, when they might not be able to leave the house because of the snowdrifts. And yet, the thick, stone walls and large fireplaces had always made Grandpère and his three older brothers feel cozy and protected. Their parents read them most exciting stories to them every night, and created scavenger hunts and other games to keep them entertained.

Grandpère, Emile had told her, loved to talk about those old days, about how much fun he'd had with his brothers. On rainy evenings when they were teenagers, they'd all invite their girlfriends over and gather around the fireplace to tell ghost stories or play silly games like musical chairs. Or they'd sing songs, accompanied by the oldest brother, Raimond, who played the harpsichord and made up bawdy lyrics for well-known tunes. Grandpère had bought out his brothers' shares of the house and then left it to Emile, his only grandchild, when he died. Although Emile hadn't visited in many years, the house had never been far from his thoughts. He'd told Celina about the long visits he'd had with his grandparents as a young boy, when his parents traveled abroad for his father's government work. There'd been picnic dinners and fireflies lighting up the atmosphere during summer, and bonfires in the fall. And most of all, Emile remembered the feel of his grandfather's strong arms carrying him up to bed when he had come close to falling asleep downstairs.

Emile had hoped that when he and Celina had saved enough so he could leave his work as a magazine illustrator and illustrate children's books full-time, they would move to the house for good and recreate a bit of what his grandfather had so enjoyed. Celina had agreed because it sounded like such a romantic and special way to live, although she made him promise that they'd spend the harshest winter months elsewhere.

Celina reached the top of the hill and stood for a moment, catching her breath. It hadn't been easy to walk up the steep incline in her good shoes, not to mention with a baby in her arms who, though petite, now felt as heavy as a packed suitcase.

Looking around, she spotted a group of about a dozen children —they seemed to be young, around five or six years old— arranged in a circle near the side of the house, playing with a large red ball. A few yards away on a step that led to a side porch, a young woman was watching the children and calling out directions. The kids were laughing and clapping their hands and jumping up and down as they waited for the ball to come their way. They looked like they were having oodles of fun.

Of course they were, Celina thought. What child doesn't love recess? In Paris, she'd worked at a primary school while she completed her teacher training, and before that, she'd been a teacher's assistant for a kindergarten class—the one job her father had allowed her to take while he tried to find her a suitable man to marry. At both schools, the families didn't have a lot, but the children were joyful and engaged. They loved the games she taught them and worked hard to learn their letters and numbers. They loved dancing and singing and playing dress-up, and giggled with abandon when she invented funny-sounding words or described imaginary animals—birds with paws or hippos with feathers or elephants with pouches like kangaroos had. It seemed inherent, her students' proclivity for happiness, and she drew inspiration from them every day. She was sure that the world would be a far better place—more giving, more caring, more peaceful—if people simply spent time with children.

With Brielle still asleep in her arms, she watched the group for a moment more and then proceeded up three stone steps to the narrow front door. There was a large wooden knocker in the center and she moved the baby to one side so she'd have a free hand to tap it. The little girl opened her eyes and stirred a bit, stretching her legs up from beneath the pink blanket. She was probably hungry, Celina thought, and likely also needed to be changed.

The door was opened by a woman with a round face and

wispy blonde hair pulled back into a bun at the nape of her neck, wearing a blue pullover sweater and baggy, gray trousers. Celina was surprised at her appearance. Back in Paris, most women wouldn't dream of answering the door in what looked like men's clothing.

"Good morning, may I help you—oh, madame, you are bleeding!" the woman said in French. "Please come in. I will take a look at that."

"It's nothing," Celina said, her gloved fingers going to her forehead, glad that unlike her brother, she was fluent in the language. She immediately felt comfortable in this woman's presence. It was a nice change from the tension she'd felt speaking to the policeman a few minutes ago. "We just had a small car crash down by the road. But I'm fine."

"And your baby? She was in the car, too?"

"No. Oh, no. She's not... my baby." She looked at the woman, trying to speak very deliberately. The farmers had indicated she should bring the baby here, but they hadn't told her what she should say. Celina was cautious. If she was right and this baby was a Jewish refugee, then it was important not to divulge where she'd been found to just anyone.

"She is not yours?" The woman looked confused.

"There were farmers who helped us with the car—my brother and me, he's still there with them. And the farmers said I was to bring her here..." She felt a touch of relief that Max wasn't with her. It would have made things even more difficult and awkward if she had to translate this conversation for him.

"Oh," the woman said. They looked at one another awkwardly, as though they suspected they could trust one another but weren't entirely sure. "So this baby belongs to..."

Celina started to speak, her mouth poised to say something while she decided what that something should be. "I don't know," she said in measured tones. "What I know is that her name is Brielle Aimée—"

"Ah, Brielle Aimée!" the woman exclaimed, clapping her hands together. "*Dieu merci!* We have been waiting for her to arrive, we didn't know what could have happened—here, let me have our new little resident." Before Celina knew it, the woman had taken the baby out of her arms and was rocking her gently, as Brielle scrunched up her face again and this time let out a loud wail.

"Oh, pretty girl, you are home now," the woman said. "You've traveled far, you have a right to be fussy. No worries, my dear little darling. I will get you settled in. We have bottles and clothing and toys…"

She started for the staircase at the rear of the front room, which had a sofa with a floral back and wooden legs, as well as a large, upholstered armchair and round end tables with wooden bases and white stone surfaces. Everything looked a little worn, maybe second-hand. There was a fireplace to the side with a strong fire burning, and a dark red circular rug on the floor.

"We thought you were arriving by train this morning," the woman said as she carried the baby upstairs. "That's why we were so worried when you weren't on the platform. There must have been a miscommunication. But all's well now. Please go ahead into the kitchen, right through the dining room. That's where you'll find Rémy—he's the director here, you know that, yes? He'll want to personally thank you. And there's some food for you, and I'll tend to your forehead before you are back on your way to Lyon."

"No, I—" Celina tried to get her to stop, but the woman was already up the stairs and out of sight. It was clear that they were expecting someone else, someone whose job was to bring the baby here. Celina didn't know what to make of that, and there was no one else to talk to. She decided to follow the woman's instructions. She wanted to meet the director of this place, this orphanage, if that was what it truly was. Her arms felt light and empty, and she was sorry to no longer be holding the baby. She didn't want to leave until she knew Brielle was in the right place and would be well taken care of.

With her arms now free, she pulled off her gloves and unbuttoned her coat, then smoothed her hair and re-pinned her bangs to the side, away from her face. The dining room was cozy and inviting, with sconces on the walls and chair cushions upholstered in a sweet toile pattern. In the center was a large wooden table, and on the wall was a chart with six names. She pushed a swinging door behind the table, which took her into the kitchen. It was a long, narrow room, with the oven and icebox along one wall and tall storage cabinets along the opposite one. Through the panes of the window near the cabinets, she could hear the children playing outside. Paris had been so tense ever since the Nazis had arrived, and everyone was scared. It was nice to hear unabashed joy for a change.

Across the room, a man was washing dishes in the deep sink, his back to her. He wore a white shirt and black trousers, with a long, white cotton apron tied at his waist. She figured he was a worker, maybe a janitor.

"Excuse me?" she said.

He turned, grabbing a yellow dishtowel from the sink to dry his hands. "Good morning," he said, rolling down his sleeves and buttoning the cuffs. He was tall, with broad shoulders and a trim waist. He pushed his thick brown hair away from his forehead with his wrist. "May I help you?"

"Yes... I'm looking for... the director?"

"You found him," he said, holding out his hand. "Rémy Tremblant."

"Oh. I..." She paused, dumbstruck. In her experience, people with the title of director didn't wash dishes. She moved forward to shake his hand. "I'm sorry, Monsieur Tremblant. I didn't realize you'd be—"

"Working in the kitchen? I guess you don't spend a whole lot of time in Paillettes. We don't stand on ceremony in this town. Too much to do, especially with winter coming. And call me Rémy, please. Now, you are…?"

"My name is… well, I brought the baby here just now. Brielle Aimée."

"Yes, I assumed so. Wonderful to see you. You weren't on the train platform, so we were getting concerned. You're with one of the American relief agencies, right? Say, that looks like a nasty cut on your forehead. Has my sister seen it yet?"

"The woman at the door? Yes, she said she'd be down soon to take a look at it. But I'm not with an agency. I'm… well, my name is Celina Cassin. And I came upon the baby by accident… What's wrong?" she said. His smile had disappeared.

"You're Celina Cassin?" he said. "As in the Cassin family? Charles Cassin?"

"Yes, that's right." She supposed she shouldn't be surprised that he knew of Emile's family. People knew one another in small towns. And yet, his reaction was so dramatic. He looked like he'd unexpectedly been punched. His eyes were wide and his hand was now against his stomach. She couldn't imagine why. Emile had led her to believe that his grandfather had been well liked.

"Charles Cassin was my husband's grandfather," she added, because it looked like he was waiting for her to go on. "He had a house here in town that I've inherited. I came to town to sign the papers to sell it."

"I know," he said. "I planned to go downtown today to stop you."

"Stop me? Why?"

"I take it you've never seen the house?"

"I don't even know where it is, exactly. Why, is there something wrong with it?"

He chuckled. "Well, yes. There is one thing that's very wrong with it."

She looked at him, annoyed. She didn't like his knowing

one, his teasing laugh. As if he was aware of something she was in the dark about. "And that is?"

He swayed a bit, moving forward and back on his feet. "What's wrong is that his house is the very house you're building in. *This* is his house. And I can't let you sell it."

SIX

OCTOBER 2018

At work the next day, Rachel put in a request to take the following week off, and when her manager approved, she went online to make plane reservations. While she had surprised herself last night with the idea of going to France, she now saw that it made a lot of sense. Hearing Griffin repeat how he found answers by going straight to the source of the information affected her in a way it hadn't before. She wondered now if her desire to know what happened to her family had always been mixed with fear of what she might find out, since her grandfather would mutter "I don't recall" or say he was too tired to talk the few times long ago when she tried to ask about her mother. She had been scared to push harder for information. What if she pushed so hard that he decided he no longer wanted her? What would happen to her then?

But she didn't want to be scared anymore. Knowing the truth had to be better than spending her life fearing what it might be. She couldn't imagine what terrible thing either her mother or her grandfather might have done to sever their bond. She loved them both. But having read the mysterious dedication, she now wanted to know what happened before she was born—and how she could use that knowledge to shape the future she wanted and deserved.

And the added bonus of being brave, she thought, was that she might make a true connection with Griffin. She yearned to be in love instead of just dreaming about it. And what better place to rendezvous than in the most romantic country in the world? They'd have some time to spend together and hopefully find that they were right for each other. She was so ready to hold hands with someone she truly cared for, to feel his arm around her shoulders, to enjoy a long, delicious kiss. Maybe even to spend the night with him, to wake up next to him and embrace that closeness. She was tired of dating, tired of believing she could be in love but then facing the fact that she wasn't. She'd had far too many promising first dates that led to disappointing second or third ones. Long ago, she'd watched a tennis match on television with her grandfather, and they'd seen a player go from losing badly to winning the final three sets and the match. The announcer later asked him how he'd turned things around, and he'd said he'd known he had to do something different. Switch gears. His plan had simply been to change things up.

That's what she needed to do. To propel herself out of this cozy little town that she rarely left. It was worth a shot. At worst, she'd end up right back where she'd started.

At best, she'd end up walking through a wide-open door and into a wonderful future she couldn't even imagine.

She began to research flights, and realized it was going to be a complicated itinerary. The direct flights from New York to Lyon were beyond expensive, so she booked a flight for Friday evening leaving JFK at 7:30 p.m. with a stopover in Dublin. It landed at 7:15 a.m. Dublin time, where she'd have roughly two hours to stretch her legs and get something to eat. The next leg of her trip was a two-and-one-half-hour flight, and with a time change of an additional hour, she'd arrive in Lyon at 1:30 p.m. local time. From there, she could Uber to Lyon's main railway station and catch a 5:00 p.m. train to Paillettes. Turning to accommodations, she combed through a number of travel sites and found a small guest house, La Maison au Sommet, that earned good reviews. So she made a reservation for six nights. She texted Griffin with her travel information and said her train was scheduled to arrive at 8:00 p.m. on Saturday. A moment later she got his response:

I'm showing up Friday and will make a reservation at the same place and plan to meet your train on Saturday. Looks like there's a restaurant in town with amazing Provençal dishes on the menu—l'agneau, les cuisses de grenouilles, le lapin, les pieds-paquets followed by petits calissons. I'll see if I can make a reservation there, too. See you soon!

She sent back a thumbs-up emoji, glad that he was booking his own room. Despite her high hopes for the relationship, it wasn't appropriate for them to share right off the bat—and she was happy he apparently saw things that way as well. Curious, she then went to look up the dishes he'd named. The first one, lamb, she could handle, but the next three—frogs' legs, rabbit, and the feet and belly lining of a sheep—sounded far less appetizing. She didn't know how she'd be able to stomach all that, especially since she'd probably be queasy already from lack of sleep and all that travel. But she vowed to be open-minded. After all, this trip was a reset, a chance to discover if she was, or could be, someone besides the desk-bound Rachel she'd been for so long.

She returned to the airline page to double-check her flights just as Nick, the library's rare books curator, wandered past her desk. An older man with a squiggly gray ponytail at the base of his neck, Nick had become a good friend since he was hired over the summer. He'd been wonderful to her when she'd needed to unload these last few months after visiting her grandfather and seeing his decline.

"Going anywhere special?" he asked, looking over her shoulder at the screen.

She nodded. "France, actually."

"Very nice. What's in France?" She told him about the strange things her grandfather had said yesterday and then pulled her copy of the book from her bag to show him the dedication.

"Wait, this is the book you told me you had been researching for your Ph.D., isn't it?" he said, lifting it and carefully thumbing through the pages. "It's great that you're getting back into it." Nick was a Ph.D. candidate in classical literature, and he'd been working on his degree for almost a decade. He'd been sorry when she told him she'd abandoned her research.

"Well, it's not about the degree," she told him. "It's about my family. What my grandfather was talking about yesterday and whether he knew this author and why this dedication has my mother's name."

"I get it. Although you might still want to consider... Say, wait a minute," he said, his eyebrows rising. "Isn't that where the guy is?" She'd confided in Nick about Griffin, and he was totally intrigued by the romance. He'd said it had an old-fashioned quality about it, although with texts and videochats substituting for love letters sent by mail.

"No, that's not where the guy—Griffin—is. He's in Geneva." She paused and looked down, feeling herself blush. "Although he's meeting me in France."

"So you're going there for the guy—"

"No, I'm not going there for the guy," she said, standing so she could make her point more forcefully. "I decided to go on my own. He offered to meet me. He's a journalist, you know. He knows how to track down information. Maybe he can help me."

She paused, then shrugged. "Okay, I'll admit it, I'm glad he's coming," she added. "I like him. Why are you looking so suspicious? I thought you approved of this thing we have going. I thought you said it felt like a novel."

"Yeah, but that was just when it was texting. Now you're leaving the country to meet him. You don't even know him."

"That's not true. We know a lot about each other. Lots of people meet online these days."

"Maybe, but do you want to be chasing him all over the globe? I thought he said he was coming to New York to meet you for the first time."

"Well, things changed—"

"Apparently. Look, I want good things for you. I want it to work out. But I don't know... roaming through the French countryside on your own—"

"Stop," she said, holding up a palm. "I'm excited about this. Don't ruin it for me."

Nick pantomimed locking his lips with a key and then sat back down at his desk. Rachel stayed where she was, not wanting to leave this way. She trusted Nick. He had a good head on his shoulders. And he was a romantic, like she was. He'd told her how he'd proposed to his wife on a helicopter as they circled the Hawaiian Islands because he wanted to be close to heaven when he popped the question. But what she was about to do—to him, it was a bridge too far. How could she explain herself to him? Something had brought her and Griffin together for that program she'd organized. Not that she believed in destiny, not really, but she did believe in following her instincts. Even if that meant traveling alone and meeting him in a foreign town where she knew no one else.

She walked over to Nick's chair and nudged his shoulder. "You don't have to be completely silent," she said. "You could tell me to have a good time and that you hope I find what I'm looking for. Don't you think it's better that I'll be with someone when I'm there, rather than being alone? I think it's safer if someone is waiting for me."

"Someone you barely know—"

"But someone, at any rate. Someone that my friend Nancy knows. She recommended him for my panel, you know."

"And she told you she didn't like him."

"Well..." She paused. It was true, Nancy had said Griffin was smart and charming but not the guy for her. "It's not that she doesn't like him," she said. "She only said he wasn't the settling-down type. But she knew him a long time ago when he worked at her TV station. He's probably changed a lot since then." She sighed. "Nick, I really think he could be the one."

Nick softened. "What makes you so sure?"

"He's sweet," she said, pulling her chair over and sitting down next to him. "And he's thoughtful. You should have heard him last night. He wants to help me. I told him about my grandfather, and he understood. He really did. He told me his grandmother had had dementia."

Nick looked at her sideways. "Did you check out his story?"

She scowled and looked away. She wanted him to agree that she could take off on Friday night and come home a week later with a new love as well as a new understanding of herself created from whatever she was able to glean about her grandfather and her mother. It was possible. Of course it was. Sometimes she saw her life as a movie—didn't everyone? And why couldn't her life be a movie that goes right? She wanted exactly what Nick had with his wife. Someone to go home to at night. Someone to snuggle with under a warm blanket and watch TV and drink hot cocoa when it snowed outside and there was nowhere to go. Who made her feel that she mattered. Who would look at her and think, I am so lucky that I'm with Rachel.

Someone who could make her feel exactly the way she'd felt last night when Griffin recognized that something was wrong and urged her to tell him what it was. She was tired of being alone, an aloneness that was getting more and more intense the more her grandfather drifted away.

"I want to believe that sometimes things do work out the way the romance novels say they do," she said. "Can't you understand that?"

He stood, and she rose to hug him.

"Be careful," he said. "Stay in touch. Call if you need me, okay?"

"I will. Thank you. And don't worry, I truly believe this is the best thing for me. This book, this guy, this author... it's all coming together. And nothing was coming together before for me. Sometimes the universe is telling you something."

He squeezed her hand, and she nodded and went back to her desk to power down her computer. She was so tired of the guys she'd dated over the years, guys who didn't touch that place in her heart, in her imagination, that Griffin did. She remembered how Nancy had once suggested that she liked Griffin not in spite of all his traveling but because of it. That she was scared of getting close to anyone so preferred to find someone she could literally never be close to. She'd thought about that theory for a while. But she knew Nancy was wrong. She wanted to connect in person with Griffin. She wasn't avoiding that; she was reaching for it. Why else would she be making this trip? It was time to finally grasp everything she was due. A new meaning to her life. A new way forward. A new discovery. It was all possible, a complete love story and a complete life story, right there in the sun-kissed mountains of southern France.

She turned off her desk lamp and headed down to the first

floor. She needed to pack since she was leaving tomorrow night, but decided to first go see her grandfather. She felt bad that she'd miss a week's worth of visits. He probably wouldn't understand when she tried to explain that she wouldn't be there for several days, but she couldn't leave without a goodbye. It was impossible to know these days how his mind worked, which words and sentences made an impact and which were just sounds. Maybe some of what she said would penetrate, and in the coming days he'd remember why she wasn't showing up.

At The Bremson, she went to the memory care unit and knocked on the door. Kate answered, and when she explained why she was back, she led her to the solarium, a wide oval room lined with tall windows, the landscape outside glowing golden. "He's better than when you saw him yesterday, although he was a little agitated in the morning," she said. "Let's see how he's doing now."

Her grandfather was sitting on a hard-backed chair near one of the windows, staring outside. He was still but also looked very engaged, as though he were watching something important. Or maybe it was something inside his own mind. It was impossible to tell.

"Henry, look who came back to see you," Kate said, tapping him gently on the shoulder. "It's Rachel. Two days in a row. You're a lucky grandfather."

"Hi, Papy," Rachel said, bending down to kiss his pale, dry cheek. She pulled another chair close to him. "How are you?"

"Ah, good," he said, smiling, his teeth yellowed but his blue eyes clear and sparkling. "Brielle, yes? Brielle Aimée?"

"It's Rachel," Kate said. "Your granddaughter."

"My... what?" he said.

Rachel pressed her lips together. He'd never thought she was someone else before. "It's me, Papy," she said. "You know. You call me Rachelle."

"No, don't fool with me. You're Brielle Aimée. The little girl from the storybook."

Rachel unbuttoned her jacket and sat down next to him. She suspected she should humor him, but she couldn't bear letting him think she was a storybook character. "No, I'm not *in* the story," she said. "Brielle Aimée was the girl the book was dedicated to. And it was also my mother's name. Your daughter, remember?"

"Yes, I remember," he said, his tone soft and kind. "I was there when it all started." He shook his head, and a huge grin spread across his lips. "My, it's good to see you."

She hoped that his smile meant he recognized her after all. But there was something about his eyes, a lack of focus, that was frightening. And what did he mean, he was there when it started? She wasn't at all sure he realized who she was.

"Papy," she said. "Listen, okay? I'm traveling for about a week, so I won't be coming by for a little while. But don't worry or get upset. Papy, try to hear me. I will come to see you as soon as I get back. Do you understand?"

He looked at her and nodded. "You are back. You came back!"

"Yes, I was here yesterday, and now I'm back."

"Because I thought you died," he said. "We were told you died. You and Cece. I felt awful. But here you are."

Rachel looked up at Kate, who raised her palms and shook her head. She sighed and looked again at her grandfather.

"Papy, listen. I'm going away for a short time," Rachel said with more force in her voice. "I'm leaving but I will be back."

He sighed. "I'm so relieved. Because I–" Then he looked more closely at her, and his smile disappeared. "No," he said. "No. You're not her. You're not little Brielle. She was a baby."

"And now she's grown," Kate said. "You know that, Henry."

"No, this isn't Brielle," he said, his voice low and stoic. "She died. The baby. And the mother. And the other ones, the children, so many." He shook his head. "I couldn't help them. There was always someone making you do things or you'd be killed, too..."

Rachel watched him rub his chin hard and then look out the window. He didn't want to talk to her. He was shutting her out. As if being with her was too painful for him to bear.

Kate motioned to her, and Rachel followed her to the hallway.

"I can't believe this," Rachel said. "He's never talked about the past like this. I wanted to have a nice goodbye. And make sure he knew I'd be back. Now I don't even know if he'll remember me."

"Don't worry. We'll remind him."

"And maybe I'll call a few times? And you can bring the phone over to him?"

"Of course. Now go ahead and have a good trip. We'll take good care of him."

Rachel started to follow Kate to the door, then stopped to take one more look back into the solarium. Her grandfather was staring out the window again. What was going on inside his confused head anyway? Here he was, talking about people who died and a baby who died, and children who died. And something he had done because he'd been forced to do it...

Oh my God, she thought. Had he been responsible for the death of a baby? Or several children? Was that what he was saying in his odd, confused way? Was that what had been haunting him all these years? Was this how he was connected to the secret orphanage and Cece?

She thought about the things she'd said to Nick just a little while ago. How optimistic she was about France. How excited she was to be meeting Griffin. She'd been practically giddy. She'd even pictured her life as a movie. But now she felt a chill. Was Nick right? Was taking this trip a bad idea? Were there too many unknowns? Too many things that could hurt her?

No, she thought. Now the trip was more important than ever. Because now it was even bigger than the dedication. If her grandfather felt guilty about something, she needed to know what it was. Maybe it wasn't as bad as he was thinking. She wanted to put his mind at rest. He looked so sad. She couldn't hide at work or in her apartment anymore.

She needed to find Cece and learn the truth. And then she would find a way to move forward, whatever she discovered.

SEVEN

NOVEMBER 1942

"Please. Let's start over," Rémy said, as he untied his apron and slipped the loop over his head. He adjusted his shirt, tucking it more neatly into his trousers. "First things first. How did you hurt your forehead?"

Celina instinctively touched the spot. It stung, and she winced and took her fingers away. "My brother and I—our car ran off the road and rolled over."

"Good lord! That must have been terrifying. If that's the only injury you got, I'd say you were lucky. Adele is a nurse, in addition to being my sister. She'll fix you up." He hung the apron on a hook by the sink, then gestured toward the swinging door. "Now, let's have a seat out in the living room. And—ah, what's wrong with me? Please let me take your coat. And I should have offered you something to eat. Are you hungry or thirsty? Can I get you anything?"

She shook her head, so he led her back to the room where she'd entered. The living room, she thought. *Emile's* living room. She could hardly believe that she was standing in the house he'd spoken so affectionately about. It wasn't quite what she'd visualized. With all the talk about months of snow and cold, she'd imagined it damp and gray and cavernous, made cozy and pleasant only by the loving family that lived there. But this house wasn't that way at all. Yes, the walls and floor were stone, and the windows were small. Through the panes, she could see the last few orange leaves on a nearby oak, still clinging to the branch as though reluctant to admit their day was over.

But still, there was something lively about the place—the red rug and colorful upholstery printed with roses and lilies and green foliage. And there were crayoned drawings tacked around the windows and placed along the mantel of the fireplace, pictures of snow-capped mountains against blue skies and flower gardens with daffodils and poppies.

Monsieur Tremblant—Rémy—took her coat and draped it on the stairway banister. He waited until she was seated on the sofa before sitting on an armchair opposite her. He had a tender, easy smile that made him look approachable, along with a broad forehead and firm jawline that gave him a capable appearance. His thick, light brown hair was combed to the side and back from his forehead, a little longer than she was used to seeing on men. His dark eyes tilted slightly downward at the corners, which made him look vulnerable, while his mouth curled upward in a warm, inviting way.

He had a youthful gait, but she could also see a kind of gravitas in his face. It made her think of how childlike she and Emile had been in Paris. She knew she'd aged in the last year, affected by all that had happened. But this man didn't seem to be aging from stress. She imagined he was by nature an old soul. And that his maturity only deepened as he got older. She wanted to be suspicious of him—after all, how dare he move into Emile's house? *Her* house? And yet it was hard to regard him that way. He looked like the kind of person who could come up with a reasonable explanation to any question, a practical solution to any problem.

"We've been talking with the children about nature," Rémy said, evidently noticing that she'd moved her gaze away from him and back toward the decorations on the walls. "For some of our children, this area is very new. They haven't seen the amount of snow we often get. We are trying to prepare them for the coming winter, so they won't feel scared or—"

"Wait, wait," Celina said, holding up a hand. The conversation was confusing, and his possessiveness toward the house absurd. "*This* is my husband's house?"

"If you are Emile Cassin's wife, then it certainly is."

"I don't understand," she said, her voice rising. "Why are you here? This house is supposed to be empty. It's been empty since my husband's grandfather died a decade ago."

"Well, clearly not," he said, his tone calm and somewhat amused. "I can see why you'd be surprised, but it's not like we haven't tried to make contact. I reached out to your husband several times since we started up last year. I was hoping he'd come visit so we could talk. Is he here with you? I'd like to speak to him."

"He—" She looked down at her hands on her lap. "My husband died last fall," she said.

Rémy was quiet for a long moment, and she could see he hadn't expected that news. "I'm so sorry," he said. "I had no idea. Celina, I'm very sorry to hear this."

She looked up at him. She'd become used to hearing such apologies, so much so that they had started to sound rote to her. And her gratitude had become perfunctory. But the words sounded different coming from this man. He seemed sincerely moved, and his tone reflected deep caring. She was touched, too, that he'd used her first name, and spoken it with such tenderness.

"I know there is probably little I could say to make you feel better," he said. "But perhaps it would help to know that there are some in the town who knew your husband as a child.

They knew his grandfather, too. The family was loved very much."

"Thank you," she said. "It's been almost a year, but it's..."

She paused. The mention of Emile still brought tears to her eyes. She felt this man looking at her with sympathy, and she appreciated his kindness. But she still couldn't make sense of this situation. Nobody was supposed to be here. She recalled seeing correspondence for Emile originating from this town. But she hadn't been able to bring herself to open any of it. She'd thought it would be too sad to see notes to Emile from people lucky enough to believe him alive. And besides, she'd assumed that many would be routine, form letters and such. Max had promised to read all the accumulated mail once they got back home.

Just then the woman who'd answered the door came back downstairs. "Marie is tending to the baby, warming her up and changing her clothes, and in a little bit we'll try to give her a bottle," she told them.

"How is she?" Celina asked. Her arms felt empty without the baby in them.

"She's doing wonderfully. You did a good job with her," Adele said. She turned to Rémy. "Did this lady tell you it was she who brought the baby here? She carried her all the way up the hill from the meadow."

"So I'm just beginning to hear," Rémy said.

"And now I want to tend to your forehead," Adele told Celina. "My kit is in the back office." She walked down the hallway, disappearing into darkness. Celina couldn't help but flinch at her use of the word office. This was a home. Her husband's home. There was no office.

She looked back at Rémy. "I don't have a lot of time. My brother and I are supposed to see the lawyer here in town so I can sign the papers giving him power to close on a sale in my absence. My brother already found a potential buyer for the house—"

"So how *did* you end up with the baby?" Rémy said, standing up, his hands in his pockets. "As you're clearly not the person designated to bring her here." His tone was friendly but firm, and not nearly as happy-go-lucky as he'd sounded in the kitchen. He'd brought her out here and sat her down, and politely taken her coat and offered her food, all to establish goodwill before launching into his questions. Still, he was so likable. It was hard to take offense that he'd ignored what she'd just said.

"I found her under a bush after our car crashed," she told him, thinking it was in Brielle's best interests to give him the full story. "There was a note pinned to her blanket. It said her name and *cachée,* and I knew what that meant from—"

"Did anyone else see the baby?"

"My brother. And the farmers who were helping with our car. They told me to bring her here."

"Anyone else?"

"There was a policeman—"

"Red? Was it Red? The one with the red hair?"

"Yes, I think he had red hair."

He moved in closer, and she felt like an accused criminal in an interrogation room. The only thing missing was a bare light bulb overhead, the harsh light shining into her eyes.

"What did you tell him?" he asked.

"I said the baby was mine. That seemed to be what the farmers wanted me to do."

"And he didn't dispute that?"

"No, he believed me."

Rémy looked upward and sighed. Then he returned to the armchair and sat—or more accurately, flopped—back down. "That's good," he said, his friendly tone returning. "It could have been disastrous if you'd said otherwise."

"Rémy... Monsieur Tremblant—" she started.

He sat up straighter, pulling himself together once more. "You were right the first time. Rémy—"

"Okay, Rémy. Please," Celina said. "Why are you here? Do you live in this house, my husband's house... well, my house now? Do the children I saw outside live here? Are they all..." She lowered her voice. "Are they all Jewish?" She saw him hesitate. "My husband was half Jewish," she said, her voice stronger as she spoke about Emile. "He had false papers and was part of the Resistance. That's why he was killed. I lied to the policeman and brought the baby here. I think I deserve the truth."

He nodded, then stood again and walked over to the wall near the fireplace. He turned to her, his arms crossed over his chest.

"Yes, you do," he agreed. "You're one of us, too, now. Six of the children you saw outside are secretly living here. They were brought here from Paris last spring. The official line is that they are children from the village, and that this is a school. But the truth is, they are Jewish children whose parents were rounded up. Which is what we know happened to this baby's parents as well."

Celina thought of Brielle and the note pinned to her blanket: *Please care for my baby girl until we are together again.* She couldn't imagine what that poor mother had gone through, how awful it must have been to write those words. Where was she now? Was she even alive? And if so, how worried she must be. How awful not to know if someone had indeed saved her baby.

"Your car crash—it must have disrupted the transfer of the baby from the train station," he continued. "Whoever had her must have known the police were around. So I assume they decided to hide the baby and hope the farmers discovered her once your car was moved."

"So what... what will happen to her now?" she asked.

"We hope we can keep her and the six others safe until France is liberated," he said. "The children who live here all have a counterfeit home in the village. Each child belongs, so to speak, to a family that claims to be... well, their actual family. That's the story we put out to the authorities. And it's the story we'll tell if the Nazis show up. We'll continue like this until the war is over. And then we will try to find their parents. If any are still alive."

He returned to the armchair. Clasping his hands together, he leaned forward, his elbows on his knees. "It sounds dangerous to you, I'm sure. And it is. But you should know that we have a good life here. We make the children's lives as normal as possible. The upstairs bedrooms are where they sleep, and the dining room is where they have their meals. We use the carriage house out back as a classroom."

Adele returned with a basket containing towels and first-aid supplies. She sat down next to Celina and began applying ointment and a bandage to her cut. Before long, a young woman in jeans and a short-sleeved, button-down shirt came downstairs. She was carrying Brielle, who was freshly wrapped in a pale blue blanket.

"All warm and clean," the young woman said, addressing Celina. "I'm Marie, I help Adele with the kids. I thought you'd like to say goodbye before you go." She put Brielle on Celina's lap.

Celina held the baby under her arms. "My goodness," she said as she bounced her softly up and down. "How are you, little girl? Glad to be safe and warm now?" The baby watched her wide-eyed. Celina looked at Marie. "How old do you suppose she is?"

"I'd say three months, maybe a little less," she said. "She's a smart one. You can tell by those bright eyes. It'll be a joy to watch her grow."

Adele pointed to Celina's forehead. "Keep that covered for

two days, and it will heal nicely." She gathered her first-aid supplies and Marie picked the baby back up.

"Come on, little one," Marie said. "Let's go get you a bottle."

Celina thanked Adele and watched the women leave for the kitchen. When she turned back, she saw Rémy looking at her, his eyebrows raised. "Well?" he asked.

"Well, what?"

"I want you to tell me we can stay," he said, his tone pleasant but firm. "This house has been empty, and we need it. You have to understand that I did try to contact your husband. We knew about the brave work his group was doing. We thought he would want his grandfather's house to be put to such use."

Celina nodded. Emile had been brave. He'd told her he would give his life for France to be free again. And Rémy was right. Emile would have gladly given this house over for his purposes. He'd have wanted the two of them to do even more.

"As I said, we have six children living here and now one baby," Rémy said. "If Germany ends up occupying all of France, it's going to get harder to keep them safe. The police here are already cooperating with the Nazis. There are Jews hiding in private homes around town as well.

"We have nowhere else for these children to go," he said.

Celina nodded again. She was aware that the free zone here in the southern part of the country would very possibly soon cease to be. This was why Max was so determined to leave France immediately. It would get significantly harder for Americans to leave if the Nazis took over the whole country. As it was, it had cost Max a great deal of money in administrative fees along with, most likely, a not insignificant number of bribes, to expedite their passage out this week.

It was also why he wanted her to sell the house quickly. Owning property in France could get very complicated if Germany took over the whole country, he'd said. That's why he had already identified a buyer. He thought it would be best for her to cut all her ties to France and live back home free and clear. She'd thought that was a good idea, too.

But all that was nothing compared to what was going on here. This was what Emile had lived for, what he'd died for.

She lifted her gaze. "Of course," she said. "It's yours for however long you need it."

He sighed. "Perfect!" he said with a smile. "That's the best news I've heard in a while. You won't regret it."

"I can see that," she said. She stood and went to get her coat from the banister. "I should be going. My brother will be wondering what's taking me so long. He's anxious to get back to Lyon this afternoon. With any luck, he's gotten the car to start. We're supposed to go home to Maryland later this week." She looked in the direction of the kitchen. How she wished she could be the one taking care of the baby.

Rémy helped her on with her coat. "Well, you have a lot of travel ahead. It's probably unnecessary to mention this, but please be careful about what you've seen here. It could put us at risk if the wrong people find out."

"I know," she said. "Remember, my husband was in the Resistance. He was part of an underground newspaper. They distributed plans for sabotaging the Nazi-controlled railways. He was doing that when... well, when they were discovered."

"Of course," he said. "I meant no offense."

She fastened her coat. "May I ask you a favor?" she said.

"Anything."

"Is there any way you can write to me? And tell me how the baby is doing?"

He looked at her, his eyes sympathetic. "I wish I could say yes. But it wouldn't be safe, would it? I don't think you can trust that mail won't be examined these days. If it even could get through."

She nodded. Of course, he was right. She felt foolish for even asking.

He walked her to the door, and she turned and looked around. "You've got quite a wonderful set-up here. Your sister and Marie—do you all live here?"

"I do, along with my sister and her husband," he said. "Robert maintains the house and the grounds, and Adele does the cooking and helps take care of the children. My job is to procure food and supplies. Marie comes when she can, but she mostly helps out on her family's farm nearby."

He chuckled and lifted his palms. "I don't know how, but it all works pretty well."

Then he grew serious again. "The only thing is... well, it's going to get a little more complicated. It occurs to me now that you told Red you were the baby's mother. That was the right thing to do. Except that he does check in on us. Often. It's going to be hard to explain to him why you left and the baby's still here. He's going to be suspicious, which is not a good thing.

"Celina... would you possibly consider staying a while? Not forever, but maybe just until we can figure out a story that he'll believe? He's aware of the baby's arrival now. We need some time for him to turn his attention to other things."

"What? Stay?" she said. It was an impossible proposal. Even though the idea of being here to take care of the baby did appeal to her heart. "But how? I mean, what would I do here? How would you explain my even being here?"

"Well, the one thing we are missing is a teacher. You see, we've started having children from the village come here each day, to try to appear even more like an actual school. The kids are young, but they need real lessons. We all pitch in, but it's not the same."

"I'm a teacher," Celina blurted out. She didn't know why she'd said that. Except that it was the truth—she had worked in schools, both in Paris and back home. But more than that, the idea of staying here and raising Brielle and teaching the other children sounded like something she was meant to do. As soon as the words came out of her mouth, though, she knew it couldn't be. This so-called school was built on deceptions that could subject them all to Emile's fate. She wasn't as brave as her husband had been. She didn't think she ever could be. It would be so much easier to go home and let her mother take care of her. To go to dances and parties and help out with bake sales, as she used to. Her parents would want her to forget ever having been in France. Wasn't that best?

"I don't know," she said. "Like I told you, we're sailing home this week, my brother and I. We're going home—"

Just then there was a clatter from the back door, and a cluster of children came rushing down the hallway behind the staircase. Celina watched them hang up their coats on a coatrack and then head to the dining room. Evidently it was lunchtime. She wondered which of them had real families in the village, and which of them only appeared to. Her heart ached for those ones, the Jewish ones. How was it possible that they lived here, without parents or siblings? What terrible things had they witnessed?

She turned and, through the front window, she saw Max coming up the hill. She knew his gait so well—that bold strut. It was a defense, she'd always thought, his unspoken assertion to the world that he came from money so no one should mess with him. But the world was messy. How had she grown up in a family that didn't want to face that fact?

"I understand," Rémy said. "We'll figure it out. Good luck, Celina, and thank you for bringing the baby here. We won't forget what you've done."

She turned the doorknob and went onto the porch. From the high vantage point of the house, she could see the line of trees in the distance and then the steep drop-off to the gorge below. Max waved to her, a cigarette in his hand. She walked to him, and he threw his cigarette butt onto the driveway and rubbed it out with his foot.

"You okay?" he asked. "I see they bandaged you up. The car seems to be working. There's a café in town, I'm told. We can get a quick bite, do our business, and then be on our way."

She looked at him.

"You sure you're okay?" he asked.

"I'm fine."

"And you found where the baby belonged?"

She nodded. The baby was exactly where she belonged.

The only question was where *she* belonged. And she had precious little time to decide the answer.

EIGHT
OCTOBER 2018

Rachel arrived at the airport on Friday in plenty of time for her flight. She hadn't slept much the night before, feeling anxious about both traveling to Europe by herself and her visit to her grandfather. He'd had so much on his mind, so much she wished he'd been able to tell her. But although his words were lost, his meaning was indecipherable.

And it had all begun when she'd shown him the dedication in the book. *For Brielle Aimée.* Maybe there was no meaning at all in his words. Maybe it had simply been the reminder of his daughter's name that had riled him up and confused him. After all, she was *his* baby. Yes, they apparently hadn't spoken for a very long time, but that didn't mean he hadn't loved Rachel's mother or wasn't devastated when she died. Maybe the dedication had upset him because it brought back memories of his estranged daughter.

Or maybe it had brought back memories of his wife, Rachel's grandmother. Rachel knew so little about her. Once at the playground she'd heard her mother talking to her friend about losing Rachel's grandmother to cancer just after Rachel was born. That word, "losing," had haunted her for weeks.

She'd imagined her mother always looking around, hoping her mom would reappear and no longer be lost. Rachel had crawled into her mother's lap and wrapped her arms tightly around her waist that evening. It seemed to her at that moment that the best way to avoid losing someone you loved was to hold on as tightly as you could.

But a few months later she discovered that she hadn't held on tightly enough. Because then it was her turn to lose a mother. Just like her own mother had.

Of course, Rachel was lucky to have had Mrs. May, her grandfather's housekeeper, in her life while she was growing up. A short woman with sturdy legs and a crown of short, silver hair, Mrs. May had continued in the job until last year, when Papy became too much for her to handle and she decided to move in with her sister in Tucson. The mother of two boys who were grown by the time Rachel moved in, Mrs. May had been delighted to have a little girl to help take care of. It was Mrs. May who taught Rachel where babies came from and helped her navigate the intricacies of growing up so she didn't have to discuss anything embarrassing with her grandfather. It was Mrs. May who took her out for ice cream every year on Mother's Day, to distract her from the celebrations her friends were having with their own mothers.

It had never occurred to Rachel that her grandfather might have been grieving for his wife and daughter each year on Mother's Day. But seeing her grandfather's reaction to the dedication, she couldn't help but wonder if he'd been grieving in silence for years, and if she might have helped him if she'd only recognized the signs.

She was making her way to the gate area when her phone rang. Looking at the number, she saw that it was Griffin calling on FaceTime. She ran her fingers through her hair and then answered. He was sitting at a bar, a nearly empty glass of red wine and a half-eaten tin of French fries in front of him.

"Hey, Sherlock," he said. "Here I am, landed in Les Pail—whatever it's called —about an hour ago."

"So what's it like?" she asked as she found a seat by the gate. She was glad that he'd called. His timing was perfect. She needed a smile or a laugh.

"Tiny. The center of town is, like, two steps from the train station. And very European, at least from what I can see in the dark. Winding streets, lots of hills, mountains in the distance, and the buildings all look hundreds of years old. Our guest house is very central, just past this old stone clock tower in what looks like a town square."

"Sounds pretty," she said.

"You'll love it. It's amazing, especially the people. There's this little tavern with a bar that stays open late—I guess there's not much to do here at night other than hang out at a bar. Anyway when I got here, the kitchen was closed—I mean, it's after midnight here—but the owner went to the back and made this whole meal for me. Steak au poivre—do you know it? Steak with this fantastic, creamy sauce, with string beans and French fries, best fries I ever tasted. And an amazing red wine. What a meal!"

She smiled as she watched him take a few skinny French fries and press them into his mouth. It was so in character, so *Griffin*, for him to be out once again late at night, making the most of his time in a new place. Even though she'd only known him for a short time, and only through phone calls and such, she felt like she got him, inside and out. He was like that—a fabulously entertaining open book, a road that took you to the most fascinating places, a train you yearned to board not because you loved the destination but because you knew that wherever you were heading, it would be an incredible ride. She loved how he could be so overjoyed at an unexpectedly delicious meal, how his upbeat responses to life's various situations knew no bounds.

And somehow his attitude was contagious—what other

person on earth would get a restaurant owner in a small village to reopen his kitchen for a guy who'd stumbled inside after midnight? And make him a huge, delicious meal? She had no doubt that the restaurateur also enjoyed the encounter, and rather than being annoyed at the late hour, he was pleased that it was his establishment Griffin had entered. She was sure she'd be a much happier person if she could be more like that. Less inside her head all the time. More determined to let life happen, to seek new experiences, and to believe things would go her way.

"Sounds great," she said. "I'm excited."

He reiterated that he'd be at the station when her train arrived the next evening. "Have a good flight," he said. "Think you'll recognize me? It won't be hard. Not exactly like Grand Central Station, here. Just look for the one guy hanging out on the platform!"

She nodded, and as she ended the call, she promised herself that she would try to soften her fears about what she might learn and be open to what positive things might come. This was the boldest thing she'd ever done, impulsively traveling to a remote village in France to explore the past but also possibly begin the next chapter of her future. It was thrilling that Griffin would be there to meet her. And it made her feel good, that he wanted to help her explore her roots.

What would it be like to wander around town with this handsome man, to see those bright eyes and attractive smile in person, to feel his warmth and relish the live effects of his charisma? She loved his sun-kissed hair, his cute nose with a slight upturn at the tip, his big eyes that truly taught her the meaning of "piercing." She loved the short, well-groomed stubble that lined his chin, and she loved the way he'd look sideways at her, and sometimes wink, when he wanted to challenge her or convey that he knew her almost as well as she knew herself.

When the plane boarded, Rachel settled into her seat, picturing meeting Griffin at the train station the next night. What would he be wearing? What kind of smile would he have when he first saw her? Would he say, "Hey, Sherlock!" as he always did when they spoke? Or would their first sighting of each other in person call for something different? She wondered if he'd say something memorable, something about time and distance, or expectations finally realized, or something about how his priorities changed the moment he saw her standing there in front of him. She thought of the kiss they'd share when she arrived, how soft his lips would feel, how his grasp of her shoulders would be both strong and tender. She imagined telling people how they'd met, how they both knew they were made for each other, and how right it was that fate had implausibly brought them together.

"You are completely hopeless," her friend Nancy, who had suggested Griffin for her library program, had told her on the phone when Rachel had recounted their first phone call. "Yes, he's charming, he's handsome. Yes, he's probably going to be on the national news before long, and millions of women will fall for him. And at his core, he's a nice guy. But he's not interested in what you want.

"I know you want your Prince Charming," she'd said. "But Griffin Reynolds isn't him."

Rachel had heard Nancy out. She knew her friend had her best interests at heart. But Nancy had married her college boyfriend before she'd even graduated and now had three school-age kids. Nancy wasn't reading the situation correctly. She didn't understand what dating was like these days. She didn't know how easy Rachel found it to be with Griffin, no matter that they were in different states or even countries. She didn't know how interested Griffin was in Rachel, how he was always asking questions about her life and her work. She didn't know that to Rachel, speaking with Griffin was like unwrapping the most surprising and amazing birthday present. Every time.

As the plane taxied on the runway and then took flight, Rachel reached into her carry-on and took out her copy of *The Little Lost Fish*. It moved her to think about the book in the context of what she'd reviewed in the research notes on her computer—how the author had worked for the Resistance, how she saved Jewish children by helping to take care of them, how her life and death were a mystery, how some thought she'd been killed by the Nazis. Could Papy possibly have something to do with her brave acts? She put the book on her tray table and turned to that special page again, the page that had driven her grandfather to tears two nights ago:

The baby fish searches with open eyes
I'm going home, home now, his song
To the place where my heart lies
To the home where I belong...

The words were even more haunting as she thought about the kind of Resistance work C. Tailleur had done. Had she been predicting her own death with these words? Or was she imagining how the children felt, the Jewish children she was trying to save, who must have desperately wished they were back home? She remembered crying in her grandfather's arms whenever he read this page, even though she knew the little creature would be safe in the end. It always struck her as so sad. The poor baby fish searching for all that he'd lost.

She turned the page and studied the next picture. The fish, still in the sea, was lit from behind by some unknown source of light. And because of that light, his shadow appeared, colored in black and dark blue, on the water. Below the picture was the next verse:

*The baby fish sees colors, light rays, shadows chill
And where the dark ghosts curve or lie,
But he's so far from home, so very far still
And doesn't understand how or why...*

Rachel sat back in her chair. While her grandfather's favorite verse had been the previous one, she'd always loved this one the most. The colors, the rays of the sun, and the interplay of light and dark had always fascinated her. She remembered playing in the backyard, jumping from the patio to the lawn, trying to make her shadow look as dark as the baby fish's silhouette in the illustration. What were the rays of light the baby fish saw? A place of freedom, like Switzerland or America? A symbol of faith like the Star of David? What were the shadows and ghosts? The swastikas on the armbands the German officers wore?

In later pages, the book took a decidedly more upbeat tone. A little girl appears toward the middle of the book and becomes the protagonist for a time. It seems that the baby fish becomes her pet, and when she leaves on outings, she hides the fishbowl on a shelf in her closet, blocked by coats and old toys. On one adventure, the little girl goes boldly into the forest and gets lost for a time among the tall shrubs and thick vines, each of which is numbered from one through six. At one point, she comes to a crossroads and doesn't know which path to take. But then a voice inside her head—a voice she believes is that of the fish—leads her back home and to the closet.

Many scholars had come up with interpretations of this part of the book. She hadn't recorded them in the file she'd saved about C. Fauteur on her computer, but reading the verses again now, those interpretations came back to her mind in sharp detail. Some researchers had hypothesized that there were clues for Resistance members nestled in the story, that the words and numbers corresponded to different addresses in Lyon where meetings were held. Others said the colors in the pictures stood for different buildings in Lyon where plans were being developed to double-cross the Nazis and send them into the sightlines of armed Resistance fighters. And there were also some who thought that the verses on these pages contained passwords for admission into Resistance meetings.

Of course, Rachel had never thought about these things when she was growing up. She'd seen the book in a whole other way. She'd found it so wonderful that the fish loved the little girl, and that his love was what kept the girl safe. She remembered how relieved she'd felt when the girl and the fish were reunited, and later when the fish finally found his mother. That's what this book had always reminded her: that it wasn't pointless to hope for better things and to believe that love could cause them to happen.

She wondered, too, if her mother, as a young girl, had had a book or a toy or something that could make her hopeful. Or had it been the birth of her daughter that had made her truly believe in the promise of the future? That seemed likely. Her mother had loved her so much.

When her plane touched down in Dublin, Rachel disembarked and headed for the next gate on her itinerary. But as she approached it, she saw on the large departures board that her flight was delayed by an hour due to poor weather. She wasn't too concerned, since she'd allowed herself plenty of time to get to the train station in Lyon. With a shrug, she changed direction and went to the food court near the security checkpoint to get a sandwich and some coffee.

But back at the gate a little while later, the news was not good. The storm that had caused the original delay was letting up, but according to the gate agent, there was a mechanical problem with the plane, and the flight would not take off for at least an additional two hours. Now Rachel felt herself grow anxious. She didn't want to miss Griffin, didn't want him to go to the train station and find her not there. She found a seat and sent him a quick text: *Looks like I'm delayed. First weather and now something's wrong with the plane. I hope I get there tonight. I'll keep you posted.*

She watched her screen for a bit, waiting for the three dots so she'd know he was responding. But they didn't appear. She told herself that didn't mean anything. After all, it was a Saturday morning, and he was probably sleeping. She found a bookshop in the concourse with a small fiction section. She bought a novel, brought it back to her gate, and tried to lose herself in the story.

The three-hour delay turned into four, and then five, and then the announcement that she'd been dreading came: the flight was canceled. She followed all the other distressed passengers to the boarding counter. The upheaval in her plans was disorienting. She was all alone with no control over her whereabouts.

She eventually made it to the front of the line, and the agent rebooked her on the same flight the next day. Then he directed her to a shuttle bus that would take the stranded passengers to a nearby hotel for the night. On the bus, she sent another text to Griffin, and when he didn't answer, she tried to call him. After all, it was now the middle of the afternoon. He had to be up. But her call went to his voicemail. She tried again a few minutes later.

Again, no response.

At the hotel, she checked into her room and considered calling Nancy or Nick, just to hear a familiar voice. But then she changed her mind. They'd both tell her they'd told her so, that she'd set herself up for this, that maybe she was finally seeing Griffin's true colors. They'd tell her to continue with her trip. Forget him, they'd both say. You can do this yourself.

But she didn't believe Griffin was ignoring her. Or had changed his mind about her. She texted him and updated him with her flight info. And then she decided not to send any more texts or make any more calls. She didn't want to appear as desperate as she felt. She would go ahead with her new itinerary. And she would trust that he'd be there waiting for her, just as he'd promised, despite the changes.

Exhausted from the time change and the stress, Rachel had an early dinner in the hotel café and fell asleep right away when she returned to her room. After a quick breakfast the next morning, she reboarded the airport shuttle. Fortunately things went much smoother at the airport, and her plane took off for Lyon on time. When she arrived, she was glad to see that her suitcase had survived the delay and was right there on the baggage carousel. With her belongings in hand, she found a helpful English-speaking man at the information desk who pointed out where she could get an Uber. The car drove her to Lyon's main transportation hub, where she waited to board the train to Paillettes, twenty-four hours after she'd originally planned to do so.

The train left on time, and after transferring to the local line one hour into the trip, she reached the foothills at the base of the mountains. The train sounded rickety and the mountain was steep, the tracks winding along curves that seemed mere inches from the edge of the cliffs. In the beginning she feared that they would sail right off the edge and down into the water. But she grew calmer and more used to the position of the rails, and soon found herself marveling at the stunning mountainside and glittering stream below. She noticed houses built into the mountains, and wondered who lived there and how they got groceries or other necessities. From time to time, they passed abandoned train stations, stone structures that sparkled in the sunlight, their wooden doors red or blue. They were so picturesque that she took some photos with her phone. The whole route began to strike her as exotic and extremely romantic. She now understood why Griffin had sounded so entranced.

At some point she must have fallen asleep, because she woke with a start when a conductor walked through the train calling, "Paillettes, *prochain arrêt.*" It was almost eight o'clock, and the sky was darkening. She shook awake and rose as the train slowed and then stopped alongside a long stone platform with a wooden sign that read PAILLETTES AU SOMMET. The Glitter at the Summit.

She proceeded through the train and grabbed her suitcase from the luggage rack as the doors slid open. She took a breath and proceeded out of the car. Here it was, she thought. The moment of truth. Either he was there or he wasn't. Either he'd paid attention to her texts and listened to her calls or he hadn't. Either he wanted to see her or he didn't. It was out of her hands.

She stepped off the train and stood still. There weren't many people disembarking, and even fewer were on the platform waiting to greet the people arriving. The mountain air was chilly, and she pulled her coat closer to her neck and looked around. Within a few minutes, she was the only one on the platform.

He wasn't there.

She checked her phone. No texts. No missed calls. No voicemails.

She thought now of her sick grandfather, her lonely life, her questions about her mother. The things in her life she wanted to change. The things she thought this trip could solve. What was she going to do now?

NINE
NOVEMBER 1942

"Jeez, that's quite a bandage," Max said, reaching over the square wooden table to touch her forehead.

She drew back in surprise. She'd forgotten about the cut. "It doesn't hurt anymore," she said, touching the spot with her fingertips.

"It was a nurse you saw?"

"That's what they said."

"I hope she knew what she was doing. Maybe we can get a doctor to check it out before we board the ship. I'm not sure anyone here knows what they're doing."

They were sitting in a café near the center of town, both of them having a baguette filled with alternating tomato slices and mozzarella chunks sprinkled with basil. Celina had fallen in love with French food from the moment she'd set foot in France. It was remarkable that even a small café like this could make a simple sandwich taste so good. But she hadn't been the one to choose her lunch. Max had chosen for both of them, the option he felt would be served the quickest. He was determined to get to the lawyer's office right on time. He didn't want to spend a more than necessary in this, as he put it, "backward town."

They'd walked in silence from the house to the café. As he'd approached the village center, she'd stumbled on a cobblestone underfoot and had to grasp Max's arm to stop herself from falling. She wasn't appropriately dressed for this aged town with its uneven, hilly streets. Her skirt was too tight, her heels too narrow. But then again, she hadn't planned on doing very much other than stop for a quick bite and step into her new office. She found herself thinking of Adele's clothes. She supposed there had to be a place where she could buy slacks like the ones Adele had been wearing. And sensible shoes. She did own some comfortable clothes, but they were packed up in her flat.

Max finished his sandwich and lit up a cigarette. "You were in there a while," he said. "What were they doing?"

Celina hesitated. *Please be careful about what you've seen*, Rémy had said. *It could put us at risk if the wrong people find out.* She remembered the fear on the farmers' faces when the policeman showed up and looked at the baby in her arms. She knew Max wouldn't intentionally put this village in danger. But she wasn't sure she was ready to tell him everything.

"What were they doing?" she repeated. "I don't know. Mostly they were looking for bandages. I think."

"And were you right about…"

She looked up. "Hmmm?"

"You know… were you right about the baby being—"

"It's all fine," she said. "The baby is fine."

"She's going to stay there?"

Celina stayed quiet.

"Okay, you're right. Let's not talk about it anymore." He pushed his plate away. "Let's forget it all happened. Come on, finish up. We need to get going."

Celina put her elbows on the table and rubbed her eyelid with her fingertips.

"Cel, what's going on?" he said.

"Hey, Max," she started. "What... what would you think about staying overnight? There has to be an inn where we could stay."

"Stay?" he asked. "Why on earth would we do that?"

"So I can rest? I mean, yes, that's what I need. It's been a rough morning with the crash and all. I could use a rest," she said.

Max stamped his cigarette butt in the ashtray on the table. "No, we are not staying. You can sleep on the way back. Sir—um, monsieur?" he called to the server. "Uh, check?"

"*L'addition, s'il vous plaît?*" Celina said when the server looked over.

Max stood and reached into his trouser pocket for his wallet. "I still can't believe we even came here," he muttered. "What was that husband of yours thinking?"

"He wasn't thinking anything," she said. "He didn't buy the house. It was an inheritance."

"Yeah, well, he should have sold it a long time ago. Ridiculous town."

Celina looked around, glad that there were only a few other people in the place and they didn't appear to understand English. She wouldn't have wanted them to hear Max's insults. It was a pretty town. Emile had spoken so lovingly of it, and of his memories of coming here as a little boy. The happy games outside, the warm fires inside at night. He'd even drawn pictures of the place for a children's book he wanted to write someday. He'd shown them to her the first time she'd set foot in his apartment. She remembered one drawing he'd made of himself as a little boy. He'd drawn a frown on his face, an upside-down U, because the summer was over and he had to leave. She'd fallen in love with Emile that night. With his eye for beautiful things, his ability to infuse them with love and make them even more beautiful. A stone fireplace. A pile of autumn leaves. An ocean. A family.

"It's not a ridiculous town," she said. "Especially not now."

"What do you mean?"

She decided she wanted him to know the truth. She was mindful of Rémy's words, but she knew she could trust her brother. "They explained it to me when they took the baby. Max, this isn't just some random mountain town. Maybe it was when Emile's grandfather lived here. But it's more now."

Max sat back down. "What are you talking about?"

She lowered her voice. "Max, you have to keep it to yourself, what I'm going to tell you. Because I don't want to lie to you. But the place where I left the baby—it's not just any house. It's Emile's house. My house. They moved into it because it was empty. The director there—he'd been trying to get in touch with Emile.

"Max, they're hiding Jewish children," she said. "It's disguised as a school to throw the Nazis off. But it's not. It's a secret orphanage. And they need the house. So I'm not going to see the lawyer. I'm not going to sell it."

Max let out a harsh breath. "So that's what you've decided, have you?"

She nodded.

He shook his head. "You realize, of course, that if you leave things like this, you may not even have a house to come back to. If the Nazis take over this part of France, they're sure to confiscate any property owned by Americans. They'll arrest this guy, take all the kids, and house their own people here."

"I guess that's a chance he's willing to take," she said. "If I sell the house, they'll be kicked out right away. I guess he thinks it's safest his way for now."

Max rubbed his chin, then sat back in his chair, throwing up his hands. "Fine," he said. "That's fine, if that's what you want to do. It's your decision, I guess. I can't make you sign those papers if you've already decided not to. But that doesn't change the fact that we need to leave here right now. Let them do whatever they're doing with those kids. We don't need to know about it. I don't want to get involved. I don't want you involved either."

He reached into his shirt pocket and then patted his jacket pocket. "Damn, I'm out of cigarettes. Where can I get a pack, do you think? Never mind, I'll ask the guy. Wait here."

She watched him approach the server and show him his empty cigarette package. For a moment, she felt sorry for him, for not being able to communicate in French with ease. He had such a hard time feeling comfortable. And sometimes it seemed he hated himself for being weak like that. When they were young, he hadn't been good at math and hated doing his sums, and he'd throw toys and books, anything he could get his hands on, across the room even when their parents were trying to calm him and help him. He didn't want their help; he wanted to do it himself. Then he'd withdraw, his eyes lowered, his chin down. She'd often thought he'd missed out on so much in life because he was so defensive. Never taking a chance. And mad at himself for being that way.

Max returned to the table with the check and a fresh pack of cigarettes in his hand. He tossed some cash on the table and helped her on with her coat. "I gave the waiter a little extra to call the lawyer and cancel the appointment. Not a good idea to just not show up. Now's not a good time to make anyone angry." He took her protectively by the elbow and guided her out the door.

Outside, the sun was sitting atop the glistening mountains in the distance. She thought about the way the baby had looked up at her as she lay there beneath the bushes. How she'd fixed her eyes on Celina's. How she'd kicked her feet in anticipation of being picked up. Her willingness to trust had been so sweet.

Celina imagined feeding her a bottle, watching as she drank, her lips clenching and releasing rhythmically with every sip. She imagined lifting the bottle from time to time to check how much was left. "What a good eater you are!" she'd say and return the nipple to the baby's mouth.

"What's wrong?" Max asked.

She looked toward the mountains. "I keep thinking about that baby. The children. She has no one. None of them do," she added.

"And that's why they're here. You got her where she needed to be. Put it out of your mind."

"It felt so right to be holding her."

"But she's not your baby."

"It felt for a minute like she was."

He stopped to light a fresh cigarette and took a pull, then continued speaking as he exhaled, the smoke exiting his mouth and nose in ugly, chaotic spurts. "For God's sake, Cel," he said. "Now you're making me worry. I'm concerned about you, that bump on your head. You need to be checked out. Look, you've been through a lot. You've been living too long with war and death. It was a bad idea, coming here. Trust me, we need to leave."

He took her elbow again and led her toward the field where the car had crashed. As they walked, he talked about their parents and their older brother, Carl, whose wife was expecting her fourth child this winter. How Mom was preparing for the new baby, how Dad was buying a train set, how they were all so hopeful for a boy, surely it would be a boy this time. Max's grasp on her elbow was tight, and for a moment it made her feel safe. It sounded nice, what Max was saying. It was true, Paris had been horrible—the soldiers, the roundups, the killings. Nothing like when she had moved into Emile's small flat, their life together fueled by their love and their dream to create children's books. She'd written home about their marriage, even though her letters likely never made it there. She'd imagined her parents coming over one day. She knew they'd love him once they'd adjusted to the marriage. He'd always been so likable, so enthusiastic, so loving. And he'd been so excited about starting a family. He'd built a rocker, even though he was far from handy, and she'd picked the fabric for the cushions—yellow with butterflies and carnations. Soon after, she'd begun to feel a fluttering in her belly that felt like nerves but wasn't nerves at all. It was her baby saying good morning to her, to the world. Celina had adored that feeling. She'd look out the window at the streets of Paris and feel the flutter and think she was the luckiest woman who ever lived.

She now stroked the area of her abdomen that had been starting to swell. It was flat now. She could barely remember how that fluttering felt. She only knew that it was different from anything she'd ever felt before. Sometimes she couldn't even summon any recollection of how it had all been. But today, she felt it. Today, when she was holding Brielle, she remembered how it felt to be someone's mama.

"The car is just ahead," Max said. "We drove it off the field and parked it on the street. It works fine. Although I'll probably have to drop the price to sell it before we leave. Nobody's going to pay top dollar with all the bodywork it's gonna need."

The one thing we are missing is a teacher, Rémy had said. *We all pitch in, but it's not the same.*

Celina slowed and looked up. She gestured with her chin toward the blue sky and the orange and gold leaves on the tall trees. "It really is beautiful here," she said.

Max nodded, clearly placating her to get her to keep walking. She held onto his arm as they started down a rocky slope, tripping and righting herself by leaning on him.

"Emile wanted to show this place to me," she said. "He'd described the mountains, the trees, the sparkling water below. The narrow train tracks. The stone buildings..." She didn't now why she was saying all this, listing the town's attributes. She supposed it was because she was leading up to something. And she wanted acknowledgment that she'd lost someone very special and was entitled to grieve. Max saw her grief only as something to be fixed.

Maybe, she thought, she was also looking for acknowledgment of who she was. Of her thoughts. Her need to choose her own next step. She'd been younger and stronger when she'd moved to Paris. She was wiser and sadder now. But she wasn't broken. She could be strong again.

"Emile loved visiting here when he was a kid," she continued. "He said he couldn't wait to bring a baby here. He wanted so much to be a fath—"

"There it is," Max said, pointing to a ridge just beyond a small church. He peeled her hand from his elbow so he could go there.

She watched him, wondering what Emile would say to her if he were here. Would he be disappointed if she got into the car? If she forgot about the children, pushed all this out of her mind until Rémy's words no longer replayed so clearly in her head? A neighbor had told her that if she concentrated hard enough, she'd hear Emile in her heart. That was what it meant, that people live on. She wondered if Emile knew, somehow, what she was facing. She looked skyward again.

What would you have me do? she asked.

Max circled the car, checking out the damage for what she was sure was at least the tenth time. From her vantage point, she could see that the right fender was scratched and the roof was dented. They were lucky the edge of some boulders hadn't cut right through the metal roof and sawed their skulls in half. Max had been right—it was best to leave town as soon as possible. They shouldn't drive on these roads after the sun started going down. They hadn't even been able to make it up here just in the light of day. There were risks all around. The funny thing was that if you didn't know the truth, if you could only see the shops along the main street, it would be easy to believe that you were somewhere safe. In a village just like any other village, if you didn't try too hard to see behind the facade.

But then again, as she'd learned, that was when the danger came. When you weren't looking closely enough.

"It'll get us back," Max said. "It could have been worse." He looked at her, exasperated. "Celina, get in the car!"

"She needs me, Max," she said. "She's a baby without a mama. And I'm... I'm a mama without a baby."

He scowled at her. "What are you saying?"

"I want to help."

"But she isn't your baby! We don't even know where she came from."

"Does that matter?"

"She's not yours!"

"I know, but... she kind of is. She's everyone's. Isn't that what we learned from the farmers today? When they wouldn't give her to that policeman? That we're all... involved?

"I know you think I'm not making sense," she said. "But I have a feeling this is what I'm supposed to do. This is what Emile would have me do."

"We're going home."

"No, you're going. I need to stay."

"You can't take care of her. You don't know how to be a mother." His words were like a punch. He stopped and shook his head. "That's not what I meant—"

"No one knows how to be a mother until they become one."

Max gritted his teeth and took a few steps away from her. Then he walked back. "What about Mom and Dad? How are they going to feel when I show up and you don't? Do you know how that's going to make Mom feel? You're her only daughter, for God's sake."

"I'll write to them. They'll understand. Or they won't. It doesn't matter now."

"Look, this is getting us nowhere. I'm going in the car and counting to ten. You have until then to get in the car with me."

"I'm not going to."

"Fine. You're a grown-up. Do what you want. But don't change your mind and start calling me. Don't expect me to come back for you."

"I won't."

Max waved her off and slid behind the wheel. He started the motor. She expected that he'd drive off, probably going way too fast out of frustration and anger. But then he rolled down the window.

"You're sure you want to do this?" he asked gently.

She nodded.

He looked away from her. "You're as stubborn as all of us in this family," he said. "Come on in. The least I can do is give you a ride up the hill."

She smiled and climbed in, and they started up to the house.

When they arrived, he put the car in park and took her elbow. "Wait," he said. "I didn't mean it. You can call me if you need me. You know I'll come back for you. Daddy's princess."

She leaned over and kissed his cheek, and he hugged her harder than he ever had before. She left the car, then gave a small wave as she watched him drive away. When he was out of sight, she turned toward the front door.

Standing on the top step was Rémy.

"I heard you had a job opening for a teacher," she said.

He nodded. "Come inside. Let me tell you more."

TEN
OCTOBER 2018

Rachel stood on the empty train platform, not knowing what to do next. She'd been so sure Griffin would be here as he'd promised. Yes, she was a day late, but she'd updated him several times about the change. And if he'd missed her texts and had shown up yesterday, he could have easily looked online to see what had happened. He had all her flight information. And it wasn't as though she had begged him to join her. He had offered to! It had been his idea. He'd suggested the timing because he was waiting for new instructions for his project and had a few days off from work.

Still, the platform remained empty. Except for her.

Her heart started to race and she felt her cheeks flush, even though the night was cool. It was an uncomfortable feeling, and yet it was also familiar. She was no stranger to being abandoned, as her father had done it to her when she was a baby. Her mother had never said anything about him, and Rachel had been too young and too content when her mother was alive to raise any questions. When she was in fifth grade and working on a family history paper for school, she had no choice but to ask her grandfather about her dad. She suspected he wouldn't provide many answers, and she was right—he told her he'd never met her father and had no idea where to find him. She explained the situation to her teacher, who said not to worry—Rachel could focus her paper on the aspects of her family that she knew. It was a kind response, and yet Rachel could feel the pity in her teacher's voice, and the shame she felt from that encounter never let go. Her father's abandonment felt like a punishment for wrongs she didn't even know she'd committed. And the best way to deal with it, she found, was to ignore the unknown, as her grandfather did.

Of course her mother hadn't left her intentionally; still, it had felt to Rachel like being abandoned when she had to leave her home and her familiar apartment complex to go live with a grandfather she'd never met or heard about before. Back in those early days, she'd often tell herself that her mother was still alive. Sometimes she imagined that her mother had been kidnapped and hidden in the tower of a gigantic castle, and she was the one who'd save her. She envisioned her mother hugging her and thanking her for being so brave and never giving up.

Other times, she imagined confronting her mother in a far-off palace, where her mother had run off to: "Why did you leave?" And staying angry until her mother broke down in tears and begged for forgiveness.

Rachel dropped the handle of her suitcase and put her hands on her waist. It was just plain wrong, what Griffin had done. If his plans had changed, the decent thing would have been to reach out to let her know. It wasn't as though he'd stood her up at a restaurant, which would have been bad enough. No, he'd abandoned her in a remote village in a foreign country after making concrete plans to meet her. She was mad at him, but more than that, she was mad at herself. She'd been so sure he was sincere. After all she'd been through in her life, she should have been smarter. How had she fallen for his lines? How had she let herself become a fool?

The platform was dark, with just a few lampposts throwing tiny ovals of weak yellow light on the stone walkway. It felt eerie, standing here by herself in this strange town. She needed to pull herself together and go to the guest house she'd booked. She was foggy from all the travel and couldn't think anymore. All she wanted was some comfort food and a bed where she could sleep.

She went down the steps and left the station plaza. Fortunately the center of town was close by, as Griffin had said. At least he'd given her that helpful tidbit. And it appeared the way he'd described it as well—winding, hilly streets with stone buildings that looked ancient. She'd never been anywhere like this before. She walked along a stone path that led to what seemed to be the main street of Paillettes. A few blocks uphill was a tall clock tower on a stone quad from which narrower streets emerged like spokes of a wheel. Griffin had said their guest house, La Maison au Sommet, was just beyond the clock tower, and again, she was glad the information was accurate. It was a two-story gray stone building with a sign hanging from an iron post that said it was erected in 1729.

Wheeling her suitcase behind her, she went up the three steps. The red wooden door was unlocked, and she pressed down on the brass lever to let herself in. The lobby was small and quaint, with two wood-frame sofas on either side of a square dark-wood coffee table with carved legs. By the wall was a curved, shoulder-high wooden counter with some pamphlets in a pile. Across from the counter, the lobby opened up on to a tiny bakery, which seemed to be closed for the day, its lights dimmed and the tables empty.

There was no one in the lobby, so she stepped into the bakery. Behind a display counter filled with pastries and chocolates, she saw an older man with a shock of white hair cleaning the spout of an espresso maker with a pink rag, while a woman with equally white hair in a low bun was stacking plates and bowls on a shelf along the back wall.

"Um... excuse me?" she said. "*Excusez-moi?*"

The man looked up, startled.

"Um, hello," she said. "*Bonjour.* I mean, *bonne nuit. Je suis... j'ai...* checking in?" she said, finally giving up.

"Ah, of course, welcome," the man said, and she was relieved that his English was easy to understand. In a tiny town like this, it would have been possible—likely, even—that people would speak only French.

"Is there someone at the front desk to help me?" she asked.

"*C'est moi.* I do it all," he said with a smile, tossing his hair back from his eyes, which were heavily lidded. His face and neck were deeply wrinkled. "Allow me a moment, *s'il vous plaît.*" He rinsed the rag in the sink, looking over his shoulder. "May I offer you something to drink? Water, tea? Or a coffee, maybe?" He had a gentle, tuneful voice, and she liked him immediately.

"Coffee sounds nice," she said, thinking she could use a shot of caffeine as she navigated the evening and ultimately found a place to eat. The man prepared it for her in a china cup on a saucer. He carried it over to her. "*Voilà.*"

"Thank you. *Merci,*" she said and took a sip. It was rich and nutty, and just the right temperature, not too hot. She remembered what Griffin had said about how delicious the food was here. She was looking forward to a good meal. It had been a long time since she'd eaten.

"Follow me," the man said. "Bring your coffee. We'll get you settled. Where are you traveling from?"

"New York."

"That's a long way. What brings you to our little village?"

"Well..." She didn't know what to say. Should she mention Jane? "A few reasons," she answered.

They reached the counter in the lobby, and the man walked

behind it. He put a file folder on it and removed some papers. "Your name, mademoiselle?" he asked.

"Rachel Eggerton."

"Welcome, Mademoiselle Eggerton. I am Claude, your host. I'm glad you made it. We were expecting you yesterday."

"My plane was delayed. I did send an email—"

"No problem. It's all good. And your credit card?"

She put her coffee cup on the countertop and reached into her bag for her wallet. She handed him her card and watched him copy the number onto a form. It was so strange to see him doing the paperwork by hand. She couldn't remember the last time she'd seen that.

He returned the card and gave her a pen to sign the form. "So I see you are planning to stay with us for six nights—well, five, since you were delayed," he said.

She nodded. She wasn't sure she'd stay that long, with Griffin not here. But she would worry about that later.

"Your room is 201," he said. "It's up the stairs to the right. I can help you with your luggage."

"That's okay, thank you. I've got it. But... there was someone I was supposed to be meeting. His name is Griffin Reynolds. I think he arrived here on Friday."

"Monsieur Reynolds? But he left this morning," Claude said.

"He left *today*?"

"He said something about his work."

"But..." She didn't know what to think. She couldn't believe he'd left when she'd texted that she was arriving tonight.

"Although he did tell me, mademoiselle, that he was supposed to have met someone here," Claude added. "He said she never showed up."

"What?" she said. "But that's me. I'm the person he was meeting."

"He was expecting you yesterday, as we were. He said

maybe you decided not to come. He said he was... what's the expression? Stood out? Stood over?"

"Stood up?" she said. "Why would he think that? I texted him about the plane. It was delayed because of a storm and then a mechanical problem. I emailed here, too—"

"And that is the problem," Claude said. "That same storm. It blew through here, too. The internet has been down ever since."

"You have no internet at all?" He shook his head, an apologetic smile on his face. "Not at all?"

"That is correct, I'm afraid. No phone service either."

"So he didn't get my texts? And you didn't get my email?"

He shook his head. "That's why I am handwriting," he said, gesturing toward the paperwork on the desk. "It happens occasionally. More often in the winter, when the snows come. I know it must sound shocking to you. But we are used to it."

"So he didn't get my messages? He thought I changed my mind and decided not to come?" That explained why he hadn't responded to her. She felt horrible for the things she'd been thinking. He was probably thinking bad things about her, too! But had he really thought she'd change her mind and stand him up? She wouldn't have done that. Although she'd been thinking that was exactly what he'd done. They didn't know each other very well yet. It was easy to imagine the worst.

"Oh, no," she groaned. "Did he say where he was going?"

"No, I'm sorry."

"And the internet is still out?"

"All communications are. As I say, it happens here."

"So no phone calls or anything?"

"Not for now. It won't be long. Maybe another two or three days—"

"Two or three *days*?" She didn't want to be rude. It was all just so hard to believe. Back at work, sometimes the library was knocked offline, but that was only for an hour or so. And even then, people flipped out at the inability to get online. Typically they'd all use the cell service on their phones. It was unheard of to be out of touch for days at a time.

"There's nothing to be done, I'm afraid," Claude said. "Except wait it out."

"And there's no way I can reach him now? Or he can reach me?"

"I suppose you can take the train back to Lyon and try to reach him from there. Although it sounded like he was going to stay up here in the mountains. And if he's up here, you probably wouldn't be able to reach him even from Lyon. When our town goes down, usually all the towns around here do as well."

She groaned and threw her head back. One delay at the airport and now everything had fallen apart. He hadn't heard any of her messages, and he hadn't been able to send any to her. And it seemed he thought she'd decided to bail on him. She wouldn't be able to correct the error for as many as three days—and she couldn't try to find him because she had no idea where he went.

And it was even worse, she thought, even bigger than just Griffin. She was isolated from the rest of the world. No way to reach anyone unless she took the train back to Lyon. She had hoped to stay in touch with her grandfather during the week, to call a few times and ask Kate to bring the phone to him. What if he wanted to hear her voice? What if he thought she'd abandoned him?

"Oh, damn it!" she said, the "d" explosive coming from her mouth. She was surprised at her behavior. She never acted this way in public. But what a mess this had turned into! She knew she should control herself. But she thought Claude might understand. She probably wasn't the first tourist to be thrown by this very situation. "I'm sorry," she said, as she placed her bag on the countertop to put her wallet back inside. "It's just... oh damn it, I'm just so—"

Suddenly the sound of china shattering overtook the area, the clatter echoing on all sides. She looked down to see that her bag had pushed her coffee cup and saucer off the counter and onto the stone floor.

And that wasn't all. Next to her, a young man had arrived, handsome, with curly dark hair. He had on a light blue shirt and white slacks—and he wasn't just wearing that. No, now he was wearing her coffee. He was covered from his chest to his shoes.

"Oh no! Oh, I'm so sorry," she exclaimed. She couldn't believe she'd done that. She'd never let her anger take hold like that. She'd never spilled coffee all over someone before. "I don't know what came over me. I'm so sorry—"

Claude rushed over with a small broom and dustpan, while the elderly woman who'd been stacking plates in the bakery now came running with a mop and bucket, along with a couple of white cloth napkins. She handed them to the coffee-covered man, who proceeded to try to dry himself off, though his shirt now had a huge cloud-shaped brown splotch across the chest, and his pants were spotted down both legs. Rachel squatted to help clean up the broken china, but the woman tapped her hand and shook her head, squeezing her eyes and repeating, "Oooh, oooh," clearly trying to say that she'd hurt herself by handling the shards.

Rachel rose and watched the activity. She felt embarrassed and awkward, especially since there was nothing for her to do except continue to repeat how sorry she was. She regretted even more that she'd ever agreed to come here. She never did well when she left her familiar surroundings, which was why she so rarely did. Being out in the world, away from home and among strangers, was fraught with risks. She thought she should try to make arrangements to go home tomorrow, but then realized that without internet or cell service, she couldn't even do that. She supposed she would have to make her way back to Lyon by train and then book a flight. She hoped that this place had a paper schedule of train departures.

Finally the cleaning was done, and the floor was broomed and spotless. The only remnant of her outburst was the man's stained clothing.

"I'm so sorry," Rachel repeated. *"Je suis... je suis..."* But the man wasn't listening to her, and she didn't know what more to say. She couldn't keep apologizing, but what else could she do? All she wanted was to go to her room and try to pretend that the whole thing had never happened.

"Don't feel bad, mademoiselle," Claude said. "What is the English expression? No harm, no foul?" He went behind the desk and handed her the key, then motioned toward the staircase. She looked back at the young man. The woman now brought over a damp cloth, and with everyone's attention fixed on the stain, Rachel took the opportunity to rush to the stairway.

She climbed to the second floor, dragging her suitcase behind her. She would leave tomorrow for sure.

She only hoped she wouldn't have to see this man again before she made it out of town. Although in a town this small, that didn't seem likely.

ELEVEN

NOVEMBER 1942

By the end of her first week in Paillettes, Celina felt fully a part of the household. Rémy had put her in a comfortable bedroom on the second floor, with a single bed covered in a warm feather cover and a small bathroom next to the closet. The walls were old and thick and the window small, but it faced east so let in the morning sunshine. Celina didn't have any clothes with her, but she borrowed from Adele while she waited for her former landlady to send her the few boxes that remained in her apartment, after she'd sold her furniture and packed up her photographs and keepsakes with Max's things. In addition to her clothes, the boxes contained the initial drawings and verses that she and Emile had been working on for the children's book he'd wanted to write. She was glad she hadn't sent those drawings home with Max. They made her feel close to Emile, and she wanted to keep them with her.

Her room also contained a simple wooden crib that Rémy had salvaged from the attic, where furniture donated by owners of the surrounding farms was stored. Celina had insisted on her first night in the house that Brielle not sleep with the other children. She was just a baby and needed someone to pick her up and cuddle her if she cried at night.

"Besides," she added, "that policeman—Red, did you call him? He thinks she's my child. It would make sense that she and I would share a room. He'd think something was up if he went upstairs and saw otherwise."

She watched Rémy consider this. They both felt sure that Officer Dumont—Red—had suspicions about the house. He showed up there frequently, ostensibly because he liked Adele's cooking, but Celina knew he often wandered around the house and even eyed the upstairs bedrooms, which were furnished with beds and storage cabinets holding clean, folded clothes. The pretext for these furnishings, Rémy had explained to her, was that the rooms needed to be ready in case the children had to sleep there should a heavy winter snowfall make it impossible for them to return to their "homes" in the village after school. Adele and Marie made sure to make the beds and straighten up the rooms early each morning after the children were dressed, to bolster the charade.

"That does make sense," Rémy had said as they'd sat in the living room that night while the fire burned low. "We'll keep the baby in your room." Celina was glad he agreed. Despite his often easygoing demeanor, she was finding him to be an unusual and complex person. He was charismatic and charming to outsiders, and so good with the children. And yet, at his core he was a man of few words. She knew he carried the weight of the world on his shoulders. He worried about procuring enough food to keep the children nourished, and enough clothing and shoes to accommodate their growing bodies, and enough firewood for the fireplace to help the old, lumbering furnace keep the house warm. He was grateful to the townspeople who would drop off food from their farms and clothing their children had outgrown. And he left town to go to Lyon every few weeks, always returning with warm clothing and dry goods and books and games.

But first and foremost, he was concerned about the children's safety. He drilled them to make sure they all knew their fake names and the addresses of the houses where their pretend families lived. She admired how he turned these critical lessons into a game, giving the children a tiny piece of candy he'd stashed from his trips to Lyon each time they answered correctly—and an extra piece if they said it calmly and while looking him straight in the eye. And one of the initial things he told her when she moved in was to never ask questions of anyone other than him.

"Take a lesson from the farmers who helped you with your car," he said. "Be discreet. We have workers coming in and out all the time—landscapers, doctors, couriers, occasionally a plumber or tradesman. Many are with the Resistance. Some are just pretending to hold these jobs. Let people carry on with their business. If anything looks odd to you, let it be."

"But what does that mean—looks odd?" she'd asked.

"Anything that feels unexpected," he said. "A letter that shows up and then goes missing. A plumber who spends no time on the pipes. An inventory of supplies or a weather forecast typed up and left out on the bookshelf. A book that isn't put away. You'll see what I mean. You can put lives at risk if you upset the codes they're leaving for one another. These people have work to do. Don't get in their way."

She'd felt a chill as she'd absorbed his words. The cheery pictures on the walls and multiple pairs of shoes warming by the fire belied the danger infused in the house. They made her shudder, paradoxically reminding her that this was anything but an ordinary school.

Nevertheless, Celina quickly acclimated to the layout and routines of the place. Not counting Brielle, the six Jewish children living in the house were evenly divided, three girls and three boys. With Brielle in her arms, Celina watched them take their seats at the table in the dining room every morning and enjoy the breakfast Adele prepared for them, usually baguette slices with jam or cheese if it was available, or an omelet made sometimes with fresh eggs from a neighboring farm and other times with the powdered variety Rémy was able to bring back from Lyon. They were just like any children. They quarreled, they teased, they stained their clothes or neglected to use their napkin and left the table with a crumb of bread or dot of jam on their chin or cheek. They struggled to lace up their shoes or button their clothes, they forgot to clean their hands after playing outside and needed to be sent to wash up before they were allowed to eat.

But there was something else she sometimes noticed, a touch of weightiness in their eyes. They all seemed a bit older than five or six. She couldn't imagine what they'd seen or the fear they'd felt, the horrific memories they might have of their parents being beaten and arrested. And yet, they made funny faces and loved to giggle and enjoyed getting new—albeit second-hand—clothes, the boys in trousers that were often too big, the girls in smocked dresses, all of them wearing warm cardigans as the weather grew colder. Their delight in what each new day would bring showed a resilience that often brought her close to tears.

After breakfast, several children from the village would arrive at the house, helping to further the ruse that the orphanage was a regular school. They would all gather in the living room, and Celina would escort them to the carriage house out back, which had once been the stable for Emile's family's horses and now was a makeshift classroom. Adele or Marie would tend to Brielle while Celina conducted lessons. She would divide the children according to their abilities and tailor her instruction to their academic level, teaching some their letters and numbers and helping the more advanced ones begin to read from storybooks. She loved watching the children learn and play, building with blocks and painting with watercolors or playing ball outside when it was time for recess.

Then came lunch, and then rest time, and afterward her students went outside again. Rémy insisted that the children get a lot of fresh air now, as once winter kicked in, they might not be able to go outside for days on end. When the afternoon sun had lowered in the sky, Marie would take the village children back to their homes, and those that remained would have their dinner —often bread and soup with vegetables like carrots, cabbage, and parsnips, thickened with cornstarch. On lucky nights, there was chicken or pork. Celina loved watching the children's faces when they spotted meat on their plates, since it was so rarely available. She loved seeing them filled up and well nourished.

The week after Celina arrived, the inevitable happened: Germany dissolved the free zone and took over all of France. Now the situation in Paillettes was even more dangerous: not only did they have to worry about French policemen like Red; they also had to face the possibility that Nazi soldiers would show up in town.

Celina was often on edge now, especially when Red showed up at the house. Sometimes he'd come to her classroom, and she'd do her best to stay calm. She'd smile and welcome him, and she always had the children greet him respectfully: "*Bonjour*, Officier Dumont." Still, it unnerved her when he stayed to watch her conduct her lessons. She knew he was doing his job, walking his beat as police officers did in any city. But there was a big difference. Red wasn't simply writing parking tickets, rescuing stray cats from trees, or chasing down a shoplifter. No, he was scrutinizing everyone in the house and waiting for someone to slip up, to say something they shouldn't. She knew that if he caught her in a lie, they could all—children and adults alike—be turned over to the Germans. She watched the children closely when he was there, ready to interrupt if a child started to talk about their past life or mention a Jewish holiday or ritual.

Sometimes he'd stay for lunch, and she'd offer him whatever there was—usually meatless stew or pâté, maybe an omelet—while Adele saw to the children in the dining room. He'd ask her innocuous questions—how her family back in America was, what her life had been like there, how she was enjoying working here as a teacher—and she'd cuddle Brielle in her arms, saving her own portion for when her appetite would return later. Sometimes he'd tell a riddle or recite a limerick, and she'd laugh out loud to please him. She barely breathed until he was finally out of the house.

One morning Rémy came to the classroom to drill the children on their names and addresses. He liked to drill all the children together—both the Jewish children and those from the village—so all were comfortable with the responses. As the exercise began, Celina's eye caught sight through the small oval window of someone approaching, and she quickly realized it was Red. She knew it could be catastrophic if Red saw what was going on, so she gave a quick wave to Rémy and exited the classroom.

"Officier Dumont," she said, smiling brightly. "How nice to see you."

"Madame," he responded. "You are leaving the classroom? I was coming to observe your lesson. I can see that my friend Rémy is conducting class this morning. That seems quite unusual..."

"He's giving me a little rest," she said. "I had trouble sleeping last night, a slight headache. I'm not quite myself this morning and was going to fix some tea. Would you care to join me?"

She hoped he'd say no. He made her so nervous. But he

THE SECRET ORPHANAGE 107

greed, and she had to admit it was best to entertain him here and keep him away from the children. Trying to appear confident, she gently took his elbow and led him back inside the house and to the kitchen. She should have known he'd choose it over the classroom, as he never said no to food or to tea, which was in such short supply these days. She put on the kettle and took plates, cups, and saucers out of the cupboard, as he seated himself at the table. "So how long have you been here now?" he asked.

"Two weeks tomorrow," she said, looking toward the cabinets, knowing that she'd come across as less ill at ease if she wasn't looking at him. She went to get spoons, willing her hands not to tremble.

"And you are happy here? Won't you miss your family in America, with Christmas coming next month? Won't they miss seeing you and your daughter?"

She paused, looking down at the silverware drawer as she formulated her answer. She'd explained to him the week she arrived that her husband had unexpectedly died—something she said was too personal to reveal when he showed up at the scene of the car crash. She'd added that she had been a teacher before she came to France and was happy to stay here. She'd given a fake name, Tailleur, which she'd thought up on the spur of the moment. She didn't want him to investigate and discover that her husband had been with the Resistance and the two of them had never had a child. She also didn't want him to figure out that she was the owner of the house—she remembered how Max had warned that the Nazis would confiscate properties owned by Americans. To her relief, he hadn't questioned her further. She had the feeling that he liked her and didn't want to make trouble for her. But having him like her scared her almost as much as if he hated her.

"Of course, I will miss them. But I'm a teacher, and I have a job to do. And this is a lovely town. I think it's a marvelous place to celebrate the holidays with my daughter."

He nodded as she poured the tea and then brought over a basket of baguettes and a tin of breadcrumb cookies that Adele had baked early that morning. He took one of each and accepted the pot of jam she offered.

Just then she heard the outside door opening. Daniel, one of the boys who lived in the house, skipped into the kitchen.

"Madame!" he sang out. "Madame! Monsieur Rémy said he left the candy here and I can ask you for one! I said my whole new name without even a little mistake! The best I ever did—"

Celina gasped and ran over to him, clutching his shoulders and squatting down to look directly into his eyes. "That's wonderful," she said. "But you know you're not supposed to interrupt adults when they're speaking to one another. Apologize to Officier Dumont, and I will give you a bowl of candies to take out to the classroom."

"But I did so good—"

"Apologize, Daniel. Now," she said firmly.

The little boy sighed. Celina felt horrible that she couldn't praise him for saying his assumed name correctly. He'd had trouble remembering the last name, Archambeau, and Rémy had been working extra hard with him. But Red couldn't know anything about these fake names. She only hoped she'd stopped him in time.

"*Je vous prie de m'excuser*, Officier Dumont," Daniel said.

"Very good," Celina said, handing him a small bowl with pink candies. "Now you bring these out to Monsieur Rémy. You tell him very clearly that Officier Dumont is here having tea with me. No more children are to disturb us. Can you tell him that?"

Daniel nodded and headed out the door.

She waited until he closed it, then turned back to the table.

"These children, what a handful!" she said. "No manners at all!"

Red eyed her pointedly. "The boy. What did he mean by 'new name'? What is Rémy doing out there?"

"Oh, it's... a game," she said, nodding. "A new way of teaching them letters. He makes up names with different letter combinations, and if the children sound it out correctly, they get a treat. We differ about this. I'm more traditional. But if it works... I mean, why fight him? I've asked him to record his observations so we can begin to assess—"

She was stumbling along, making up this explanation on the spot and willing her voice not to quiver, when Rémy came rushing into the kitchen. He was breathless, his eyes wide. She knew he had understood the message she had asked Daniel to convey and was panicked, as he otherwise never would have left the children in the classroom unsupervised. She suspected he'd envisioned her, Adele, Robert and Marie standing against the wall, waiting for Nazi officers to arrive and pull them out of the house and into waiting cars. She knew he'd have sacrificed his own life before he'd have let the Nazis take them or the children.

She watched Rémy spot Red at the table. Then he turned to her. "Everything okay?" he asked. She could hear his quickened breath.

"What, you mean Daniel?" she said. "Hopefully he wasn't too upset at the way I scolded him. But he has to learn to be more respectful. I was just explaining to Officier Dumont about your lesson, if you can call it that. You know, sounding out made-up names and such. I told him I'm not a fan of such games..."

Red shrugged and spooned jam from the pot. Fortunately he seemed much more interested in his treat than in any new teaching method.

Rémy exhaled, and Celina could see the tension drain from

his body. "So, my officer friend," he said, walking over and patting Red on the shoulder. "What brings you here? Are you eating our food again?"

Red chuckled, wiping his mouth with his napkin. "I'm afraid I am. It's amazing what your sister can do. Does her husband realize they could make a fortune by opening their own restaurant? Why they stay here and work for you, I'll never know. Where is she? Maybe I should suggest that to her."

Celina laughed politely, and Rémy did, too, although she could see there was still a bit of fear remaining in his eyes. He wiped his forehead and exhaled again. She smiled and excused herself to go back to the classroom, glad that Rémy was there to finish entertaining Red. She couldn't wait to leave the kitchen.

Bullet dodged, she thought. Hopefully there wouldn't be any more close calls.

TWELVE
OCTOBER 2018

Rachel entered her room still reliving the awful moment when she heard the cup smash and turned to see the poor man next to her covered in coffee. Leaning against the door, she squeezed her eyes shut, as if that would make the moment stop replaying in her head. She was so embarrassed. How had she let herself lose it like that? How had she forgotten that her coffee cup was right there?

She shook her head to clear away the memory once and for all, and then took a look at her room. It was small and simple, with a double bed, a four-drawer dresser, and a tiny desk near the window. The stone-floor bathroom had a shower stall and a sink with separate hot and cold taps. She wondered if this was the room Griffin had checked out of this morning. After all, the guest house wasn't that big. Of course, the room was clean, with the trash emptied, the floors spotless, and a neatly folded tissue sticking up from the tissue box on the dresser. The pillows on the bed stood upright against the headboard, and the comforter lay uncreased, its edges tucked neatly under the mattress. The bathroom fixtures were gleaming, and the bedroom furniture, though worn, was well polished. A part of her wished she'd find something of his, maybe a coat or a sweater left behind, a business card, or even just a pen slightly askew on the desk. Or better still, a note to her that he'd meant to drop off at the front desk. But there was no trace of him. It almost felt as though she'd invented Griffin. Was he her imaginary friend?

She put her suitcase on the bed and unzipped it. Even though she wasn't sure how long she'd stay, unpacking seemed the most logical thing to do. She examined each item as she lifted it from her suitcase: the blue dress she had packed for tonight's dinner. The tops and nice jeans for the days she'd anticipated spending with Griffin, appreciating his presence and encouragement as she sought to uncover the answers about her mother and grandfather. A pair of dress pants and her favorite blue blouse for another dinner. A pair of joggers and a sweatshirt in case they explored some remote areas. It was just her luck that this perfect rendezvous was never going to happen. And it felt so wrong, that he was gone. It wasn't her intention to miss their arranged meeting time. Things happened sometimes—often, rather—when there was travel involved. He apparently knew that the town was completely cut off. Hadn't he realized that she'd have tried to connect with him, that there'd be messages from her that he couldn't access? Why hadn't he had faith in her? Why hadn't he figured out that something had gone wrong, something she couldn't prevent? Why hadn't he waited even one day more?

With each item she hung up in the closet or placed in a drawer, she felt more and more foolish. Had Griffin even cared when she didn't show up yesterday? Maybe yes, maybe no. Maybe he was too involved in his own life, his own work. Or maybe he'd met someone else in town and decided he'd just as soon travel with her. One of those scenarios had to be accurate. That was where the evidence seemed to lead. When she failed to show up, he'd probably shrugged and carried on. Yes, he'd mentioned her absence to Claude downstairs, but it didn't on d as though he'd been particularly worried or upset. He probably was joking when he told Claude he'd been stood up. It was just a thing that happened. She hadn't shown up. Whatever. He'd moved on.

But still... a tiny piece of her hoped that Griffin was sad when she didn't show up. That same piece imagined that he was somewhere in a neighboring mountain town confused about what had gone wrong between them. Or maybe he was just arriving back in Lyon now, intending to fly somewhere else, and had finally seen the texts she'd sent. Maybe he'd decided to stay overnight in a hotel. Maybe he'd be back here tomorrow, relieved and excited they were soon to be face to face.

She sat down on the bed, a sweater halfway folded on her lap. Of course that fantasy was not how this would play out. Why did this always happen to her? She trusted people too much. She made them out to be better than they were. Why was she so gullible? All she wanted was to be in love with someone who loved her back. That shouldn't be so hard to find. And she'd honestly thought Griffin could be that person. Yet here she was, alone, when she'd been looking forward to having him with her as she plumbed the secrets of her past hidden in her own.

What if she found out something awful? Or shocking? Or wonderful? Anything was possible. It struck her now that her mother had never once read *The Little Lost Fish* to her—and yet her grandfather had read it to her every night. What did that mean? Other than her, the only person that united her mother and grandfather was her grandmother. And although she'd never met her, Rachel had been under the impression that her grandmother had lived her whole life in Brooklyn. But was it possible that the truth was different? That her actual grandmother was... Cece? And that this was something her own mother never knew?

Rachel wanted so badly to have the answers. And she'd

been hoping to unearth them when she was in the company of someone who truly cared about her. Someone who wanted her to muscle through the discoveries and emerge intact and with a new, clear understanding of herself and of what had happened to her family.

"Is it crazy to want to be in love forever?" she'd once asked Nick after a guy she'd met at a work party and dated had turned out not nearly as perfect as she'd initially thought.

"No," he'd said, leaning back in his office chair, his hands cupped behind his neck. "It's not crazy. But the problem is it doesn't last. Not the kind of love you seem to want. You know that floating-in-air feeling? If you want that forever, I think you're looking for the impossible."

"But isn't that what love is?" she'd asked.

"No, it's unsustainable—the dreamy thoughts, the gazing off into space, the racing heart every time you hear the guy's name. You can't feel that way forever, and no guy can feel that way forever about you. Be realistic, Rache. Or resolve to spend your life disappointed."

She hadn't wanted to believe him. She liked to think that people could be wildly in love forever. Yet here she was, alone again. Someone whose happiest moments of love existed only in her head. Who twisted things in her mind, turning the wrong people into the right people who then became wrong again. Who imagined love instead of actually having it.

She put the remaining clothes from her suitcase into the drawer and shut it firmly. She knew she had to put Griffin out of her mind. She had made the plan to come to France by herself—it was only after she'd announced it that Griffin had suggested joining her. But it was a casual, impromptu offer. She'd probably been thinking about him all this time, and missing him now, more because she was scared of what she might learn than because she needed him. The truth was, Griffin was nobody to her or her family. He had no role in this search. This was her life, her past, her work. She would carry on without him. And be better off for it. He would have been a distraction—and she didn't need distractions. She couldn't return home with nothing more than the information she'd had when she left home two days ago.

With the unpacking finished, she looked over at the door that led to the hallway. It was after nine o'clock, and she hadn't had any food since this afternoon. Griffin had said that the restaurants in town stayed open late, which was a good thing because she needed something to eat. She didn't relish the thought of seeing Claude again, but she couldn't hide in her room indefinitely. Hopefully there'd be no one in the lobby when she got downstairs, and by tomorrow, the coffee fiasco would be a distant memory for her and everyone else who'd been there.

She took a quick shower and put on a fresh top and a pair of jeans. Pulling on her jacket, she left the room, closing the door softly behind her. Walking stealthily down the steps, she peeked down the stairwell to make sure Claude wasn't in sight. She wondered if she could avoid him for her entire stay. Maybe she could find a back door. She'd have to check out by placing a handwritten note on the counter telling him to go ahead and put the charge through on her credit card, but that was okay. She smiled, thinking it ironic that she was trying to stay out of sight as she hunted down an author whose fate had remained hidden for more than seventy years.

Thinking she was in the clear, she reached the lobby and headed for the door. But before she could grasp the handle, it opened toward her, and Claude stepped in, a paper bag with groceries in his arms.

"Mademoiselle," he said, his tone warm. "Good evening. I trust you found your room satisfactory?"

She nodded, still intending to leave quickly. But he looked so kind. She was touched by his too-big clothes, his large, sparkling eyes. He reminded her of a mythical creature, an elf or a sprite. But it was his demeanor that made him even more enchanting.

"Yes, it's very nice," she said.

"I'm glad you think so. Please let me know if you need anything."

"Thank you," she said. He moved aside so she could step out, but she didn't budge. He was just so pleasant, and she felt the need to say something about her entrance earlier.

"I'm so embarrassed," she told him. "I can't believe I spilled the coffee. I feel terrible."

"It's okay," he said with a chuckle. "What does it matter? Just a shirt. He has others."

"But still—"

"Believe me. It is fine. We don't take offense that easily around here. We have a long history in this town of knowing when to hold others responsible and when to say... pfft!" He lifted his arm and flipped his hand back, as if waving away a speck of dust in the air.

"It is deep in our DNA," he continued. "This understanding of what matters. It is something we never stop living with."

"You mean... because of the war?" she asked.

He nodded.

"You've lived here all your life?"

"Not my whole life. But I was here as a young boy. I don't remember much, but I do know it was a very hard time."

"I'm sorry," she said.

He laughed. "Ah, again with the apology! No need for that. Now, what can I do for you? Are you looking for a meal?" He pointed to the paper bag in his hand. "I would invite you to dine with me, but I'm preparing only soup tonight. You probably would like to be out and about anyway. Too much alone is not so good. Maybe a bit of comfort food, as you Americans say? And a little music? I have the perfect place."

He opened the door and pointed down the street to a lit-up storefront on the next block. "We serve delicious meals here in the mountains," he said. "Make the most of it. We always do."

Before long, she was seated at a corner table in a dimly lit bistro, listening to a jazz quartet play.

Claude was right, it felt good to be out among people. The server came over, and she knew just enough French to order a glass of red wine and *"un hamburger avec frites."* She was sorry to be missing the Provençal cuisine Griffin had mentioned in his text, but she didn't have the patience now to try to translate the whole menu, and besides, that food had sounded good because she was going to be dining with him. She'd never been one to yearn for fancy items on a menu. She preferred, as Claude had put it, comfort food.

Comfort food, she thought. Her favorite meal in the whole world was the French toast her grandfather used to make on snowy mornings when school was canceled. He'd bathe the bread in egg yolk and fry it in butter until it was the perfect texture—crunchy on the outside and soft and custard-like on the inside. He'd warm the syrup before pouring it for her, and he'd serve it alongside a large mug of hot cocoa with whipped cream. She'd loved putting her face close to the mug, and making him laugh when she lifted her head and showed him the big blob of whipped cream atop her nose. Then she'd watch him sit opposite her at the round kitchen table. He'd breathe in the steam from his piping hot coffee before taking his first sip. And then he'd sigh with pleasure—"*Ahhh*"—before returning the cup to its saucer.

Her order arrived, with a small bowl of ketchup on the side, and she put some on the burger and took a bite. It was flavorful and chewy, the meat rich and juicy. The fries, too, were delicious, warm and crisp with just the perfect amount of salt. She took another bite and ate a few more fries, then picked up her wine and took a long sip. It was peppery and spicy and felt pleasingly warm going down. This meal was definitely what she needed to get through the evening, and she felt her body start to relax. She returned the glass to the table and was about to enjoy a good, long exhale when a blast of cold air slapped her face. She looked up to see the bistro door open and someone with a black overcoat and red scarf walk in. He unwrapped his scarf and scanned the restaurant. She caught her breath.

It was the guy from the guest house. The one she'd spilled coffee on.

Instead of a pleasing exhale, she felt herself let out a low groan.

Undetected for now, she observed him stroll to the bar and shake hands with the bartender, who greeted him warmly. He gave a wave to the female singer who'd joined the stage, and she blew him a kiss. Then he turned toward her, and she saw the spark of recognition in his eyes. She lifted her hand to wave hello and waited as he came to her table.

"Should I be scared?" he asked in English, with just the merest hint of a French inflection. "Is it all beverages you use as a missile? Or just hot coffee?"

His smile was wide and she knew his joke was good-natured.

"I am so sorry," she said. "I hope I didn't ruin your clothes. I'm happy to pay to clean them or replace them."

He laughed. "It's no problem. The students are used to me looking like a slob. Even if I never changed, they wouldn't notice anything amiss."

"You're a teacher?" she asked.

He gestured toward the chair opposite her and she nodded that he should sit. "Yes. My name is Alain."

"I'm Rachel," she said and shook the hand he'd extended. As he pulled out the chair, she studied him. He looked to be about her age or a little older, maybe in his mid or late thirties. She knew that most would consider him quite good-looking, with his lush, dark curls, thick but short and well-groomed beard, and dark eyes. Yet she was more taken by the calm energy he gave off. His forehead was broad, his nose slender, and his jaw strong. He came across as serene, unflappable, and incredibly approachable. So different from Griffin's "catch me if you can" energy.

"What do you teach?" she asked.

"Young children. Preschool classes. And I occasionally lecture at the college in Lyon."

He waved to the waiter, then pointed to Rachel's wine to indicate he'd have the same. "I have to confess, it's not by chance I'm here," he said. "Claude told me he sent you here, and I decided to stop by. I wanted to make sure you were okay."

"Okay?" she said, not sure what he meant. "I'm fine. Just upset about what happened."

"No, not about me. You seemed distressed back at the guest house. Before the coffee."

She looked down with a small laugh that was mostly due to embarrassment. But she was also touched by his concern. And grateful, too, to have been noticed like that. "I'm fine," she said. "It's just that I was supposed to meet someone here yesterday, but my flight was canceled and I had to stay in Dublin overnight. I was texting him with updates but he never received them because of the outage. I feel bad that I have no way to reach him."

"Is he a friend? Family?"

"Neither, actually. Well, kind of a friend. Almost... I mean, a new friend. We don't know each other very well."

"Ahh," he said, and she had the feeling he was looking right through her. That he could tell, without asking, that this was a romance she'd been pursuing. But it didn't make her uncomfortable. She was glad for someone to talk to.

The server arrived a moment later, and the two men exchanged a few words in French. "That's Raoul," Alain said when the server left. "I told him that your meal looks good and that I'd take the same."

"It's very good," Rachel said.

"The connection should be back to normal pretty soon—the phone lines and all," he said. "And I hope you'll get a chance to enjoy a bit of the town while you're here. You'll find it's a very special place. It took me a while to get used to, but now I don't think I could ever leave."

"So you're not from here originally?" she asked.

"Well, no. But part of my family is."

"Oh?"

"They moved away for a time, but some of us have been making our way back. To try to recapture what was lost. This town suffered a great deal. World War Two—it was a long time ago, but it still lives with the people here. Surprising how long pain can last, even when the pain is not your own. Sometimes that makes it even harder to let go."

His words made her think of her grandfather. She knew what he was talking about. That was the pain she'd felt since she was little—the pain of all her grandfather had suffered. It didn't matter that she never knew what caused it. She just hurt for him because he seemed to hurt so much.

"Claude mentioned that he was here during the war," she said.

"Yes. And he bears the scars. But that's his story to tell." The waiter arrived, and Alain dug into his burger. "So, what do you do?"

"I work in a library. In a town outside of New York City."

"I love New York. I lived there growing up," he said. "How is the Big Apple these days?"

She laughed, hearing that expression in such a far-off setting. "Probably just like you remember it. Crowded and busy and exciting. I wouldn't know, really. I spend most of my time in the town where I live. But you actually lived in New York? How is it that you came to live here? This place—it's so different from a big city."

"I could ask the same of you," he said. "Why would you choose to meet a new friend... here? Wouldn't it have been fun to meet in New York?"

"Well, I seem to have a family history here, too."

His eyes widened.

"Yes," she said. "I think my grandfather may have lived around here during the war, and may have even known an author who once lived here, too. His memory is not good, and it's hard to get much information from him anymore. But there's a children's book that seems to be the key. It's a popular story, at least back home, and the author goes by the name C. Tailleur. Or Cece. I came across our old copy of the book, the one my grandfather used to read to me—"

"Oh, no—it is late and I must get up early," he said. "Dinner is on me, let me get the bill. And look, the music is about to start up again. You should stay and listen, they're very good. Maybe an aperitif? Or a coffee? Let me buy you a drink. Don't miss this next set, it's sure to be wonderful."

He stood and flagged down the server. Reaching into his pocket, he pulled out his wallet and settled the bill, then grabbed his coat and scarf from the back of his chair. He'd barely eaten more than a few bites of his burger. "Enjoy our town," he said and, with a wave, headed to the door. He didn't even take the time to put his coat on.

Puzzled, she watched the closed door where he'd exited. How strange, she thought, the way he'd left so suddenly. Had she been talking too much? She didn't think so. They'd been discussing their work and then New York. It had been pleasant.

He'd been friendly. But then something had happened. His face had changed. For someone who came across as quite easygoing, he'd looked almost panicked.

It happened when she'd mentioned her grandfather, she thought.

But no, she realized. That wasn't it.

It happened when she'd mentioned Cece.

THIRTEEN
DECEMBER 1942

With the memory of that close call with Red still fresh in their minds, Rémy created new rules for the household. He assigned Adele the task of making sure he, Celina, Marie, and even Robert all knew when Red showed up and paid extra attention to the children until he left. No child was to be left alone for even a moment, and all were instructed to say nothing more than '*Bonjour*, Officier Dumont' when they were in Red's presence.

Nevertheless, Celina felt changed after that morning. She didn't think she'd ever feel entirely at ease in the house again. Still, for the children's sake, she tried to appear upbeat and relaxed, to appreciate the bright spots where she could find them. The truth was, there were plenty. The children were playful, friendly, and bright. The house was always full of energy and light, even though the dead of winter was approaching and the weather was increasingly cold and gray.

The evenings held a special charm. The children would sit in a semicircle on the rug while Rémy sat on the armchair and she took a seat on the sofa, Brielle in her arms. Rémy would push his hair away from his forehead with the third and fourth fingers of one hand—a habit that Celina found tender and sweet—then take his wire-rimmed glasses out of his shirt pocket and place them on his face, adjusting the temple tips around his ears. He'd pick a picture book up from the stack in the basket beside his chair and proceed to read it aloud, stopping with every page to show the pictures. Usually they were adventure stories—children scaling rocks or steering ships or exploring the forest. His reading voice was clear and dramatic, and the children were transfixed.

Celina found it hard to take her eyes off him. She knew he lived every day with worry, but he made himself sound encouraging and positive. She was glad he was in charge, and not her. She yearned to have as much inner strength as he did. Everyone felt better when he was around. It seemed as though nothing could go wrong when he was there, smiling or laughing or reading aloud, his eyes crinkling behind those slim wire-rimmed frames.

Still, those moments of tranquility were short-lived. As she watched the children hang onto Rémy's every word, Celina often found herself thinking of what they had gone through. She knew so little about them. Rémy didn't want them to share too much because he felt that the less they all knew, the less there'd be to hide should Red or anyone else ask questions. Yet the small bits of information she'd gleaned from observing them were so revealing. And sad. There was Lawrence, the six-year-old who'd kept a small hand-drawn map of Belgium in his shirt pocket until Rémy decided it was too dangerous and convinced him to surrender it. He later burned it in the fireplace. But that hadn't quashed Lawrence's love of drawing. Celina had noticed that he often drew pictures of a family—a mother, a father, a little boy, and two baby girls. Had they been his sisters? Maybe twins? Often the father was holding something large that appeared to be a stack of books. Had his father been a scholar or professor at one time? Had he dreamed of being one, too?

And then there was Claire, the four-year-old who always carried a baby doll with her, even bringing her to the classroom every day. At night as she listened to Rémy read, she'd settle the doll next to her under a blanket and kiss her two cheeks. Had this been the way her own mama had said goodnight to her? Violee, who spoke Spanish as well as French, was a whirling bundle of energy, spinning in circles and then stumbling and tumbling, never stopping until she'd made the other kids laugh. She loved to entertain them, but there was a hint of desperation, a wildness, in her actions. Was she trying to shake away all the sad memories in her head?

It broke Celina's heart to see them all listening so politely to Remy, just as they listened politely to her lessons each day. They'd been taught so well. What else had their parents taught them? To say please and thank you? To shake hands with grown-ups? To wash their faces and lay out clothes each night for school the next day? What else would they have wanted to teach them? Where were those parents now? Had the children seen Nazi soldiers pull their parents from their beds? Had their mothers had a chance to hug them or say one last loving word?

Those mothers—had their eyes been full of tears? Or had they kept their emotions in check so the children would stay strong, too? Would any of these little boys and girls remember the dress their mother had been wearing the last time they'd seen her, plaid or gray or maybe a skirt with roses or lilies? Or would they remember her perfume, sweet like lilacs or vanilla? Would they remember the last breakfast she had cooked for them, eggs or porridge or crusty bread with cheese or jam? The breakfast they had gobbled down, unable to even imagine the nightmare that was to come?

She wondered, too, how many times they'd ended up in a new place before arriving here? How many people had turned them away? How long would it be until they could remember their families not with pain but with smiles?

She remembered the stories Emile would tell her about the people he worked with in the Paris Resistance. He helped produce the underground newspaper at night, and then would sneak away from his day job to hand copies to couriers to distribute. She'd offered to help, but the others had said that as an American, she would attract attention, and besides, she wasn't proficient enough in French at that point to write up calls to action or interact with the couriers. Emile also said that he'd worry about her, and he didn't want to be distracted as he carried out his tasks. She'd given in, realizing that she'd probably be too scared anyway to be of much help. How foolish and cowardly she'd been back then!

But he loved her anyway, and she knew he needed her at night to tell his stories to. The couriers he encountered were young men and women who took off on foot or by bicycle to make their deliveries. He'd told Celina that he could see so much in their eyes—fear, anger, determination, and often, too, a yearning for connection, a plea for reassurance. He would try to offer a smile or a quick nod, although sometimes the need to separate quickly left little time for that. While he felt bad for their pain, he also told Celina that he was relieved to see they were still feeling something.

"Physical injuries—hopefully these can be overcome," he said. "But if we lose our ability to *feel*—I don't know if that can ever be recovered."

Celina wondered now what these children would feel once the war was over. Fury over what had happened to them and their families? Despair that wouldn't let up? How long would it take until they forgave the world and accepted there was kindness to circumvent the pain? Or would they never reach that point? Worse, would they lose the ability to feel anything, as

Emile had feared? Would they soon simply turn off their feelings, finding that the only way to endure?

One night about a month after she'd arrived, when the children had gone upstairs to bed and Brielle was asleep in her crib, Celina came back downstairs and sank onto the bottom step. It all felt too much for her that night, and she closed her eyes and pressed her hand against her mouth. She didn't want to cry. She didn't deserve to cry. She'd grown up in comfort, with parents and siblings and a house and friends. She'd had crushes on movie stars, gone to see films, been escorted by dates to school dances, spent hours shopping for clothes and records with friends. Life had been so easy, with plenty of room to grow. She'd felt nothing but love and support, and when she'd left home to go to Paris, she'd done it fully understanding that she could always go home if she chose to.

Even when she'd stayed far longer than the year she'd expected to stay, and she'd married Emile without her parents' knowledge, her family had still been her safety net. When she'd sent word to Max in Switzerland that she wanted to go home, he'd come right away to accompany her. She knew that should she ever decide to leave France, Max would find a way to come get her, and her family would welcome her back.

But these children—they had no such safety net. The whole set-up could be dismantled in a moment should Red sniff out or anyone else divulge what was really going on here. The cruelty of the Nazis was unimaginable. Could things ever return to normal?

She wiped her eyes with her fingertips and pulled herself up from the step, then turned to see Rémy coming down the staircase. She touched her nose with the back of her hand, taking a second to pull herself together.

"Are you okay?" he asked, his tone soft but direct.

She wished he sounded more tender. More than anything, she wanted right now to be comforted. But she wasn't his family and she wasn't a child. She had to be strong because he couldn't waste time saving her. There were children who needed him.

She nodded. "I'm sorry. I'm fine. Just a little... It's nothing. I'm fine."

"Good," he said. "It's getting late."

She nodded and watched him head to the back office. He probably had paperwork to do. She had much still to do tonight as well. Check that the children had clean clothes to wear tomorrow. That their boots were dry and lined up by the door. That their assignments from this morning had been completed in their composition books. The children didn't need her to feel sorry for them. They needed her to do her part to keep them safe, to keep them growing and learning as all children should do. She would do her chores. She would shake off her tears.

But the thing she couldn't shake off was her loneliness.

She had never felt so lonesome in her life.

As December unfolded and the temperatures dropped, the frigid winds making the windowpanes tremble, the children spent more and more time indoors. Celina realized that Rémy was showing up more in her classroom. At first she thought it was simply because he had more time available, since he wouldn't need to help Robert attend to any plants or fruit trees until the spring. Then she wondered if maybe he was concerned about Red showing up and asking more questions, so wanted to make sure he was there to forestall any slip-ups.

But soon, she realized that he simply liked being in the classroom. He liked being near the kids.

She thought he also liked being near her.

She loved how he'd smile at her when he came into the classroom in the middle of a lesson, waving to her to continue.

He'd sit on one of the child-sized chairs near the wall where she hung the children's handwriting exercises, the letters resting securely on the horizontal lines of the paper, the curves shaky in spots and the pencil marks dark, reflecting the pressure each child used and the effort they made to showcase their emerging skill. From there, he'd watch her talk about the weather or the climate or the topography of southern France, chuckling as she paused strategically at the end of her sentences so the kids could sing out the correct answer: "Mountains!" "Gorges!" "Winter!" "Cliffs!"

"You're so good with them," he said one morning when lessons were complete and the children were putting on their coats to scamper across the yard and back to the house for lunch.

"It's not me," she'd said. "It's them. They're so sweet. They appreciate school in a way I've hardly ever seen before. I'm so glad to have this class to teach."

"And I'm so glad you're here to teach them," he said. Then he shrugged and raised his eyebrows, as though surprised at himself for saying that. She watched him toss on his coat, challenging the kids to a race to the house. She stayed behind as the children tagged along, until the room was empty. Then she stared at the door, the silence leaving his last words echoing in her ears. He'd never said something like that to her before.

And she wanted it to happen again.

The next morning she began a new unit on animal names, and as she invited the children to call out the sounds of the animals listed on the chalkboard, she found her gaze moving again and again toward the classroom door, hoping to see the knob turn. She had the sense that her students would like that, too. Rémy had such a way of bringing lightness to a room, and now that he'd been showing up more often, his absence was more noticeable. Halfway through the lesson she was about to give up when she heard footsteps on the outside steps. A moment later it opened, and Rémy walked in. The children's delight was palpable. *"Bonjour,* Monsieur Rémy!" they all sang out, and he acknowledged them with a playful bow.

"Bonjour!" he said cheerfully. "I must be mistaken, but I thought I heard strange noises coming from here. Are there animals joining you today? Tigers, bears, snakes? Have they come inside to get away from today's frosty weather?"

The children laughed and made growls and roars and hisses to demonstrate that they were the source of the noises.

"C'est magnifique!" Rémy exclaimed, applauding to show his appreciation of their talents. The children continued hissing and roaring until he patted the air to quiet them down. "Now I have an idea," he said. "If it's okay with your teacher, how about we play a little game? I'll pretend that I'm a certain animal, and you guess what I am." He looked at Celina. "Is that acceptable? Can we play that game for a little bit?"

"Of course," she said. She would have agreed to anything. She was just so happy to have him there.

He began playing the game, extending his arms and making a fist with both hands to simulate an elephant, and then stretching his neck high, waiting for the children to call out "Giraffe!" Celina was surprised at first that all the children knew the names of so many jungle animals, but then she realized that maybe this shouldn't have been so unexpected. The Jewish children in the group had been just like any other children up until a few months ago. They'd gone to school near their homes and played with friends and been read to before they went to bed, tucked in tight as they snuggled close to their mama or papa, with maybe a tiny lamp casting a warm shadow over the bedcovers. Of course they knew about animals, the same as their classmates who lived in the village. She was glad they could participate in this game, that the Nazis hadn't deprived them of their innate ability to play. She thought of Brielle, looking forward to the day she could read

read from a picture book and hear Brielle make animal sounds.

But then again, no, she thought. She didn't want to be the one to share picture books with Brielle. That was something her mama should do. She couldn't give up hope that Brielle would one day be back with her family.

The game continued, as Rémy got down on his hands and knees and lifted his chin, then made his lips into an "O," and the children correctly guessed he was a wolf. At that point he rose to his feet and put a hand on his back. "Oh, I am too old for this kind of game," he teased. "I think I'll let you go back to your lesson while I get a hot-water bottle for my poor old bones."

The children begged him to stay, and little Daniel got up and took his hand. "Please, Monsieur Rémy," he said. "We don't want you to go."

Celina watched Rémy look down at the little boy and gently push his curly hair away from his eyes. The tenderness of the gesture touched her heart. At that moment, she saw Rémy as more than just a strong and moral man. She saw him as a sensitive soul. A soul who kept his distance as best he could because he couldn't be seen as fragile or vulnerable. There was too much at stake.

"I must go," he said. "I have so much to do to keep our little school running. But I will see you all for lunch. Thank you for your warm welcome, my friends!"

He left the room, and Celina directed the children to go back to their tables and draw their favorite animal. As they followed her instructions, she took a moment to let her breath settle and her mind refocus on the lesson. She felt just like Daniel. She was sorry to see Rémy leave and couldn't wait to see him at lunch. She replayed in her head the sound of his warm words to the children. The truth was, she didn't know much about Rémy at all. She believed he'd never been married and didn't have children. The only thing she knew was that

Adele was his sister. But she had no idea where he'd grown up or how he came to lead this dangerous venture.

She only knew she'd come to feel a great deal for him. She'd never expected it. She'd never thought she'd care for anyone else after Emile died.

And yet here she was. And though she knew it was dangerous to care too much at a time like this, she couldn't help but hope he was feeling the same way.

FOURTEEN
OCTOBER 2018

Alain left the bistro, and Rachel decided to stay for a bit. He'd been right, the music was mesmerizing. The singer, a beautiful woman with straight, chin-length hair, had a velvety voice, expressive and flexible in range. Some of the songs were in English, but one melodic ballad was in French, and she recognized a few words—*guerre* and *jamais, au revoir* and *mon amour*. It seemed to be about lovers separating, hoping for a time when war would no longer force them apart. The singer's voice conveyed a profound sense of dread and tragedy, and the music, coupled with the effects of the wine, transported Rachel back to mid-century Paris. She wondered what it would have been like to live here during World War Two, or to live here now, when the war was more than seventy years in the past but still cast a dark shadow. It was different back home, she thought. Here, many people were descendants of those who'd lived here and directly witnessed so much horror and experienced so much fear and loss. And it wasn't just descendants. Alain had said last night that Claude had been here during the war. That he still had scars. That he had a story.

And so did her grandfather. She loved him, and more than

that, she knew from the time she was very young that he was all she had. A piece of her had always feared he would abandon her if she upset him or made him mad.

When the set was over it was nearly midnight, and she put on her jacket and left the restaurant. Even though it seemed there'd be another set after a break, and plenty of people were staying on, she was exhausted. Back at the guest house, she let herself in with the front door key attached to her room key. The lobby was empty and there was just a dim table lamp to light her way to the staircase. It was strange, the way the town was so empty except for pockets like the restaurant where she'd just been. This seemed to be a town with a code, a way of operating, that would take time to crack.

Back in her room, she changed into a tee shirt and a pair of pajama pants, turned off the table lamp, and slipped into bed. In the darkness, her thoughts turned to Alain, and the way she'd gone from feeling alone to enjoying his company. She'd felt that she didn't have to impress him to keep his attention—and that was not a familiar way for her to feel when meeting someone new. She often gravitated to people like... well, Griffin. Men like Griffin, who came on full of confidence and charisma. "I'm not slowing down for anyone," they seemed to say, the subtext simmering below the surface: "Prove that you're worth my interest, or I'll leave you behind."

And she had tried to do exactly that with Griffin, believing there was nothing wrong with a relationship where one of the people was simply too busy to make time for the other. It was normal to her because it had seemed normal to him. But surely there were ways to start a relationship that didn't involve struggling over where and how to meet in person for the first time. Yes, she was somewhere she didn't belong, a place where she knew no one and didn't even speak the language—but still, she had made a connection tonight. Alain had come to the restaurant to see how she was. They'd eaten together, and he'd been gracious and attentive. She didn't worry that he'd find her lacking. She'd simply had a nice conversation with someone new.

Although then, of course, the evening had come to a crashing halt when she'd mentioned C. Tailleur and her grandfather. She had said something wrong—but what? She would have loved to talk to someone about what had happened. Nancy. Or Nick. Or maybe even Papy—maybe just explaining what had happened would have helped, even if he couldn't respond directly. But with no phone and no internet, she was on her own.

A piece of her wondered if this was what it was like to be her grandfather right now. His connection to the outside world was so tenuous. He was being drawn more and more inward, experiencing things that no one else could see or hear or touch. Whatever he was thinking deep inside, he couldn't convey it to anyone else.

Through the small window, she heard the wind kicking up, making a low, murmuring sound, causing the tree branches to tap against the glass panes. Sitting up in bed, she reached for her phone. She had to communicate. Or at least pretend to. She had to connect with someone, if only in her imagination. She opened her mail app and started an email, even though he couldn't receive it—and wouldn't understand it even if he could.

Dear Papy,

I'm here, in this region of France where you once lived. When you were... what? A child? I wonder how you felt when you lived here. I wonder if you still feel it. Why did you leave? Were you scared? In danger? Hurt? Is that why you spent so many years not being able to love anyone?

And if you knew Cece, how did you meet her? How well did you know her? Was she lonely like the baby fish in her

> story? Was she writing about herself? Or about you? Who was Cece's Brielle?
>
> The man I had dinner with tonight was so warm and kind until I mentioned Cece and you. It's made me wonder something new. Were you important here? Did you play a role in the story of this village? What do you remember that I can only wish I knew?
>
> Papy, what are the secrets in our family? What happened before I was born, and how did those secrets make you who you are? And make me who I am? Am I...

She paused, not wanting to finish the thought, not wanting to document the question in her head. But then she took a breath and continued to write. Because it needed to be said:

> Am I just like you? Have I spent my whole life chasing the wrong people because it's easier to stay apart? Even with me in your life, you always seemed so alone. With only the possibility of withdrawing further as you grew older...

She stopped and closed her phone. There was comfort in knowing that no one would ever see what she'd written. Although she saw it and could see it again if she chose to. Was it possible that she was writing to herself all this time? Was formulating words even more necessary than having someone read them? She wasn't the kind to keep a journal, even though she'd researched many journals when she was working on her Ph.D. But she'd always had the feeling the authors were writing for an outside audience. She wondered now about Cece, writing about the baby fish during the war. Had she expected it to sell and be read around the world? And if she was alive when it became so successful, why did she never take the credit? Who had she been writing for?

It was all so confusing, with no apparent path to clarity. Could she really break through the mysteries in the next week?

She slept deeply and didn't wake until nine o'clock the next morning. Then she dressed in another pair of jeans and a light sweater, grabbed her jacket, and started out the door, hoping to get some breakfast and set a plan for the day. She decided to put her doubts from last night out of her mind. There had to be answers here. Her grandfather's desperate rantings led straight to that conclusion. Before she left her room, she slipped the copy of *The Little Lost Fish* into her shoulder bag.

Downstairs, Claude was seated at a table reading a newspaper. He smiled when he saw her and motioned to an empty chair near him, then went behind the reception desk, which now held a coffee pot and some platters with pastries, fruit and glasses. He brought over a cup of coffee and a plate with two croissants alongside a few slices of cheese and some berries.

"*Bonjour*, mademoiselle," he said as he served her, then went back to the counter to bring her a small pot with butter and another with jam. She hated that she was making him go back and forth, as she now saw that he had a pronounced limp and moved slowly, dragging his right foot behind him. But he seemed to enjoy being the host, and she worried that she'd insult him if she tried to interfere.

"I trust you slept well?" he said.

"Yes, thank you," she said. "I was very comfortable."

"And what are your plans for today?"

"I'm not entirely sure. Claude, can I ask you a question?"

"*Bien sûr*."

She took the picture book from her bag and showed it to him. "I don't know if my friend told you this before he checked out of his room or not, but I have a kind of personal connection with this book."

"Yes, *Le Petit Poisson Caché*!" he said.

"So you know the book?"

"Everyone here knows the book. It's a popular birthday gift. All the parents read it to their children. This is an English version, I see. Is it famous in America?"

"A little bit," she said. "It used to be, I think, for many years. Maybe not so much anymore. But isn't the French word for lost *perdu*? Why does the French title have the word *caché*?"

"*Caché* means hiding, hidden," he said. "That word means something here because the fish seems to... you know, for the Jewish people here. *Symboliser...*"

"A symbol?"

"That's right. Because, you know, the book was written here during the war. Cece, that's the author's name."

"Yes!" she said. "Cece! Although we know her this way." She pointed to the author's name on the book. "C. Tailleur."

"Cece's hidden fish," he said. "She was involved in the Resistance, you know. She helped out at the secret orphanage. They pretended it was just a normal school and she was a teacher. That's how they got away with having the Jewish children there."

Rachel nodded, moved that Claude seemed to take such pride in this local history. She opened the book to the dedication. "And this name, Brielle Aimée," she said. "Do you know who that is?"

"It's the little girl she tried to save. One of the hidden children. Her mother had to abandon her. She left her under a bush, and Cece found her."

"So Brielle was Jewish?" she asked.

"*Oui*. That is why she was here."

Rachel looked down at the book. At least his answer solved one mystery. If this was the genesis of the book's dedication, then it was certain that the dedication wasn't to her mother. The news felt like a let-down. She'd wanted to have a personal connection to this beloved author. Although, she realized, it was still possible that her mother was Cece's daughter. And that

Cece had intentionally given her daughter the same name as the little girl she'd saved.

"Was there anything else, mademoiselle?" Claude asked. He looked around. A few other guests were now sitting at the café tables. She didn't want to stop him from welcoming and serving them. But he seemed willing to answer her questions, while Alain definitely wasn't.

"One more thing," she said. "Do you know what happened to Cece? I read she may have died in the war."

"I'm afraid I don't know for sure. It's believed that she may have been captured and killed as she tried to help the little girl, Brielle, escape to Switzerland."

"But no one knows for sure? You see, I think she may have known my grandfather. I think he lived somewhere around here for a time. He seems to have cared for her a great deal."

"I'm afraid there's little I can tell you. Cece was... *une solitaire*. What is the English word? Recluse? She never wanted attention. There's no information about her at all other than the time she lived at the orphanage with the children. Perhaps you might want to go there and see it for yourself."

"I can go there? It's still around?" She took out her phone to search for it, then set it on the table, remembering about the internet.

Claude went back behind the counter, emerging with a postcard. It had a picture of a pretty stone building, with small windows, a large garden, and a narrow, red door.

"Yes—it's a school now. An actual one, no longer pretend. For little ones. And you can walk there. It'll take about twenty minutes, a little uphill but it's a nice day. There's a library nearby you may want to visit as well. It has a fine collection of historical documents you might enjoy. Give me a moment to serve these people some coffee, and then I can draw you a map."

She smiled. Nobody she knew read or used maps. Everyone got directions on their phone. But she had no choice. She finished her breakfast as he served the other guests and then went behind the counter again. A few minutes later, he returned with a drawing on a small sheet of paper. There were intersecting streets and a red line presumably indicating her route, with stars designating the library and the school.

"Thank you," she said. "But will the school let me in? Is it open to the public?"

"Not really. But you have an in, I'd say. You know the director."

"I do?"

"Yes, he's..." He pantomimed spilling coffee on himself.

"Alain is the director of the school?" she asked.

He nodded.

"But..." She paused. She'd been talking to him about Cece last night. And he never said a word about any of this.

"Thank you," she said again and offered to help him clear her dishes. He waved her away, so she put the book in her bag, grabbed her jacket, and headed out. She didn't know why Alain hadn't said anything about the school when she'd mentioned Cece. Why did he hold back like that?

She was going to find out.

FIFTEEN

DECEMBER 1942

Several weeks after Celina moved into the house in Paillettes, a farmer arrived steering a horse-drawn wagon filled with the boxes from her old apartment. He and Robert helped her bring them into the house and, kneeling on the living room rug while Brielle napped nearby in a small wicker bassinet, she untaped and opened them. She was so glad to finally have her things, her clothes and shoes and coats, and the warm scarf Emile had given her last Christmas. But what mattered most was the large white envelope with Emile's artwork for the book they'd most wanted to write together. While Robert brought the boxes upstairs to her bedroom, Celina slid the pages from the envelope and spread them out in front of her. Twelve beautiful images bursting with color and vitality.

They'd started the book soon after they were married, working on it in the evenings before they went to bed. Emile had created a delightful main character—a baby fish. It was the size and shape of a goldfish, but with a purple opalescent body, oversized fins covered in silver sparkles, and huge, expressive eyes. They'd agreed that the story would be told in rhyme, and they'd envisioned several volumes, with each one following the baby fish on a different ocean adventure. Emile had used pastels to create stunning pictures of the elegant baby fish aglow against the blue ocean background. Celina had offered to try her hand at the verses, imagining what kind of being the little fish would be and how he'd change and mature as each volume concluded.

The last evening she and Emile had spent together, they'd sat at their small table eating a dinner of thin vegetable soup and bread—food was scarce in Paris because of the war—and Emile had imagined one day bouncing their daughter on his lap and reading their storybooks to her.

"I'll ask her, 'Aren't Mama's words beautiful?'" he said.

"And I'll say, 'Aren't Papa's drawings brilliant?'"

"She'll love the stories. She'll be so excited that her mama and papa wrote them."

"She'll be so proud. Her talented parents."

"Her famous parents," Emile had added. "Whose books are sold by the thousands all over the world!"

"Only thousands?" Celina had said.

"Fine, millions!" he'd exclaimed. "With talent like ours, there's no limit."

Emile had left shortly after to attend a Resistance meeting, which was being held that night in the basement of a tobacco store nearby that had gone out of business. He'd squeezed her hand and said he wouldn't be home late and they could work a little more on the book before bed. She'd believed him. After all, he'd always come home before. But still, she didn't have a good feeling about him leaving that night. She thought about asking him not to go, but she knew he'd say he had to, and she didn't want to argue. She believed in what he was doing and knew how committed he was to the effort. She'd waited by the window throughout the night and into the early hours of the morning. She prayed the black smoke she saw out the window and the hearing she heard down the street had nothing to do with him.

But she knew it did.

Thinking back on that night, Celina leaned against the sofa, her eyes filling at the memory. They'd been so young and so naive. Even with the Nazis patrolling their beloved Paris, they'd envisioned a future of love, creativity, and freedom. "This can't last forever," Emile would say. "It simply can't."

Just then, Marie came in from the dining room to tell her that the children had finished lunch. Celina put Emile's paintings back in the envelope and, leaving Brielle in Marie's care, went upstairs. She promised herself she would work on the book's verses a little each night. While Emile hadn't made enough pictures to fill several volumes as they'd planned, there were enough for one lovely book. No matter what, she would complete that book and get it published. She would do that for her husband and the baby daughter she had never met.

All that week, Celina returned to the drawings for an hour or two after the children were asleep and the house was quiet. She worked downstairs so she wouldn't have to turn on the light in the bedroom, knowing that she'd hear Brielle in her crib if she started to cry. By the glow of the fireplace and a weak lamp on her writing desk in the living room, she studied the pictures and tried to imagine how the accompanying story would go. While she loved all of them, her favorite was the one with the baby fish caught in a cave, unable to escape because of the strength of the ocean current. Emile had proposed calling the area around the cave Shadowland because he'd liked the idea of incorporating shadows into the blue, glistening background.

Celina was used to being alone while she worked, the only one in the house awake at that late hour. So she was surprised one night when Rémy appeared beside her. He was dressed for bed, wearing a dark blue robe that tied at the waist. She'd been so focused on the story that she hadn't heard him come downstairs. She didn't know if she was more surprised to see him at all, or simply to see him out of his day clothes.

"Rémy?" she said. "What are you doing up?"

He looked at her, his expression amused, his eyes smiling. "What am I doing up? I could ask you the same question. But I'll go first. I always get a little anxious on the night before I leave. Well, a little more anxious than usual. It helps to walk around and take stock of everything."

"Oh, that's right," she said. He was scheduled to take the train the next morning for Lyon and would be gone for four or five days, a week at the most. She hadn't wanted to think about the trip because it made her uneasy. This would be the first time she'd be here without him. He'd given no details about his plans, and she was glad because she didn't want to think about whether he might be putting himself in danger. His meetings reminded her of the ones Emile had gone to.

"Can I get you anything?" she asked. "Tea or something to eat?"

He shook his head. "No, no. Thank you. Okay, now your turn. What are you doing awake, Madame Cece?" he added, a teasing smile on his face. Rosalee had had trouble remembering her name so had taken to calling her Cece. The other kids loved the sound of that, so it looked like the name would stick. Even Red sometimes called her that.

"Me? Well, these arrived the other day," she said, pointing to the drawings on the desk. She was glad she hadn't changed into her nightclothes before coming downstairs. She would have been far too embarrassed to speak with him. Although he didn't seem to have the same qualms. He seemed quite comfortable in his robe and slippers.

"They're Emile's," she said. "We were writing a children's book together."

"May I see?"

She hesitated. The book had been her project with Emile,

and it felt disloyal to reveal it. Like opening a window into their private past. But then she relented. This was her life now. Rémy and the children.

"Of course," she said, and he surveyed the pictures. "It's a baby fish. He's lost for most of the book, but eventually he finds his way home. I know, it seems silly, this tiny fish crossing the ocean…"

"Not at all," he said and looked closer, his face near her shoulder. "He was a fine artist, your husband, wasn't he?"

She nodded.

He pulled the armchair closer to the desk and sat down, folding his hands and resting his elbows on his knees. "Tell me more about him," he said.

She turned toward him in her chair, softened by his gentle invitation to share her memories. His tone was subdued, and she remembered he'd said he was anxious about leaving tomorrow. And she was anxious for him. Emile had often told her that they needed to live in the moment. And maybe this moment, this quiet conversation, was something both she and Rémy could use.

"He is… was," she said. "He was talented and smart and kind. And silly. We were young and it was Paris and we just wanted to have fun. How can I explain? Life was fresh and lovely and vibrant and so exciting that we regretted having to waste time sleeping. The food, the wine, the scenery." She shook her head. "We were way too young to get married. We were careless. At first we didn't think the war would come to our doorstep. And then, when it did, we tried to ignore what we didn't want to accept. We should have been smarter and left Paris early on. We should have seen it coming."

"I can understand," Rémy said. "Nobody wants to believe it."

"He was like a little boy in so many ways," she continued. "He worked as an illustrator for a magazine, but he wanted to make books. I loved to watch him work. He was so serious about drawing, and yet so playful. He liked purple. And green. And he liked sweets. And he liked sometimes eating croissants for dinner. And he liked snow."

"He sounds like a man I'd have liked," Rémy said.

"I think so." She nodded. "Although he wasn't that easy to get to know. He could be moody when he was working. And quiet. But he was idealistic like a child. And trusting. Maybe too trusting."

"Oh?" Rémy said.

She looked down. She wanted to go on, to talk about the night Emile died. She'd never talked about it before. No one she knew had ever asked her about Emile's death before now. Not even Max. Everyone was too scared. But Rémy was different. She could tell that if she wanted to open up, he would want to hear it.

"I don't think he even fully realized how dangerous it was, the underground newspaper," she said. "He and some others secretly printed it at the publishing house where he worked. They met at different locations to plan each edition, and he was at one of those meetings when the building they were in was torched. I heard later that one of their group was a Nazi spy. I'm sure Emile had no idea. He never would have suspected. He never doubted that the people he worked with were... just like him.

"He never learned to be cynical," she added. "And that gives me some... well, maybe some comfort. If he had to die, at least he never had to face that kind of betrayal. At least I can remember him that way."

"Small mercies," Rémy said.

"Very small," she agreed. "And yet... they're everything. Sometimes I wonder what would be if I never came to France. My life would have been so much simpler. My family has no idea what life is like over here. But I'm not sorry I came."

She felt him studying her, the same way she'd seen him study the children as they struggled to solve a math problem or spell a new word, his face a mix of concern and encouragement and... wonder, she thought. It was the only word that seemed to fit.

"I admire you, Celina," he said after a beat. "I think you are as good a person as he was."

She shook her head. "No. No, he was one of a kind. It's what made me fall in love with him when I first came to France. I never planned to stay. I was only supposed to be here for a year, and then I was to go home and let my father help me choose a man to marry. But once I met Emile—it was at a party thrown by a friend I'd made—once I met him, I knew I'd never go back home. That wherever he was, that was where my home would be."

She looked down, suddenly embarrassed. "Here I am, making all this sound so dramatic. There's nothing all that special here. A little rich girl who went to Paris seeking adventure and got caught up in... something she never could have imagined. You're the one who made"—she opened her arms—"all this. You're the one saving people. You're the one... I mean, what it took, what you sacrificed to protect these children..."

He shook his head. "I'm not all that special either. I'm no different from you. Caught in a moment. Trying to help."

She paused, scared of the answer to the question now in her mind. "The children... when the war is over, do you think they'll be okay?"

He nodded. "I'm sure of it."

"But how? With what they've been through, what they've lost—"

"They'll grow up even stronger. And they'll build a world so much better than the one they were born into."

"How can you be so certain?"

"How else can one survive?"

She thought about his question. "I think we survive because we have to."

"And because we want to," he said pointedly. "We want to see another day."

She looked at the desk with Emile's drawings. "So frivolous," she said. "A children's book. Such an inane thing, a silly baby fish."

"No," he told her, sitting upright. "No. You were imagining and creating. That's what human beings do. What else do we have in these times? Let's not let them take that away from us, too."

She sighed. He was right. Creating—that was what she could do. What the children could do, too. Because it felt good to create. She felt happy when she was working on the book. And fulfilled. She looked at Rémy now, at his kind face and sincere brown eyes. He was regarding her with sympathy, as though he knew much that she was just discovering. Although she could have construed his look as patronizing, she didn't take it that way. He didn't look down on anyone. He was inviting her to uncover more about herself, to think more, to decide where she thought she fell in this universe. He respected her. She'd never experienced that before. Emile had been more of a dream come true, someone she clicked with, someone she adored, someone she loved to make love to. But Rémy was older. He was a serious man. And she felt serious when she was with him.

"I think I'm ready for bed," he said. "Are you going to stay up?"

"Maybe a little longer," she said. "This is the only time I get to work."

He rose from the armchair and approached her, and for a moment she thought he might kiss her head or her cheek. But instead he simply squeezed her shoulder. Somehow it felt even more intimate than a kiss.

"Goodnight, Celina," he said.

From her chair, she watched his shadow float behind him on the staircase until there was nothing more to see.

With Rémy gone, Celina distracted herself with school during the days that followed—teaching classes, helping Adele with the meals, gratefully accepting food donations from neighbors, and keeping a close eye on the children when Red showed up. The cold days were approaching, and the air smelled like snow. Celina had been through harsh winters back home, and Paris was cold in the winter, too. But here, the wind was sharper. It delivered a fierce, electric snap to your ears, the tip of your nose, the slice of skin between the top of your gloves and the bottom of your coat sleeve, and anywhere there was a morsel of exposed skin. Celina made sure to keep the fireplace in the living room stoked, as the winds howled among the trees, causing twigs and dead leaves to swirl by the window. She had the children change out of their frosty clothes as soon as they came in from outside. They bundled themselves up for the evening in sweaters and thick socks, wrapping themselves in blankets as they gathered after dinner for storytime.

But most of all, she took charge of making sure Red continued to stay in the dark when it came to the true identity of the Jewish children. One morning when she came downstairs with Brielle to greet the children having breakfast, she heard his voice in the kitchen. She was surprised, as he never showed up this early. She quickly handed Brielle to Marie and pushed past the swinging door. Red was facing Adele, his hands on his waist, his posture threatening, and Adele was looking at him, pale and trembling.

"Officier Dumont," Celina said as she approached the man, trying to approximate Rémy's casual way of greeting him. "You're here early. Extra hungry this morning?"

"I'm hoping to get a straight answer," Red told her. "I

merely asked why some children are already here this morning and eating breakfast. Don't the children all have breakfast at home? And this woman here has worked herself into a panic. What is she hiding?"

Celina stalled, trying to think what Rémy would say. How could she explain why the Jewish children were here early in the morning while their classmates were not?

"It's really... it's quite simple," she said, coming up with the words barely before she said them. "Some of the families in town don't have enough food. We are lucky that Adele can make so much of so little, so we invite those children to have breakfast here. Adele didn't want to tell you because it's embarrassing to the parents. Nobody wants to admit they can't feed their family."

She turned to Adele. "It's okay. Officier Dumont's job is to keep watch over the village. I know he will keep our secret and not make the parents feel bad. Now go ahead, Adele, and give our guest something to eat. Have a seat, monsieur, and enjoy whatever delicious creation Adele has baked this morning."

Red shrugged and went to sit at the table, evidently satisfied with the explanation and never one to pass up food. Celina longed to leave the kitchen and give Brielle a hug. She didn't want to be around Red a moment longer. But she didn't dare leave. Adele wasn't up to dealing with this man on her own. She knew Rémy would stay until Red left, and so she had to do the same.

From that morning on, Celina missed Rémy even more. She knew the children missed him too. No matter how hard she worked to keep the house warm, there was still a chill in the air, and Celina knew it was at least partly due to the absence of Rémy's big personality, his enveloping smile, his resounding voice. She tried to approximate his reassuring tone and confident air with the children, as she had when addressing Red, but she knew that to them, she was a weak substitute. Each night as she put Brielle down in her crib, she said a little prayer that Rémy was safe and would be back the next day.

And then, she'd distract herself with her book. Back at the writing desk by the fireplace, she tried to come up with verses that would reflect the dark, almost mystical look of the shadow against the water in Emile's paintings, and the way it could both entice and repel the little fish. But it was hard to write without Emile's presence and his encouraging smile urging her along. He had helped her a lot, giving wonderful suggestions for words or phrases, and she feared the parts she wrote on her own would never be as good. On the third night Rémy was gone, she completed a new verse and then sat back to read it over:

The swells and waves of Shadowland call,
Where to go, how to go, the darkness is stealing
They beckon the fish who wants Mama, that's all!
Mama's warm hugs and her love and her healing...

She liked the mood of the words, especially the idea of a mother who heals. But overall, she found the stanza too cryptic. She didn't even really know what any of it meant. She decided to put the pages away in her closet upstairs and look at them with a fresh eye the next night.

She didn't get back to it the next night, however. The days were so busy and she found the stress of Rémy's absence exhausting. But two nights after that, she brought the envelope from her bedroom down into the living room. Sitting at the writing desk, she slid out the pages, found the one with the newest verse—and gasped at what she saw.

It had been altered. Someone had crossed out some letters in the first line and added a replacement above.

witzer
The swells and waves of S~~hadow~~land call,

Where to go, how to go, the darkness is stealing
They beckon the fish who wants Mama,
that's all!
Mama's warm hugs and her love and her
healing...

She pressed her hand to her mouth to keep herself from crying out. Someone had gone into her room, searched her closet, and found the envelope. Someone had seen the drawings and her verse. Someone had changed "Shadowland" to "Switzerland."

Who would have done that? Who would have looked through her personal things?

She rose, thinking to wake up Rémy right away and show him this. Then she remembered he wasn't back yet. And more important, she remembered what he'd told her on her very first day here: *If anything looks odd to you, let it be... You can put lives at risk if you upset the codes they're leaving for one another.*

She stood motionless, thinking this through. It felt like a violation, that someone had entered her room and handled her things. And not just any old thing; it was her book—the most personal thing she owned. She reminded herself that there was no privacy here. The rules were different. She had made herself comfortable, but this was not her home. As Rémy had insisted, there was important work going on in this tiny village to thwart the Nazis and their activities. She was not to get in the way.

Still, she wondered, how could changing this one word have anything to do with the Resistance? And even if this was some secret code, why would anyone think to hide it on a page in an envelope deep in her closet? Who on earth would be searching for it there?

She gathered up the pages, slipped them back in the envelope, and went upstairs. In her room, she put the envelope back in her closet, so it would be there if someone came to retrieve the message conveyed in her altered verse. She would let it be, just as Rémy had instructed her to.

She turned, and her gaze fell on Brielle, asleep in her crib. The little girl was lucky, being so young. She'd likely never know the pain the other children felt, if all this trouble ended before too long. At least there was that. But on the other hand, this poor little baby would very possibly never know her parents. Never know the love they had for her or the sacrifices they may have made to get her to safety, even if it meant losing their own lives. Never know if she had siblings or grandparents.

Brielle was wearing a blanket sleeper that a neighbor had dropped over that morning, with clowns and pink balloons. Celina put her hand on the little girl's chest, feeling her breathe in and out, the same way she'd done that first day she'd found her in the bushes.

S'il vous plaît, prenez soin de ma petite fille jusqu'à ce que nous puissons être à nouveau ensemble.

Elle s'appelle Brielle Aimée.

Please care for my baby girl until we are together again. Her name is Brielle Aimée.

She stayed that way for a few moments, listening to Brielle's breathing.

"I hope you will know your mama," she whispered.

Then she changed into her nightgown and crawled into bed, pushing her feet to the bottom and gathering the covers close to her chin. Though outside the wind howled, inside the house was warm.

And yet a shiver came over her that she couldn't quiet.

SIXTEEN
OCTOBER 2018

Rachel left the guest house and started on the walk to the school building, following the directions on Claude's map. The route was winding, the streets at odd angles to one another, but fortunately the map was detailed and accurate. The day was sunny and clear, and Rachel took advantage of the weather to look around. She hadn't seen much of the town at all yesterday, since it had been dark when her train had arrived. But now she saw the breathtaking scenery Griffin had hinted at. She crossed a small pedestrian bridge over a brook. The mountains in the distance were vast and rose to the clouds, and she marveled at the interplay of nature and human handiwork, how the stone buildings and structures blended right into the mountainous backdrop. The bridge led to a road that bordered the edge of a cliff, with only a waist-high wooden fence and a few feet of ground beyond it separating her from the drop-off. Down below, the water rushed, glistening over rocks and darting around curves.

She was struck by the permanence of both the mountains and the ravine below. How many seasons had they seen? Millions? Billions? How many feet of snow, how much wind?

how many wars, how much tragedy? And still they endured. She thought of her mother, whose life was such a mystery to her. Was it possible that she'd once seen these mountains, too? Was it possible that Cece—her mother's mother, neighbor, teacher, something else?—had shown them to her? She thought, too, of her grandfather back home. Had he once also marveled at these mountains? Or had he been too overwhelmed by the atrocities of war to even notice them? Did he see them still in his mind's eye? Or was he too haunted by memories he could never control? Memories he'd tried so hard to express to her last week but couldn't?

It was so hard to accept him this way. He'd always struck her as so strong. And not just on the outside but on the inside, as he'd had to be, to keep all his secrets holed up for so long.

Secrets about whether her mother had a connection to Cece. Rachel felt sure she was closing in on that information.

She was here. A place where she might be able to understand.

She found the hill Claude had mentioned and began the climb upward. It was a steep walk and she was out of breath when she finally reached the top, feeling both chilly from the weather and sweaty from the ascent. She unbuttoned her jacket and looked at the building ahead. It was a large ivory-colored stone house with a red front door and small windows dotting the two stories. The grounds were well-kept, with creeping bushes overflowing with vibrant orange and red berries surrounding either side of the front step. A wooden sign mounted to two wooden posts in the middle of the lawn identified the building as LA PETITE ÉCOLE. The Little School.

She knocked on the door, then tried the knob. It turned, so she pushed it open, surprised and enchanted that she could walk right in. Things were so different back home. When she was working on her Ph.D., she often needed permission or even a letter of introduction to access many databases, research rooms, and documents. Even the facility where her grandfather lived had security stations and locked doors. She knew it was necessary yet she longed to live somewhere like here, with few barriers. She wondered if this level of openness was a response to the Nazi occupation from decades ago, and the constant fear of Nazi soldiers conducting raids and roundups. Was this community determined to its core never to live that way again?

She crossed the threshold and found herself in a spacious room, with two modern sofas upholstered in a light blue fabric to the left near the fireplace, and a pretty reception table to the right. Behind the table sat an elderly woman in a red, belted dress, her white hair gathered in a bun behind her head. There were thick, knotted veins on her hands, and her face and neck sported deeply wrinkled folds of skin. But her eyes were clear and bright. A sign on her desk read MADAME GARE.

"*Oui?*" the woman asked, adding, "May I help you?" when Rachel hesitated. It was a relief that she spoke English. In fact, she barely had an accent, and sounded almost American. Rachel felt bad that she didn't speak more French. She knew some from the research she'd done on *The Little Lost Fish*. But speaking conversationally was different from reading texts with the translation app on her phone open. She would have done more preparation, maybe even taken a French class, if this trip hadn't come up so suddenly.

"I'm hoping to speak to... Alain," she said, realizing that she didn't know his last name. "Claude from the guest house said I could find him here. We met last night, and you can tell him..." She sighed. She knew the easiest way to identify herself. "You can tell him I'm the one who spilled coffee on him."

"Coffee?" the woman said with a chuckle. Her voice was soft and tuneful. "I hope he didn't say something to warrant that."

Rachel felt herself redden. "No. It was an accident."

"Thank goodness. Please have a seat. I'll be happy to see if he's available."

She pressed the desk to push herself up, and though she walked slowly, her posture was straight. She headed for a back hallway, and Rachel sat on one of the sofas. There was a casualness, a familiarity, in the woman's tone that she appreciated and that she was coming to recognize. Everyone seemed to be everyone else's friend here.

A few moments later the woman returned. "He says he does have a few minutes. Come."

She led Rachel down a dim hallway and into a small office at the back of the house. Though it was still morning and the sun was bright outside, the room was dark, and the lamps and sconces were all switched on. The building was old and clearly had been built with thick walls to ward off cold winds. Still, the darkness was disconcerting.

Alain was seated behind a simple black desk, looking handsome and elegant in a blue button-down shirt and gray slacks. He rose and gave a wave as Madame Gare left the office. Then he looked at Rachel. "Hello," he said, politely but with a hint of a question in his voice. "This is a surprise."

"Claude suggested I make a stop here. I hope I'm not disturbing you."

"Well, it's a perfectly fine time for interruptions, seeing as the internet is still out, and I couldn't make any phone calls even if I wanted to. What brings you here?"

She hesitated, feeling a little intimidated. Judging from his office, he was an important man. She had taken offense at his speedy exit last night, and she was curious as to why he hadn't been candid with her when Cece's name came up. But who was she to expect answers from him?

"I don't know if I'm stepping... I don't mean to be rude," she said. "But we were having a conversation last night, and then I mentioned C. Tailleur—Cece—and you took off. That very second. I didn't know what to think. But then this morning, Claude tells me that she's well known here in town, and that this very building was the secret orphanage and she stayed here. And that this is a school now, and you're the director. I don't understand why you didn't say all that last night."

He pursed his lips, as though considering how he wanted to respond. "I'm sorry about what I did," he said after a moment. "How I left you there all alone in the bistro. You are a stranger in town. That was rude."

She stayed quiet, hoping he'd go on about Cece. When he didn't, she decided to press further. "It seemed as though I said something wrong. Like I asked a question I shouldn't have. And I don't understand. Because Claude was so willing to talk, and he even drew me a map and told me about a library to visit, too. This seems like a town that welcomes visitors. Everywhere else, that is."

"We are a welcoming place. We love visitors," he said. "It's merely that... I guess it's the way you brought up the children's book last night, as though you were on some kind of mission. That tends to put us on our guard. Me, at least. I'm wary of people going around investigating us—"

"I'm not investigating anything. I'm curious—"

"Because you're working on a book, maybe? Doing research for an academic degree?"

"No, not at all. Well... I was, at one time—"

"As I suspected—"

"But I put that aside. It's been years. My connection here has to do with my family—"

"And that's another thing," he said, getting even more animated. "The people who come here—if they're not doing research for a book, they're searching for some nugget gleaned from a website, some DNA link that connects them to us, or to the Resistance, that they can brag about online. Why is it so hard to understand that while we want to be kind, we're a small community with a very tragic past? The people who live here and who once lived here deserve to be in charge of their own stories. Maybe we don't want our history splashed all over the internet by those seeking 'celebrity.'" He put the words in air quotes.

She hesitated, not sure how to go on. Why was he attacking her? He didn't even know her. For someone so concerned about safeguarding stories, he seemed to be perfectly happy to invent one for her. She had no idea what celebrity seekers he had encountered in the past, but he had her pegged all wrong. And it was particularly upsetting to hear him go on like this, because she'd thought he was a nice person. He was so friendly with the staff at the restaurant last night. He'd sought her out after she'd spilled the coffee to make sure she was okay—and not about the coffee. He'd come because he felt bad that Griffin had left her behind.

"Cece chose to be anonymous," he added, more quietly. "She didn't want to be famous, she didn't want to be known. Doesn't that count for something?"

"Of course it does," she said, her tone matching his. It did count for something. And yet, honoring her mother by uncovering whether, and in what way, she might be connected to Cece—that counted for something, too.

"Look, do you want to know what this town is like?" he asked. "What we're really about? What we've always been about?"

She nodded. She'd fallen in love with the town already.

"Great," he said. "Come. Let me show you."

His expression had softened, and she felt her reaction toward him softening as well. It touched her, this protectiveness he felt toward this town and its people. And somehow, his outburst just now made him even more interesting than she'd found him last night. The Alain she'd met at the bistro had been charming and engaging, but now she was seeing a complexity, too. He was the same person, and yet there was so much more to know.

He led her out of his office, opening the door for her and then gesturing down the hallway. Like his office, the whole building was a strange combination of dreary and cozy. There was a chill in the air that belied the sunny weather outside. Walking alongside him, she wondered more about him. He was young and good-looking, and sophisticated. And yet there was a tenderness to him that made him seem a little at risk, a little too vulnerable for a big city. Maybe it wasn't surprising that he'd left New York. But she liked that tenderness. Even when he'd questioned her motives, he was earnest and genuine. She couldn't help but compare him to Griffin. Yes, Griffin was fun and outgoing. Entertaining. But now she saw his behavior more as swagger, as though he was always auditioning for the TV job he so desperately wanted. If Alain was substantial, then Griffin now seemed thin, like a chocolate that turns out to be hollow inside.

Alain led her through a large and well-equipped commercial kitchen and out a back door. They passed a shrub-enclosed playground with swings, a slide, and some climbing structures. Beyond this was a small building with a sign above the narrow door that read LA PLACE DE CECE. Cece's Place.

He opened the door and stood aside to let her go forward. Inside was a nursery school classroom. The structure had clearly been renovated—while the outside was stone, the floor was covered in multicolored carpet squares, and the big modern windows let lots of sunshine pour in. There were about ten children who looked to be four or five years old sitting in a circle in the center of the room. The walls had bulletin boards filled with children's drawings of houses and families and mountains and gardens. One bulletin board had photos of each of the children, with their names written in their own handwriting underneath.

Alain waved to the young teacher, who was in joggers and a

button-down denim shirt, her hair in a high ponytail. The woman said something to the children in French and they all turned to look at her and Alain. "*Bonjour*, Monsieur Alain," they all sang out.

"*Bonjour, mes amis,*" he answered, and then put his hand on Rachel's shoulder. "*C'est ma nouvelle amie. Elle s'appelle Rachel,*" he said.

"*Bonjour,* Mademoiselle Rachel," the children said.

"*Bonjour,*" Rachel said. She understood the words and liked that Alain had called her his new friend. They both watched as the children sat back down to listen to their teacher. Rachel was charmed by the way they were all paying close attention. While she couldn't understand what the teacher was saying, she saw the children's sheer delight in being in her company. How different their experience was from hers. Back when she was five years old, she'd been the only kindergartner with a grandfather taking care of her. She hated how the kids looked at him at pickup time, how repelled they seemed by his demeanor, the way he stood apart from the other adults. She'd always felt awkward when she stood with her grandfather in the presence of her teacher and classmates. One day, she heard one of the boys whisper to his friend, "*That's* her father? He's so old!" She felt so ashamed that she didn't even want to correct the boy's error.

But more than that, she felt insulted for her grandfather. It was awful that the other children saw him as a weird old man. She had never seen him that way. To her, he was just her wonderful Papy, who showed her that just by being with her, just by loving her, he could find a way toward a bit of happiness.

Alain touched her arm. "You okay?"

She nodded, embarrassed. "They're so cute, aren't they? I haven't been in a kindergarten classroom in a very long time. Since I was a kindergartner, I guess."

"I come here a few times a week to do some art projects with them," he said. "That's why I'm here now. Want to join?"

She couldn't think of a better way to spend the morning. A short time later, she was sitting at a table and working with two little girls to cut out shapes from paper for collages. It didn't matter that she didn't speak their language. They still had fun. They spoke the language of play.

At times she looked over at Alain, who was helping another group make furniture out of red, blue, and green modeling clay for a large dollhouse in the corner. He was sitting cross-legged on the rug, totally engrossed in the project and attentive when a child would show him their handiwork or ask for some help fashioning table legs or a sofa back. She was taken by his focus on the children, his all-out concentration on their activity, his ability to sit quietly and listen. And his easy smile and encouraging nods.

When the children had cleaned up and were getting ready for lunch, Alain led her back outside. "It's a very special school we have here," he said. "Some of the children are from our community, and some are from war-torn areas or places that have suffered from natural disasters. Our funding comes from relief agencies and charities. We bring in two or three children every year and find housing for them and their families, if their families are still alive. Otherwise, we find them temporary homes, families that will take them in. That's the mission of the school. To make the world a little smaller, a little less frightening."

They reached the door to the kitchen, and now she spotted wooden beams and paint cans on the ground. Alain noticed her gaze. "Yes, we're expanding," he said. "We're reconfiguring the second floor into four classrooms. Another room for young ones, and then three classrooms for older children. I didn't teach this year because of the remodeling, but I'll have my own class again next year."

He led her into the kitchen and invited her to sit at a round wooden table. Then he went to the pantry and brought back a plate with macarons and chocolate croissants, along with a bottle of sparkling water and two glasses.

"It's a wonderful school," she said. "I love how you're bringing children from other places here."

He poured the water and popped a macaron into his mouth. He slid the plate her way, and she took one, too.

"It is wonderful," he said. "For many reasons. And it's why... well, it's why I can be a little suspicious. Like I said, we love visitors, but I'm resistant to people with some kind of agenda."

"You think I have an agenda?"

"Well, your friend seemed to. The one you were supposed to meet. I heard this morning that he was talking about coming back at some point with a TV crew. He seemed to think it could help his career."

She sighed. She could picture Griffin talking about bringing a camera crew here, thinking he had a big story. It was debatable whether *The Little Lost Fish* could actually propel his career. But it troubled her that he'd been speaking like that. She had confided in him as a friend. She hadn't expected to learn that he'd been thinking of exploiting this town's sad history for his own purposes.

"I don't have an agenda," she told him. "At least, not in the way you're thinking. I'm not like those other people you were talking about. And I'm not like... the person I came here to meet."

"So why are you here?" he asked.

She looked down at the table. "I appreciate that Cece didn't want attention. But I think her story may be my story, too. I think my mother could have been related to her. She might... she might even have been Cece's daughter. It has to do with the book she wrote. The dedication is to Brielle Aimée, which is my mother's name. That's what I was trying to tell you last night. My mother died long ago, so I have no way of asking her. But my grandfather lived here during the war, and he knew Cece. I'm sure of it—"

She stopped when she saw Alain shaking his head. "What?" she asked.

"Cece didn't have a daughter," he said.

"You know this for a fact?"

"I do."

"But how? You said that she wanted to be anonymous. Claude said that, too. It's not even clear how she died. *If* she died..."

"But that much I know," he said. "There was no daughter. You're going to have to trust me on that. What exactly did your grandfather do here during the war?"

She looked at him, at his handsome face with its strong features, that firm jaw and large, open eyes, at his broad forehead now sporting a stray dark curl he had yet to brush away. He lowered his chin and folded his arms across his chest, and he looked at her with those inviting eyes, his concentration producing a pair of tiny, vertical lines between his eyebrows. She believed that he wanted to hear her. She thought anyone would be lucky to have his attention as she did now.

She explained about where her grandfather lived, and how he raised her after her mother died, and how she now visited him a few times a week. How she'd taken to showing him memorable items to keep his mind active and how he'd become agitated when she showed him the dedication in the book.

"He's always been so sad and distracted by something in his life that he couldn't... that I don't think he could face himself, let alone share with anyone. Even me," she said. "And the only thing he loved other than me was Cece's book. He read it to me every night when I was little. And I came to love it, too."

"It's a beautiful book," he agreed softly. "All the children around here grow up having their parents read it to them."

"I was very young when my mother died," she continued. "I never even knew I had a grandfather before I went to live with him. And now that it seems my grandfather is ready to tell me why—well, he isn't capable of doing it anymore. I need to know where I come from. What I'm looking for—it's not on a DNA website. I want to know the things you can't research. I want to know... the story.

"And I want him to know that I know," she added. "And that I forgive him for holding everything back. I want him to know that I've learned where I came from and I'm good with it."

He lowered his eyes and bit his bottom lip. She didn't know exactly why, but her words had touched him.

"I know how you feel," he said.

He looked at his watch. "I have a meeting to get to," he said. "An architect and a builder for the new classrooms. But Rachel—I do want us to talk more. Can I see you again? Will you have dinner with me tonight?"

"I would love to," she said.

SEVENTEEN
DECEMBER 1942

After six long days, Rémy returned one afternoon, sitting alongside a farmer steering a horse-drawn wagon, the back loaded with sacks of dry goods he'd picked up from the market and some fresh milk and eggs the farmer had given him. The kids were delighted to have him home, and Celina was, too. Meals and classroom time took on a more cheerful tone in the following days. And yet, Celina couldn't help but notice a difference in him. He was more introspective when the kids were not around. Sometimes she caught him standing by the fireplace staring through the window at the mountains in the distance, one arm against the window frame. Once in a while he'd rub his forehead with his thumb and then return his hand to the window.

"Why does he look so worried?" Celina asked Adele one day while she fed Brielle her afternoon bottle. The weather had warmed up a touch, and Marie had taken the children outside to play.

Adele frowned. "Things are changing," she said. "Robert was getting supplies in the village yesterday, and the news isn't now. The Germans know there are Jews in these mountains. There were roundups in the neighboring towns last week. And when he heard that Red showed up while he was away and was asking those questions—he's concerned that Red will figure out the truth about us. If he hasn't already."

Listening to Adele, Celina envisioned Red and a gang of Nazi officers storming into the house and prying Brielle from her arms. Her tears would be useless, her begging for Brielle's life met with derision and taunts. The other children would be taken away, too, and she and all the adults in the house she cared for so much—Adele, Marie, Robert and, of course, Rémy would be arrested, if not tortured or killed outright. She ached for them all. And her heart broke for Rémy. She knew he felt responsible for everyone in the house, and for all the villagers who were keeping their secrets. If anyone was seized or worse, he'd blame himself. In the evenings, she found him more and more often in that position by the window, his arm braced against the frame, his face in shadow from the fire. She yearned to press her hand against his back, to let him feel the warmth of another person. To maybe give him even a smidge of comfort. There were times when she grew breathless, surprised by a desire to wrap her arms around him and press her body against his. But she couldn't let her emotions get the better of her. It would complicate things too much. Yes, they were human, and they needed affection like all humans did. But now was not the time.

So she devoted herself anew to the children, who were growing and changing, unaware of the looming threat. Brielle could now roll over and grasp her rattle, and was starting to babble, making sounds like "baba" and "ooh." Claire was starting to read, and Daniel was able to count to 100. As Christmas approached, Rémy cut down a tree from the woods and the children decorated it with paper stars and rainbows.

Celina felt bad having the kids participate in the rituals of a holiday that wasn't theirs, but Adele pointed out that it would look suspicious to Red and any Nazi sympathizers coming through town if there were no Christmas decorations or celebrations in the house.

On Christmas Eve, the children opened presents—secondhand toys and clothes donated by neighboring families, who had wrapped them as best they could with old sheets of newspaper. There were baby dolls and toy animals and wooden blocks and tea sets and even a camera, scratched and worn but still functional. Lawrence was the lucky one who picked the camera from under the tree, and he soon began documenting all the routines of the day and begging Marie to take the film rolls to the store in the village where they could be processed.

As December turned to January, Celina barely thought about the change that had been made to the pages of her book. She hated that someone had handled the drawings and verses that were her strongest remaining connection to Emile, but she was glad the intrusion had happened only that one time. She hoped that whatever the message was, it had been found by its intended recipient and the ordeal was behind her now. She never brought the matter up with Rémy even though she'd wanted so badly to talk about it. He had too much on his mind, and he had specifically told her not to speak of anything she noticed amiss.

But then, about three weeks after that first revision appeared, there were more. Celina spotted them when she went to the living room to work on the book. This time, the markings showed up later in the story, on a page with two verses that centered around the baby fish's final journey:

Then again she went to the sea.
The little fish who once swam so fast
Asking what, and where, and how can I be?

Brielle
~~The fish~~ now knew her lot was cast.

Celina froze. This revision was far more frightening than the last one. Why would someone refer to Brielle by name? In what way was her lot cast? Were the Nazis aware that she was a Jewish child? Was Brielle in danger? Should she take the baby and flee right now?

Frantic, Celina searched through the other pages and pictures, looking for more words added or changed. Most of the pages were untampered with. But then, on the last page, she saw another revision:

> *The fish was finally getting her wish*
>   *Beerli   mama*
> *Off to ~~the sea~~, where her ~~heart~~ can rest*
> *Back to the sea for the sweet little fish*
>   *safe   mama looks west*
> *Then to the ^ place where her ~~love can share~~*
>   ~~*best*~~.

And under the stanza were the words "*jusqu'à ce que nous puissons être à nouveau ensemble.*" Until we are together again. The exact words from the note that had been pinned to Brielle's blanket.

Celina blinked and read the words again. Beerli was a town in Switzerland bordering France—a town, she'd heard, where many Jews had fled in hopes of reuniting with missing relatives. That's when she suddenly knew the truth. These notes on her book's pages—they weren't messages from one Resistance member to another. No—they were intended for *her*. Someone was trying to tell her that Brielle's mother was alive and in Beerli, looking west toward France. And that it was safe to bring the baby there. There was no other way to read these changes.

She stared at the pages for a few moments. Then she gathered them and went upstairs. In her bedroom, she looked at Brielle asleep in her crib and stroked Brielle's chest, her little body snug in her pink blanket sleeper. Yesterday afternoon, Celina had come into the living room and seen Brielle in Marie's lap, the two of them playing with Brielle's Christmas present, a matted but still cuddly teddy bear. The sight had almost brought her to tears. She didn't want to give up this little girl. She loved her. She believed that they could heal together following the losses they had each suffered. But she knew what it was to be a mother who'd lost a baby. It was precisely because she loved Brielle that she had to let her go.

"Don't worry, I will bring you to your mama," she whispered. "I promise you I will. I will bring you to your home."

She waited until the next evening, after the children had gone to bed and Brielle was in her crib, to ask Rémy if they could speak. She knew Adele was upstairs so would hear Brielle if she fussed before falling asleep. The envelope with the book pages was in her hand.

"Of course," he said and led her to the kitchen. There, he put on the kettle for tea. He looked tired, his eyes sunken and red. She brought two teacups to the table and sat down. When the tea was ready, he poured for both of them, then sat opposite her.

"I'm sorry I've been so distant lately, Cece," he said. His voice was weak but he smiled as he used her nickname. "I hope I haven't made you unhappy. I honestly don't know how I'd have gotten through these last few months without you. The children are thriving because they have you as their teacher.

"What's on your mind?" he asked.

"I have something to show you," she said. She slid the pages out of the envelope and laid them on the table in front of him. "I know you said not to take note of any messages I might find. That they had to do with the Resistance. But this is different."

She showed him the changes made in her verses and the words from the note that were written on the bottom. "Someone is leaving notes about Brielle. Someone is trying to tell me that her mother is alive and in Switzerland. There's no other way to read this, is there?"

He looked the verses over, then lifted his eyes. "I don't know," he said. "There does seem to be a message here. But I'm not convinced it's what you think."

"It has to be. It's so clear."

"I don't know," he repeated. "Who would have done this?"

"Does it matter?" she asked. "I don't think so. All that matters is that someone is trying to help reunite Brielle and her mother."

"We can't be sure—"

"But what else could it be? There was someone who left her under the bushes that day with the message pinned to her blanket. Someone knows who she is. They may have even seen me take her. And now, this has happened. It's like you've said—people know all kinds of things. It's the nature of the war, of what we're living through."

"I still—"

"So what do we do? What do we *do*?" she demanded.

He reached out and touched her hand, and she knew he was trying to calm her. Then he looked at her hard. "We do nothing," he said softly.

"Nothing?" He nodded and she pulled her hand away. "How can you say that?"

"It could be a trap," he said. "It could be someone connected to the Nazis. Maybe a ruse to prove that the baby isn't yours. And get us to admit that we're hiding Jewish children here."

She considered that, then shook her head. "I don't think so.

That note pinned to Brielle's blanket—it talked about them being together again. This is the message to reunite them. To show that the mother is safe and waiting for her baby."

"Celina, you don't know that."

"But it makes sense—"

"But you don't know it." He rose and rinsed his cup in the sink. Then he returned to the table. "It's getting worse," he said. "They come to town all the time now, asking where the Jews are. They ask in the village, that's what the farmers are telling me when they drop off food. We have to hold fast to our story. We have to keep things as they are. You can't rock the boat, Celina. It's the status quo that's keeping us safe."

She sat back in her chair. She knew he had a point. And yet she couldn't stand the thought that this poor mother was waiting for her baby and had found a way to communicate her whereabouts. It would be so easy to ignore that possibility, because she wanted to keep Brielle. She wanted to raise her. She adored the little girl, the way she lit up every morning when Celina greeted her in her crib. But Brielle belonged with her mother. And if Celina could bring the two together, she had to do it.

"How can you be sure you're interpreting all this correctly?" Rémy asked.

"I ask you again—is there any other way to see it?"

"And I answer you again—it could be a trick."

"It's not a trick," she insisted. "The changes in the verse are saying exactly where to bring her. And the words on the bottom repeat what was said in the note on her blanket. Someone is sending a very specific message to me."

He looked up to the ceiling. "Celina, you don't know how things work. You've been here only a few months. You're still an outsider."

She felt her breath catch. "How can you say that to me?"

"My point is that you see things differently. Look, I know

what you've sacrificed to be here. And you love the children, and they love you. And you've put yourself in danger and estranged yourself from your family—"

"And yet I'm an outsider?"

"That's not what I meant." He shook his head. "You're a newcomer, is that better? You're an American. You weren't *here* when it all started. You don't know, you don't have the history. You were in Paris when we were setting this up as an orphanage—"

"Yes, I was in Paris with my half-Jewish husband who was working for the Resistance. And was killed for it."

"And I'm sorry." He sighed. "Look, it's possible you're right. Maybe this is someone who knows the mother and is trying to communicate on her behalf. Maybe she did find a way to tell us that she's safe. Maybe she does know that her child ended up here. But we have to think this through rationally. How would you get the baby to Switzerland?"

"I could borrow a car."

"No one has a car to lend you here. And Red would see you going. He watches our every move. He'd be suspicious. And he'd stop you."

"I could ask one of the farmers to take me. I could hide in a wagon."

"And you think they could just breeze over toward Switzerland and cross the border with no one stopping them and searching the wagon? And fine, let's say somehow you get through. What happens here? What happens to the other children? What happens when Red finds out you and the baby are missing? He'll know something's up. And everyone here will have a target on their back."

"That's not true. He believes she's my baby. He'd be surprised if I left without her, not with her."

"Exactly. So then what? Let's assume you can actually find her mother and deliver the baby. What happens to you? You're telling me you'd leave with the baby—*your* baby—and return without her? What would Red think then?"

"So I won't come back. I'll stay in Switzerland."

"And what about the children here who need you? You can just turn your back on them?"

"I don't know, I... What would you have me do?"

"I would have you stay here with Brielle," he said. "And we wait the war out. And then we go about trying to find the children's parents. All of the parents. We find out who survived."

"That could be years."

"I understand that."

"And you understand that Brielle and her mother will be separated for *years*? All the years they could have had together, they won't have? When would you propose we bring them together? When Brielle is six, eight, twelve? When she doesn't even know this woman who will insist she's her mother?"

"It's not a good option. It's an awful choice—"

"But does it have to be a choice? Can't we do both? Can't we bring Brielle to her mother and save the others too?"

"It's safest to keep things as they are. It simply is. Celina, I understand how you feel. But there's nothing more to say."

She let his words, his refusal, linger in the air. Then she rinsed out her own cup and left the kitchen. In the hallway, she pressed her back against the wall and closed her eyes. She didn't want to fight with Rémy. She knew how devoted he was to the children, how desperately he wanted them all finally to be free. But she was sure he was wrong. There had to be a way to keep the kids here safe while still bringing Brielle to Switzerland. Because there was a woman out there, a mother, who needed her baby.

And that was what Celina couldn't bear. Brielle was growing so quickly. Now she was starting to eat solid foods, boiled vegetables and fruits when they were available. Soon she would be crawling, laughing, getting her first tooth, pulling herself up. When had her mother last seen her? The day before she was hidden under the trees? Or a week before? Or longer? She hadn't had the chance to hear her baby babble, see recognition in her baby's eyes when she looked in the crib. What else would she miss? Brielle's first word? Her first time blowing bubbles? Eating something delicious, a cookie or a pastry? Drinking with a straw? Her first sentence, her first step, her first wave goodbye as she left for school, knowing her mama would be there waiting at the end of the day? How long could they make this poor woman wait?

Just then she heard footsteps coming from the kitchen. She opened her eyes as Rémy stopped short in front of her. He clearly hadn't realized she was still downstairs. The two of them stood opposite each other, their backs against opposite walls. They stared at each other for a long moment, their breathing heavy. Celina felt her heart race. Her cheeks flush.

"Celina, I can't... we can't... I don't know how..."

He paused, his body still. And then, with a burst of energy, he stepped forward, cradled her face in his hands, and kissed her. It happened so fast, she didn't even register what was going on at first. But then she noticed the feel of his mouth, warm and firm and irresistible, and before she knew what she was doing, she lifted her chin and pressed her own mouth against his.

It was over in a moment. Rémy stepped back and looked at her. His eyes were wide, and Celina was sure he'd surprised himself as well as her. He opened his mouth to speak, and she suspected he was going to apologize. She shook her head to stop him. He had nothing to apologize for. She had kissed him back. She had wanted that kiss, too.

"I'm sorry," he said anyway, despite her trying to stop him. "That was out of line. We're colleagues, we're... it won't happen again." He exhaled and walked back into the kitchen, and she turned and started for the staircase.

He was right, she thought. They were colleagues. They

lived in the same house. She was a teacher in the school he ran. There were ways they had to behave. This kiss had crossed a line. It had been a mistake.

Except it didn't feel like a mistake. And that's what made it even more dangerous.

EIGHTEEN
OCTOBER 2018

After leaving Alain, Rachel walked through the building to the front door, giving a wave to Madame Gare, the white-haired woman who had welcomed her in. She started down the hill, excited for what the evening with him would bring. Her feelings for Alain had changed so much in the last hour. She was moved by how he'd spoken so lovingly about the school, and by his commitment to welcoming children who had suffered tragedy. She loved how much he seemed to enjoy sitting on the rug and molding clay with the kids. Even here in this tiny, remote town that few had ever heard of, he was an activist with a mission. She thought of what she'd read about the Resistance while she was working on her Ph.D., how it took all kinds of people to derail the Nazis. There were activists who took up arms and activists who helped in the background. She admired Alain for his determination to make the world better in his own way.

And she admired him for the roots he'd laid down here. It made her see her own life in a different light. And she was seeing Griffin in a new way, too. What Alain had said about the film and TV crew cast a worrying light on Griffin's priorities.

Alain had offered to meet her at the guest house that evening. With time to kill before that, she stopped at a small café for a sandwich and a coffee, and then decided to go to the library Claude had mentioned. It was just up the road from the guest house, another stone building with dark, cool walls that belied the sunny day. It was open, the front door unlocked, and she made her way inside. But the signage was all in French, and without any internet or cell service, she couldn't translate the words on her phone.

A thin, older man with a name tag pinned to his white polo shirt approached her. "You are the American visitor at Claude's house, yes?" he said, his accent pleasant and his smile sweet. "You are looking for information on the secret orphanage and Cece Tailleur? Like your friend, the young man who was here earlier in the week?"

She let out a breath, disappointed that Griffin had shown up here, too. It seemed he had met nearly everyone in town during the single day he'd had here. She hoped this man hadn't also been offended by Griffin's mention of a TV crew.

"Yes—well, our reasons for being here are very different," she said and went on to explain that she believed her grandfather once lived in this town. "There's so much that he never told me about," she said. "So many brave things took place here. Like the secret orphanage. The more I discover, the more I want to know."

He nodded and led her across the room, where he pulled a slim, hardback book off a bookshelf. "Our local historian put this volume together," he said. "It's one of a kind." He placed the book on a nearby table and flipped through the pages. "About the orphanage you mentioned? It was quite a complex arrangement they had. There was a system for giving the Jewish children fake identities and incorporating them into the town. Many families agreed to pretend the children were theirs, despite the grave risks. Here—this is a picture of the children who lived in the orphanage."

Rachel was struck by the pride he clearly took in this little town. She tilted her head to see the grainy photo. There were children in front of the fireplace that Rachel remembered seeing inside the school building. She guessed it was taken in the winter, as the children were dressed in thick sweaters and pants or woolen skirts. She was surprised to see that they all appeared happy, smiling for the camera, some of the little girls with their arms around each other. They looked like any other kids posing for a class picture. It was hard to believe they'd been separated from their families. That they may even have seen their parents beaten and dragged through the streets.

The man turned the page, revealing a photo of a beautiful young woman with light eyes, shoulder-length hair curled under and pinned behind her ears, and a wide smile. She was wearing a turtleneck sweater and loose trousers and sitting on a rocking chair. On her lap was a baby wrapped snugly in a blanket.

"That's our author," the man said. "Cece Tailleur. It's believed she was an American who lived in Paris for a time before arriving here."

"That's her?" It was the first picture Rachel had ever seen of her. She looked closer at the woman.

"She had a child?" she asked.

The man raised his palms. "It's a bit of a mystery," he said. "Some believe this was her daughter."

"But Alain at the school told me she didn't have a daughter."

"As I say, the facts are unclear. Some say this was her daughter, some say this was one of the Jewish children brought here. Tailleur does not even appear to be her real name, but simply a *nom de plume*. In any case, she disappeared at some point, taking the baby with her. It's widely believed that she tried to escape with the baby to Switzerland. It's quite possible that she was followed and arrested."

"Followed?"

He nodded. "There was a local police force that supported the Nazis. And one officer in particular who patrolled this area and knew the comings and goings at the orphanage. If he arrested her for helping Jews leave France, she could have been sent to Drancy—that was an internment camp near Paris. Some believe that's where she died. But there's no proof of her being there and no record of her death. It remains a mystery. Probably always will be."

He closed the book and held it out to her. "Would you like to borrow this? There are more photos of Cece and the children. Evidently one of the children loved taking photographs. Many of the pictures here are from that collection. They were found in the school years after the war."

"I can borrow it?" Rachel asked.

"Yes, of course," he said. "You can bring it back after you've looked through it."

"Thank you," she said and headed out the door. She didn't know what to think. The baby in the photo couldn't have been her mother. That baby was alive in the 1940s, and her mother wasn't born until 1965. But could Cece have had another baby years later? A baby girl that even Alain didn't know about?

Back at the guest house, she changed into the blue dress she'd brought to go out to dinner with Griffin her first night here. She was pleased to have a reason to wear it. She was looking forward to seeing Alain again. She'd liked how he'd responded, the way he'd said, "I know how you feel," when she talked about her grandfather. She had no idea what he had in mind. But there seemed to have been some emotion in his voice, and she wanted to learn what was behind his words.

When she went downstairs, he was there in the lobby. He'd put on a nice pair of slacks and a dark crew-neck sweater. He smiled when he saw her, and she noticed the way his eyes lit up.

"It's beautiful out," he said. "Got a little warmer as the day progressed. We're lucky for an evening like this in October. Would you like to eat *al fresco*?"

"Very much," she said as she put on her jacket, and they headed outside. The soft breeze felt good as they walked across the street and past the clock tower to a tiny outdoor restaurant near the train station. Twinkling white lights were threaded into the branches of the olive trees. The host brought them to a small round table with a votive candle burning in the middle. The patrons were young—mostly in their twenties and thirties, some with baby strollers alongside their table. Several people had arms covered in tattoos or hair colored blue or orange or multiple ear or nose piercings.

Rachel laughed. "It's hard to believe all these young people have been without wi-fi or cell service for multiple days now," she said. "And they seem to be okay with it."

"They're used to it," Alain said. "This is how we live. It's true, we get used to much that others would find intolerable. And yet, look. People are enjoying one another's company. Nobody has their head down staring at their phone. That's what I found so strange when I made a trip back to New York last year. Groups of people together but really not together at all."

She smiled. He had a point. She wondered what he'd think if he knew that she'd been having a whole relationship over the internet with Griffin and had actually believed she was falling in love with him. She realized now that even though it had begun several months ago, what they had wasn't a relationship at all. It had been so easy to assume that the internet could lend itself to intimacy.

The server came over and Alain asked if she'd like some

local French wine and would allow him to order a few Provençal seafood specialties for dinner. She nodded, relieved he hadn't mentioned sheep innards, as Griffin had. Alain spoke to the server in French and a few moments later, he returned with a bottle of wine. He served some to Alain, who tasted it and nodded, and then filled both of their glasses. The wine was light and a little fruity, different from the one she'd had with her burger last night but equally appealing.

"You're in for a delicious meal," Alain told her. "I know that you came here for the history, but we are way more than that. I hate how often people try to understand others by reducing them to one thing. A sad person. A scared person. A friendly person. We are all many things at once. That's what I find with the children. It's possible to be happy and sad and lonely and to feel connected all at the same time. I think that's the miracle of people. I see so much that surprises me."

She took that in, thinking how she'd grown up with such a different perspective. She'd learned from her grandfather to hold back as a protective strategy. To appreciate the safety of familiar surroundings and unchanging routines. To avoid surprises, not to actively seek them out. But here she was, out in the world, drinking great wine and anticipating a fabulous meal and having a conversation with a very delightful person she'd just met who lived in a far-off country. She felt connected, as he'd said. And not just with a face or a text or a document on a screen.

"So how about you?" he asked. "What surprises you?"

"What surprises me?" She put her chin in her hand and thought. "I think what surprises me is how I'm feeling now. How I don't know anyone—I mean, the person I came to be with isn't here and I didn't know him very well anyway. And yet I feel so comfortable and so welcomed. I like it here. I came here thinking this would be a sad place because of its history, and because Cece's story feels so tragic, and her book feels sad, too. Even though it's a children's book, it has so much danger. It made me cry when my grandfather read it to me. But it's not a sad book in the end. And this isn't a sad town at all. It's like you said—it's lots of things. We can be lots of things. The past and the future."

He nodded and lifted his glass, toasting to what she said. She raised her glass and sipped too.

"It makes me think about New York and September 11th," she added. "The memorial where the towers stood, with the fountains of rushing water. It's always crowded, and there are people stopping to remember, but also people hurrying to get somewhere, or sometimes children running around. And some people don't like that it's not more somber. But it's outdoors, and it's New York, and isn't that what the people who died would want? Life to come back? Although... I guess it's not that simple. I've been thinking about that a lot. My grandfather—he never could get beyond his past."

"Tell me more about him," Alain said.

"I wish I knew more," she said. "I only know that he grew up in France and he was here during the war and it affected him deeply. He was always angry and he made other people feel bad, even those who tried to love him. Except me. He was great to me. Maybe because I was just a kid."

She went on to describe the nursing home where he lived and how she'd stumbled upon *The Little Lost Fish* when she was looking for things to show him—and how startled she was by the dedication. "When I showed it to him, he started talking about Cece like he knew her. He even knew that was her nickname! It made me believe there was a deep connection with my family. I mean, that dedication—that name, Brielle Aimée. I don't think it could be a coincidence that my mother has the exact same name. I mean... do you?"

She saw him look down. "I don't know," he said softly. She wondered if she'd been sharing too much.

"I'm sorry," she said. "Did I say something—"

"Oh, no. No," he told her. "I'm just... I'm touched by your feelings for your grandfather. He's lucky to have you."

"I'm lucky to have him. He's all I had growing up." She looked at him. "What about you? You said you knew how I felt when I mentioned my grandfather this afternoon. Do you have someone older in your life, too?"

He nodded. "She's haunted by the past as well," he said. "Not in the same way as your grandfather. She doesn't live with anger. She lives with... regrets. And some guilt. I want to ease her mind as much as you do your grandfather's. Funny, right? We live with the sorrows and the shame of those who came before. We talk a lot about this at the school, our faculty. How we want our young students to understand their history but not be weighed down by it."

She watched him take a sip of his wine. He was such a thoughtful, wise person. And yet, he remained so cryptic. Who was this older person in his life, and what regrets did she have? Rachel couldn't shake the feeling that Alain still didn't trust her. That he knew something that could help her but didn't want to offer it yet. He was speaking with such purpose, choosing his words so carefully—the way he'd turned the conversation to the children instead of opening up more. She'd thought earlier that it was Griffin and his mention of a TV crew that were making Alain cautious. But they'd gotten past that—at least she'd thought they had. Was there something more that she represented to him? Something she needed to explain before he could be sure about her?

The waiter arrived with their food, three steaming plates that he set in the middle of the table. She took a portion of each onto her plate, and everything was delicious—a wonderful blend of seafood and pasta and light, citrusy sauces.

"I did learn a lot today, after I left you," she said, wanting to start up the conversation again.

"Yes?"

She explained how she'd gone to the library and come away with the book of photos. "The pictures of the children were heartbreaking," she said. "Those sweet faces, and all they'd gone through."

"But many of them grew up and went on to live good lives," he said. "It's a testament to them. And to the people who took care of them."

"I saw a photo of Cece, too. With a baby girl," she added tentatively. She remembered how he'd reacted when she'd questioned earlier whether Cece could have had a daughter. How he'd declared with such confidence that no, she hadn't. She was reluctant to return to that uncomfortable conversation. But she also didn't want to hide what she'd seen. Nor did she like the idea of avoiding a topic that she cared so deeply about.

"I learned that some people thought it was her baby, while others say it was one of the Jewish children in the orphanage," she said. "It's hard for me to understand how no one knows for sure. How does a person disappear like that? How can there be no documented information about her—especially since there's the book she wrote that's been translated around the world?"

"I guess that's how she wanted it," he said.

She eyed him suspiciously, as a thought occurred to her.

"Wait, do you know more about her than anyone else does?" she asked. "Is that why you won't speak about her?"

He stayed quiet, looking at his plate.

"Why won't you tell me?"

"It's not my story to tell."

"But then... whose is it? And why—"

Just then a shadow crossed their table. Rachel looked over her shoulder to see Claude approaching. "*Salut, mes amis!*" he said. "What a nice evening for an outdoor meal. Take advantage. It won't be like this much longer."

Alain stood. "Please, join us."

"Oh, no. I couldn't."

"Yes, please," Rachel added. She was sure Alain was relieved to see him because it took the pressure off answering her questions. She would have wanted to continue talking with Alain. But she liked Claude. And she would have regretted if Alain cut the evening short again, as he did last night.

Claude took one of the empty seats at the table, and the server brought over another plate and poured him a glass of wine. He took the serving fork and put some food from each of the platters onto his plate, then drank a good portion of his wine. "You know I had dinner already, but that never stops me from eating again. Mmmm, delicious, everything! Rachel, how was your first day in our fine village?"

"It was lovely," Rachel said. "I followed your map and went to the school. Alain was kind enough to let me visit with the children. And then I went to the library," she added. "I saw a photo of Cece. And now I'm even more curious about her."

"I wish I had more to tell you," Claude said. "You'd think I would, but I don't. You see, I knew her for a time. I don't often admit it, but perhaps the wine has loosened my tongue."

Rachel looked at him. "You *knew* her?"

He nodded. "I was one of the Jewish children saved here."

She gasped. "Oh, Claude," she said. "I had no idea." She didn't want to press him to talk. She would feel terrible if he thought her intrusive. But unlike Alain, he seemed perfectly happy to offer up more.

"I was very, very young," he said. "I don't even remember what she looked like. l do remember arriving there. There was a man who drove three of us to the house."

"You must have been so scared."

"Actually, I don't remember being scared. Or sad. Maybe I was in the beginning. But I mostly remember feeling safe once we arrived. There were games and books and toys, and there was enough food to keep our bellies full. Not as much as here now. But enough." He chuckled and took a forkful of fish.

"And Cece was a marvelous teacher," he added. "I remember she and this man, Rémy, and a few others took such good care of us. It was a very nice existence. Of course, we had to memorize fake names and addresses to give if anyone asked. But they didn't make it sound scary. It was just a rule. We had to practice, though. They gave us candy if we said it correctly—and an extra piece if we said it without hesitation." He chuckled and shook his head. "They were so clever. And so... what is it in English? *Faire preuve d'un calme olympien?*"

"Olympian?" Rachel asked.

"It's an expression," Alain said. "It's like... cool as a cucumber."

"Yes, cool. Calm," Claude said. "And then... they were gone. Both of them. I didn't understand. I was five years old. But I knew we wouldn't be staying there in the house for much longer. One day a man took a few of us into the woods one night. We walked for days. I don't remember much. Somehow there was food for us. That's where I broke my leg. As you no doubt have noticed, it never healed properly. But we did make it to Switzerland, and there was a refugee camp where we stayed. Later I found out that my parents and my older sister died in Auschwitz."

"I'm so sorry," Rachel said.

Claude nodded. "I stayed in Switzerland for many years," he said. "I went back to my real name, Claude, instead of the pretend one I had to learn back then, Daniel. A very nice family took me in, and I could have stayed there for the rest of my life. But I always knew I'd come back. This place feels like home."

He drank some wine, then smiled and patted her hand. "We all have stories," he said. "I imagine you have one, too. But I think I've overstayed my welcome. I'm going to push on.

Thank you for sharing your dinner with me. Enjoy your evening."

She watched him walk away, dragging his right foot. "That poor man," she said. "He's all alone, isn't he? I saw him yesterday bringing home soup for dinner just for himself. Does he have anyone in his life?"

Alain shook his head. "The singer at the bistro where you ate last night? She's the closest one to him. They've known each other for... going on forty years."

"Does she love him? Does he love her?"

"I'll leave that for him to share."

She looked at him. "You say that a lot—what stories are yours to tell and what stories aren't. That's important to you, isn't it? People owning their own stories?"

He nodded. "At the end of the day that's all we have. We are our stories."

"I guess so." She took a sip of wine to get up the courage to say what was on her mind. "What about you, Alain?" she asked. "What is your story? Or aren't you ready to share it with me?"

He smiled. "It's complicated," he said. "And I'd like to share it with you. But not yet. I do feel for you and your grandfather, Rachel. I hope you can go home with whatever it is that will answer your questions and ease his mind. But my role in that..." He paused. "Like I said, it's complicated."

"I see," she said and finished her wine. Again he'd closed the door, and there was nothing more to say.

A short time later, they left the restaurant. Rachel was surprised when Alain took her hand as they walked back to the guest house. She didn't think he liked her that way. He'd been polite and personable at dinner, but also guarded, offering some tidbits about himself but holding so much back. Even though he'd made such a point of liking surprises, of being open to life. And yet, she welcomed his touch. His hand felt solid and cool. She hadn't held hands with someone for a long time, maybe not since she was in high school. She looked around. The streetlamps were dotting the atmosphere with diffuse clouds of light, so that the olive trees along the road seemed to be outlined in gold. It was a beautiful sight, and she felt herself falling even more in love with this pretty village. If her grandfather really had lived here, she had no idea how he could have left it behind.

They reached the guest house, and Alain paused in front of the steps to the door. He turned to face her, still holding her hand. "I'm leaving tomorrow morning for a couple of days," he told her. "I'm catching the early train out of town."

"Oh?" she said, trying to sound curious. But she couldn't help but be disappointed to hear he was leaving.

He nodded. "With my hat in my hand, actually. I have meetings in Lyon and Paris with some foundations and philanthropic groups. The renovation is proving more expensive than I'd hoped. I don't want to cut corners. The school is too important."

"Is it difficult? To get the funding?"

"Hard to say. There's money there. But I do need to make the case. Getting face to face with these groups helps. They deserve for me to make the effort to show up."

She tilted her head. "You care so much about this school, don't you?"

"It's my life's work."

She thought back to what she'd left behind at home, her own work. A failed attempt at a Ph.D. A job she liked but that didn't mean to her what the school meant to him. "It must be nice," she said. "To have something you can call your life's work."

"It is," he agreed. "Although to be honest, at this moment it doesn't feel like the center of my world at all."

"No?"

He shook his head. "Because right now, all I can think about is how much I want to kiss you."

She looked at him, startled. She hadn't expected that. Yes, he'd taken her hand, but that had felt more sweet than romantic. She was flattered by his words. She wanted to kiss him, too.

"I'd like that," she said.

He stepped closer and dropped her hand, and a moment later she was wrapping her arms around his neck and feeling his arms around her waist, and feeling, too, his warm lips on hers. It was a lovely kiss. A kiss she wished could go on forever. Their mouths fit together so well, their heads moving slightly in harmony. When she pulled back, she felt him slowly withdraw, too, and they pressed their foreheads together for a moment. He'd talked about connection, and so had she. And for a moment, she felt that together they were showing each other what true connection was.

But there was so much distance between them. He had information, secrets, that he wouldn't tell her. And he hadn't explained why. He'd simply said it was all too complicated. She'd grown up with a man who kept secrets. She didn't know if it was smart to get involved with a man who, while clearly charismatic and more engaging than her grandfather, seemed to be the same way.

She dropped her chin down, not knowing what would come next.

He took her hands with both of his, and she looked at him. The wind had kicked up, and his hair was blowing across his forehead. The expression in his eyes was warm and reassuring. "I'll be gone through Wednesday. Thursday at the latest. Will you still be here? I mean, I hope you'll still be here."

She didn't know how to answer. She hadn't decided what to do. She didn't know whether she would find the answers about her mother and Cece that she was looking for, and if the search yielded nothing in the next day or two, what point was there in staying? Just to wait for him to come back? Her grandfather was alone. And with no internet or phone, she had no idea of what was going on with him. Whether he was lonely or frightened. Whether he was missing her. She'd hate if he was suffering in any way.

"I..." She shook her head. "I don't know. I have a life... too..."

"Of course," he said. "And this, I guess, is why I don't let myself get involved. It's hard, saying goodbye. But this is the kind of place where some people stay... and others pass through."

He walked her to the door, opened it for her, and then kissed her on the cheek.

"Have a good trip," she said. "And good luck. I hope you get every dime... you need..."

"I hope you get what you need, too," he said.

He paused, then turned to walk away. She watched him disappear into the darkness. She didn't want this to be the end. They'd only just met. But what choice did she have? She hadn't come here to stay. She was the second type he'd mentioned, the one just passing through. She'd had no business letting herself start to fall for him. In a way, it seemed similar to how she'd fallen for Griffin. Both men were unavailable when you came right down to it. Was Nancy right—did she not want to meet anyone? Was she like her grandfather, too damaged to connect for real?

Was Alain just like Griffin to her? Or was this different?

That night, she stayed awake for a long time, thinking about the last twenty-four hours. The town had affected her. She thought about Claude and the singer at the bistro whom he'd known for forty years. She wished she could see them come together before she left. Because maybe then she'd see real love. What did it even look like? Was love having someone who opened the door for you? Who bought you gifts? Who stayed up at night when you were alone? Who took care of you when you weren't feeling well? Or was it about feelings and not actions? Someone who made you smile when you were low? Someone you couldn't keep your hands off of? Someone whose kisses made your heart sing and whose smile made it jump? Was love the thing that finally let you feel okay with yourself? Appreciate yourself because someone else did?

The problem was that she'd never seen real love before. Her grandfather hadn't loved her grandmother, as far as she knew. Or if he had, he'd long forgotten about it. He didn't have any photos of her. He'd never spoken about her. He had no good memories of her, at least none that he'd ever cared to share. And her mother had been alone, too.

And maybe that was why she'd always been so confused about love. Scared that it wouldn't be what she wanted it to be. To her, the promise and anticipation of love were thrilling, so she clung to it. Nick had once told her that he thought she loved the pursuit of love. Maybe he was right.

Because the only time she'd perceived anything close to real love was the time when she was little and her grandfather first mentioned Cece. She hadn't thought of that conversation in many, many years, but it came back to her now. It was one evening when she was in bed and Papy had just finished reading *The Little Lost Fish* to her. She was in second grade, at a stage when she was always asking questions, and she'd been learning in school that week about the parts of a book: the cover, the table of contents, and the title page, with the names of the author and illustrator.

"Who wrote this story?" she'd asked.

"She was a friend of mine."

"Where is she now?"

"Far away."

"Can I meet her?"

"I don't think she... I don't know where she is."

"But how can she be a friend if you don't know where she is?"

"I used to know her."

"Oh." Rachel had taken this in. "What did she look like?" she asked.

"She was the most beautiful woman I'd ever seen," he told her.

"Then why didn't you marry her?"

He didn't answer.

"Did you love her?"

"This is not a good conversation."

"Did you tell her you loved her? Did she know? Did she love you too?"

He shook his head.

"Why not?"

"Because I didn't deserve to love her," he said. "I didn't do enough. I wasn't worthy of her love."

Rachel had thought about this all that night and into the next day. "Do I do enough?" she asked him the following night. "Am I worthy of your love?"

"You're a child. Children are always worthy of love."

She'd thought then of all the books she knew—how they so often ended with a parent telling their child they loved them. Even when the child was naughty. Even when the child made a mistake. There was nothing a child in a book could do that would stop them from being loved at the end. That was the good news. Even when her grandfather was too distracted or sad to show her love, she knew she was loved.

But the adults in her life didn't always feel loved.

For a long time, this made her terrified to grow up.

In the dark, Rachel got out of bed and retrieved from her bag the hardcover history book she'd brought back from the local library. She switched on the lamp on the nightstand and climbed back onto the mattress. She opened the book again to

Cece's picture. Cece had been so beautiful. And so good, according to Claude. So good to the children she took care of.

She flipped ahead a few pages, seeing more photos of the children—sitting in a circle on the rug in the living room, displaying drawings they had made, having dinner together at a dining room table. And then she reached the next chapter, which was about the Nazi threat that loomed over the town. There were pictures of Nazi soldiers and then a page titled *Les Collaborateurs Nazis*. Nazi collaborators. Below the heading was a group picture of French policemen, four of them, dressed in uniform and standing outside a building with a sign that read POSTE DE POLICE.

She drew in a breath.

She'd know him anywhere, that man on the left. Even in a photo from so long ago. Those broad shoulders. That long, straight nose. The perfect posture. The cleft in his chin.

It was her grandfather.

NINETEEN
JANUARY 1943

In the days that followed, Celina and Rémy barely spoke to one another. They interacted only to exchange necessary information: some hand-me-down sweaters had arrived; there was no meat to be had, so the children would have to do without this week; Claire had the sniffles so she shouldn't go outside to play. Celina held classes at the carriage house in the mornings as usual, and nodded politely at Rémy when they crossed paths in the house. She hated that they were at odds with each other, despite the kiss they had shared. He was her friend, her teacher and, in a way, her savior. By opening this place to her, he had brought meaning to her life, something that had been lacking since Emile died. He had given her purpose and shown her a way forward other than returning to her childhood home and a life that no longer felt like hers. He had given her a way to pursue hope, to find humor, to embrace connection anew. The kiss had proven all that and more.

But he had pulled rank that night in the kitchen. He had shut her down, something the kiss couldn't erase. At dinner each night, she saw Adele and Robert look at the two of them doubtfully. And before long, those looks transformed into sadness. Celina understood. There was a rift in the family they had become. And she wondered if things could ever be good again.

But all that was mild compared to what happened next.

Three nights after their disagreement in the kitchen, during one of the coldest nights of the winter, Celina was awakened by the slam of a car door outside and the sound of angry German commands: "Open up! *Mach es Schnell!*" She sprang out of bed and threw a blanket over her shoulders. In the hallway she saw Adele, and when she got downstairs, Rémy and Robert were looking out the window. Celina rushed over to join them. The harsh beams of the car's headlights revealed what was happening: four German soldiers were across the road, pounding on the door of an adjacent farmhouse. When the door opened, they stormed inside. A few minutes later, she saw them dragging a man out of the house and through the deep snow. He was in his pajamas, with no coat and his feet bare.

"Oh my God," Celina murmured. It was one of the farmers she'd encountered on her first night in town. One of the two who had helped protect Brielle from Red and then shown Celina where to bring her.

Rémy rushed away from the window and out of the house. Celina and the others watched him through the window as he approached the group. "Excuse me, gentlemen," they heard him call calmly as he drew nearer, stepping through the melting snowbanks to avoid the icy walk. "Is there a problem? Can I—"

"Back away!" one of the soldiers shouted, as another landed a punch on Rémy's face. Rémy reeled and fell on the ice, and the soldiers kicked him repeatedly as he lay on his side. Celina started for the door, but Adele grabbed her arm to stop her. She turned to the window again and saw Rémy on the ground, looking their way. She knew he wanted her to stay put, to not make things worse by engaging. That's what he'd taught her. That was the only way to survive.

The soldiers pushed the pajama-clad man into their car, then climbed in themselves, and the car drove off. When they could no longer see the taillights, Robert grabbed a flashlight from the closet, and the three of them ran outside. Rémy pulled himself onto his knees. When he looked up, a thick rope of blood streamed from his hairline down his face.

They pulled him up and helped him back to the house, his legs stumbling and dragging. "I'm okay," he said. "I'm okay." But Celina heard a weakness in his voice that she'd never heard before. And it touched a part of her heart that she didn't know was there.

And that's when she knew she loved Rémy.

It wasn't right. She had no business falling in love.

But she couldn't help it. What would happen now?

The next morning, the children went about their usual routines, seeming not to notice that anything had changed overnight. Rémy's right eye was swollen, his arm was in a makeshift sling, he limped heavily as he walked, and he had a large bandage on his forehead that Adele had applied. But when he smiled at the children and told them he'd tripped on the ice that morning bringing in a delivery of eggs and flour, they believed him and continued with their day. Celina was relieved. And she wasn't surprised. Rémy had created a bubble for the children. They were insulated from the outside world, and whatever they had experienced in the past had long ago faded from their minds. Maybe in time their fears would resurface. Maybe years from now a memory of a parent being beaten or of a cold night outside or of hunger and grief would tear them apart. But for now, they were good.

The one thing that did change was Rémy's demeanor. It was a bigger change than the one Celina had seen when he returned from Lyon. In the days that followed his beating, he was quieter, and there was a shadow in his expression. He was distracted. He left the dinner table early. He still read stories to the children or admired their artwork, but his praise was softer, and somber. His face lacked the spark that had always been there before. The spark that made her believe there was a future ahead for all of them.

With Rémy compromised, she knew it was her job to step up. She helped carry in the firewood that Robert chopped, glad that the physical work in the house had made her stronger than she'd ever been. She helped Adele prepare meals that would fill the children up while making the ingredients last as long as possible. In the evenings, she worked extra hard to be cheerful and encouraging so the kids wouldn't notice Rémy's silence, the way he frequently sat still in his armchair and stared out the window. She made sure there were games and stories and songs, and lots of joyful posing as Lawrence snapped pictures with the camera he'd received for Christmas. When it was time for bed, she watched Rémy slowly find his way upstairs, stepping with his left foot and then pulling his right foot up to meet it, leaning heavily on the banister. Her heart ached as she followed with Brielle in her arms.

And so the days passed, one by one. But Celina knew they were going down a new, frightening road. They had built a household here, and it had reminded her of the children's blocks—diverse shapes and pieces coming together to create a whole. Except that the blocks all came together neatly—the square block went in the square hole, the round block went in the round one, the thin cylinder slipped perfectly through an opening in the flat block. The whole of their little community seemed fractured beyond repair. She felt horrible about the way she had spoken to Rémy about Brielle's mother, about the demands she'd made and the argument they'd had. She'd behaved like a child. She shouldn't have antagonized him, asking him to do something he believed was ill-conceived and could lead to more danger. And above all, she shouldn't have allowed the kiss to happen. It had added too much fuel to the fire. Now when he was suffering and really needed her, there was too much baggage between them for her to truly help.

"Is he okay?" she asked Adele one day as they prepared dinner in the kitchen. Marie was supervising the children's rest time in the living room, and Brielle napped in a bassinet Celina had placed where it would draw warmth from the stove.

Adele adjusted the flame under the soup pot. "He will be okay. He's strong, my brother. We grew up nearby, in a village similar to this one, but with a father who wasn't good"—she clenched her fist, and Rachel realized she meant he hit them—"and a mother too weak to stop it. I was the older one, but he was the protector. He protected me. He aims to protect anyone who is without power."

Celina nodded. She was sorry but not surprised that Rémy would have a story like that. It was the reason he'd become who he was.

Adele turned back to the boiling soup. "I know you're concerned," she said. "I'm worried, too. Nobody wants him back more than I do. Just keep teaching the children and caring for the baby. Keep your attention on them."

"I will," she said. "But the thought of him... I mean, there must be something more I can do... just thinking about..." She looked down and shook her head. When she glanced up, she saw Adele looking at her.

"Oh, no," Adele said. "Tell me this isn't so. Did you fall in love with him?"

Celina looked down at the table. "No. No, I mean... no," she insisted. But she knew Adele didn't believe her. She was sure it was written all over her face. The way she thought about him constantly. The way she yearned for him to smile again. The way it pained her so badly to see him broken. The way he'd touched her shoulder that one night when she was upset about the children and all they'd experienced. The way they'd shared that powerful, life-changing kiss. The way she'd sometimes stay awake at night wishing he would come into her room…

"It's not safe to fall in love these days," Adele told her. "It endangers us all. You must stop yourself. Nothing can come of it."

Celina felt her eyes fill. "I keep remembering him being beaten that night. He was punched and kicked, and still he said he was okay—"

"Celina, stop," Adele said. "We come from hearty stock here in the mountains. We are solid and we don't bend. Generations of us have built the little villages here, just like millions of years have built the mountains that surround us. Take a lesson from us. Stay strong now, and it will serve you the rest of your life. Trust me. You have it in you."

Celina clenched her hands together. "I don't think I do," she said, her voice shaky.

"Then you must leave," Adele said. "Get on a train and go to a new place. Find a way back to America if you can, and wait out the war there. You are free to leave here. The only thing that stops you is whether you are one of us now. Whether you want to stay and do the work."

Celina knew Adele was right. It was weak of her to fall in love here, now, when the world was on fire. It was unfair to put her own feelings ahead of the children's safety. It was wrong to be selfish when Rémy was so selfless.

Or was love the only way to make it through?

The weeks slowly passed. Every morning she helped dress and feed the children, then gave Brielle to Marie. With the temperatures so frigid, she began teaching class in the living room, so the children wouldn't have to go outside to reach the classroom. Robert had helped her bring pencils and paper and other supplies to the house. Every day she taught the children about weather and time and days of the week, about colors and letters and how to write their names. Every afternoon she brought the children to the dining room for lunch, and played with Brielle, watching the little girl grow and change, reaching for toys, laughing, making more sounds, learning to sit. Later she'd bundle the village children up in scarves, hats, and gloves and watch Marie escort them home. At dinnertime, she'd bring the Jewish children to the dining room. Sometimes Rémy would show up for meals, and sometimes Adele would carry a tray upstairs to him.

At night she would come downstairs to work on her book, hoping Rémy would join her. Sometimes she heard him walking upstairs, the sound of his limping gait distinctive. And sometimes he would come into the living room, only to murmur, "Oh, you're working. I'm sorry," and go upstairs again. She longed for him to stay. She longed for him to trust her again. But whatever he was feeling—whether it was distance because of their disagreement or his own deep concerns about what the Nazis might do next, he kept to himself. He refused to let his eyes meet hers. She'd never felt so alone since the night she lost Emile.

As the end of March approached, the snows melted, and the days lengthened. One day Celina realized she'd made it through her first winter in Paillettes. But while the temperatures started to grow warmer, the tension in the house remained. The war was still ongoing. The threat of the Nazis was unrelenting.

Then one night just after she'd put Brielle in her crib and gone downstairs, the pages of her book in hand, she found Rémy standing by the bottom of the staircase. The lamps were dark, and the only light was from the fire, which bathed him in a flickering golden glow. His gaze rose as she walked down each step, but the rest of his body was still. It seemed he'd been waiting there for her. Her heart jumped at the sight of him, of those large, enveloping eyes. It had been a long time since he'd looked at her with tenderness.

"Celina," he whispered.

She paused on the bottom step. "Did you want something?"

He put his finger to his lips and motioned to her to follow him. She put her pages down on the writing desk. He led her into the kitchen, using his palm to still the swinging door behind him. He leaned against the countertop.

"You were right," he said. "There'll be more raids now that spring is here. It's going to get harder to protect the children. Sometimes patience is what's needed, but sometimes it's not. I was wrong. We need to do things your way."

She shook her head. "I don't understand."

"What I'm saying... is that we are going to bring Brielle back to her mother."

Celina breathed in sharply. "But what about all you said? What about—"

"Those clues in your book—I don't think they're a trap. I've seen the Nazis set traps before, and this one doesn't feel the same. I believe you're right, that someone is trying to tell us the woman is alive and in Switzerland. I've given this a lot of thought. I don't know how long we can outlast the Germans. But we have a way out for the baby. And waiting... I fear it will make things worse. One less child here means one less child to feed, one less child to hide. We need to take her away. For her own sake and for the sake of the rest."

"Yes," Celina said. "Yes. But how will we do it?"

"The same way others are escaping. It's happening every night, now that the worst of the winter is over. We will cross through the woods to the Swiss border. There are people out there who will help us."

"But you can't. You're still hurt."

"I'll be fine. I can make it." He paused. "Can you?"

She looked down, feeling tears stinging her eyes. Of course she could make it. She knew what it entailed. She'd heard the stories. It would take several days, maybe even weeks. The route was strenuous. There would be little food. They would likely be sleeping out in the woods when they couldn't find shelter. Still, she was fit and strong. Strong enough to take care of Brielle. Strong enough for Rémy to lean on, too, if his injuries meant he needed her help.

But now she remembered what he had said that evening of their fight. The evening of their kiss, the same evening when he had resisted this trip. He'd said that if she went to Switzerland and found Brielle's mother, she wouldn't be able to come back. Nobody would believe she'd return without her child, least of all Ed. He would be suspicious, and ultimately he would figure out what was going on in the house. He would realize that none of the children here had real families in the village. Rémy had suggested that night that if she took Brielle to Switzerland, she'd have to stay there. Or even go back to Maryland.

But how could that be? She couldn't leave Paillettes for good. She loved it here. She loved the smell of the fireplace when it was cold outside. She loved the way a good meal, even when the food was mostly thin soup or vegetable stew with a bit of potato, could warm her belly. She loved how tired she was at the end of the day. She loved that if she was very quiet at night when she finished working on her book, she could hear the quiet, calm breathing of the children in their beds as she tiptoed to her room. She loved how she worked so hard that she sometimes felt her legs ache and tremble as she fell asleep at night. She loved that she had finally found a way to believe there was something in her life that would last. That her time on this earth would count, that these children would grow up and have children of their own and would make a difference because they had been here in this house when the world was falling apart.

She loved Rémy.

She reached out and put her hands on Rémy's waist and then stepped in closer and pressed her head against his chest, hoping for a sign that he was feeling the same way. He placed his hands on her upper arms, holding her in place right where she was. He stroked her arms up and down a few times, and she felt his tension, his desire, in his touch. And then she felt him kiss the top of her head and rest his chin there. She didn't want to move. This wasn't the passionate, desperate kiss they'd shared last time, when they were both angry and confused. No, this time, this kiss, was different. In some ways smaller but in other ways much larger. This wasn't something that happened in the heat of the moment. This was an embrace that held all that had come before, and all that the future promised. If they could just figure out how to make that promise real.

He slowly eased her away, and she raised her head to look at him. He leaned down and kissed her, and she kissed him back, and then he brought her close and hugged her against him. She breathed in the scent of his chest, she savored the warmth of his body. She knew she had to release him. She had to be brave. But how much braver could she be? She had turned her back on so much to be here. She had left behind her family. Her comfortable way of life. The large, beautifully decorated bedroom her parents still no doubt had waiting for her. She had sacrificed festive meals and dinner parties and dances.

And it was right, the sacrifices she had made. But was she brave enough, too, to sacrifice her heart? To stay in Switzerland while Rémy returned here? She had lost her first love unwillingly. Could she willingly lose her second?

No, she thought. No, she wasn't going to lose him. She wasn't going to accept that reuniting Brielle and her mother meant giving up the man she loved. She was going to find a way to hold onto Rémy. And keep the other children safe, too.

He looked at her. "Yes?"

She nodded.

"Then go get the baby ready," he said. "Pack blankets and clothes, anything she'll need. Bring food and some clothes for yourself. Be quick.

"If this is going to work, we need to go at once."

TWENTY
OCTOBER 2018

In bed that night, Rachel couldn't shake that image of her grandfather in the history book loose from her mind. Could he actually have been one of the most horrible of individuals, someone who turned people over to the Nazis? He was her grandfather, her only relative, the one who'd made her cream cheese and jelly sandwiches, who'd walked her to and from school every day without fail, who'd taken care of her, played with her, and read to her? The one who'd been the adult in her life when she had no one else? How could it be true about this person she had loved so much? She wondered if he'd been haunted all these years by what he'd done and the memory of who he'd been. Or had he hoped that his years of taking care of her and tending to her and loving her would make up for his having been a *collaborateur*?

And what made her discovery of the photo even worse was that she'd never be able to ask him about it. His mind was so muddled and his ability to communicate so compromised. She'd felt lucky that she had arranged good care for him. That he was safe and comfortable, that there were people like Kate who made sure he was well-fed and tried to keep him content and calm. Did he deserve such care when he'd committed such horrific acts? When he'd been on the completely wrong side of things, when he'd sentenced who knew how many Jewish adults and children to torture and death?

She squeezed her eyes and flinched as the image from the book filled her mind. How could this murderer be her grandfather? Could there be some error? And yet, she didn't see any way of getting around the worst possible conclusion. Her grandfather's picture was right there on the page. She wished she could be mistaken, that she could say the photo was too old or too blurry to recognize him for sure. So many men probably looked alike back then, especially when they were dressed in uniform. Maybe she had jumped to conclusions. Maybe she should go back to the museum in the morning and investigate more.

But she knew it was him. His face was so clear.

She wondered if maybe he was less guilty than she feared. Maybe he had never actually turned over anyone. Maybe he never wanted to help the Nazis. But did that make it better? Was he allowed to claim innocence simply because he'd never willingly or intentionally sent a Jewish child or adult to the camps, to the gas chambers? Did he get a bye if he'd been forced to collaborate? If he'd have been killed had he tried to save anyone?

Or was that too easy? Did his mere presence on this atrocious police force implicate him no matter what he'd specifically done?

Of course it did, she thought. So many others had played a role in keeping the Jews in this town safe. They'd kept silent about changed names and birthdays, about documents forged. All it took to destroy something so carefully constructed was one person. One bad actor and, like a house of cards, the whole thing would collapse. That's what her grandfather had been—the one bad actor who likely caused Cece's death and the deaths of other people, too.

And what of her mother? Had she known the truth about her father? Is that why she never wanted to see him? Never acknowledged that he even existed?

And what about her, now that she knew the truth? What was her responsibility? Could she go home without confessing her grandfather's sins? Or did she have an obligation to tell Alain what she'd found out? To show him the picture of her grandfather? As the descendant of someone so guilty, did she have an obligation to apologize for him and make amends as best she could? Was she accountable for what her grandfather had done—and if so, in what way? Was she guilty for adoring her grandfather? For trying her hardest to make him feel loved? For all the hugs and kisses she'd given him over the years? For doing all she could to keep him protected in his old age?

She got up and tiptoed to the window, then lifted a slat of the wooden blinds. By the light of the moon and a few dim streetlamps, she could see that it had started to rain. It was a hard rain, not a gentle, cleansing one. The drops were large and came down with such force that they clattered against the window. She trembled, feeling cold. How could this be? Her grandfather, her sweet, sick grandfather. And yet she couldn't deny that everything now made sense. The anger he'd felt. The drinking too much during his younger years, which he'd hinted about. The absence of any information or memories about his wife. The separation from his only daughter right through the day she died. His inability to befriend anyone. His identification with the lost and lonely fish in the only book he cared about.

And then, of course, his confusing words when he'd seen the book's dedication. He'd implied it when she was there—that he'd played a role in whatever may have happened to Cece. Of curse, Kate had always encouraged her to dismiss his nonsensical rantings. She said it was just the dementia talking. But maybe she was wrong. Maybe his memory was entirely intact, and it was only his inability to hide his past anymore—maybe that was the true result of his dementia. Could he really have been an agent of death? Was there nothing else he could have done?

She wished there was somebody familiar she could talk to. But she was here in this isolated bubble. She wondered what Griffin would say to her. She didn't know, because she didn't know him at all. She'd fooled herself into thinking she did. But what about the people she did know? Nancy had known her grandfather since middle school. Together they'd decided he was damaged by what he'd witnessed during the Nazi takeover of the country where he grew up. What would Nancy say now if she knew the truth?

Rachel looked out the window toward the clock tower, its stern face visible despite the driving rain. This pretty town was still healing from the pain of those years, Alain had said. Yet everyone here had welcomed her. They had no way of knowing that she was connected to their pain and the evil that had caused it. She was the descendant of someone who had committed the worst of offenses. Someone who, with his inhibitions fading, had intimated that he'd played a role in the death of the author he'd introduced to her. And now she had her own conscience to examine. For a long time, she had known there was something off about her grandfather. Had she suspected at all what it was? Had she realized on some level that it was terrible? And had she been trying all her life to protect herself from having to admit any of this? By pursuing impossible relationships? By choosing a career where she didn't have to talk to people very much? By believing she didn't deserve as much love as others did—others without her family's dark secret?

Maybe she deserved to never find a partner, to never have a

family, since any children she had would be guilty like she was. She feared she was destined to spend the rest of her life alone. Maybe she'd always known deep inside that her grandfather's lineage should stop with her. That she should be the end of the line.

Rachel slept only about a half-hour or so at a time that night. In the morning, she got out of bed, dressed, and went downstairs. She was relieved to see that Claude wasn't there yet, that the desk was being staffed by one of the café workers. She ordered a croissant and a latte but when it arrived, she could hardly touch it. She kept her head down and murmured "*Merci*" as the woman placed the plate in front of her.

She wanted to leave town. She didn't think she could stay there any longer, knowing what she now knew. But she also realized she shouldn't leave without telling Alain what she'd discovered. Maybe he would feel compelled to share it with everyone in town, to let them know what he'd learned about the stranger they'd all welcomed so warmly. Or maybe he would keep it all to himself. Whatever happened, he was entitled to the information. Even if it meant she'd have to stick around a couple of days to tell him. She assumed he'd have left already. He said he was leaving on the early train this morning and would be back tomorrow or Thursday. So she had a whole day, maybe two, to wait.

What was she going to do? It no longer appealed to her to investigate any more history of the town. She didn't even care about *The Little Lost Fish* anymore. How dare her grandfather read her this book, over and over, and share the pictures, and dry her tears when they reached the sad part? He had never had any right to care about this book. She wished she'd never heard of it.

She went back to her room to get her coat. She needed to return the history book to the library. Upstairs, she slipped the history book into her tote bag, and then put her copy of *The*

Little Lost Fish alongside it. She thought maybe she'd donate that one while she was there. She wouldn't explain anything, she'd just put it on a table near the shelves.

Arriving at the library, she saw the man from yesterday checking in books from a stack on his desk. She looked down so their eyes wouldn't meet. He'd been so nice, and she hadn't deserved it. She decided she'd come back later, after closing time. Maybe she'd leave both books by the locked front door for him to find tomorrow when he came to open again.

Back on the street, she realized with a bit of revulsion that she was behaving just like her grandfather had all his life. Avoiding contact. Keeping to himself. But he was lucky. At least he had had her, his granddaughter, in his life. Someone who worshipped him and gave him love from the time she was tiny through his old age.

But no, she thought—he wasn't lucky, he was smart. Cunning. He had engineered their relationship by showing up when she'd had nowhere else to go, no other family member to take her in. Of course she'd loved him. And he didn't have to answer for anything, the way he might have if he'd appeared while her mother was still alive. With her in his life, he could reinvent himself as a loving grandfather with nothing to hide. How very clever he'd been.

She found herself walking along the gorge. The weather was colder today, and the water below looked choppy. She remembered what she'd read about this town and its harsh winters. How people had buckled down and gotten ready for the snow and the lack of food back during the war. Of course, things were better now. There was reliable heat and plenty of food. Still, she supposed the preparation for winter that the villagers had gone through remained a part of what made this town what it was. The past never really disappeared. Not for anyone.

Soon, she was close to La Petite École. She approached the

turnoff and started along the driveway. She had to see it again, the place where the Jewish children had stayed, the place where *The Little Lost Fish* had been written. To put a final button on this ill-conceived and painful trip.

She made her way up the hill. The building appeared especially stark and cold on this gray day. She looked at the narrow red door and the small windows, which seemed designed to keep the cold outside and the warmth inside. And to keep the children insulated, too, from the evil outdoors. Had her grandfather ever gone into the house? Had he ever seen the children he would betray? Had the children been taught to trust police officers, or had they always been on their guard? Was this where Cece's fate had been determined? Was this where her grandfather had set in motion the events that would ultimately lead to her death?

She was staring at the house, deep in thought, when she heard footsteps behind her. When she turned, she saw it was Alain's assistant, Madame Gare, walking toward her.

"Good morning!" the woman said in English, breathing heavily. "Our visitor from America. I'm glad to see you—I don't often get to use my native language. Just coming back from a little walk around the grounds. It takes so little to tire me out these days. The teachers all worry when I try to tackle these hills. But I think this is what keeps my heart ticking.

"So what brings you here?" she said as she gestured with her free arm toward the door. "I'm sorry if you were coming to see Alain. He's away on a business trip. Didn't he tell you?"

"He did," she said. "I found myself heading here anyway."

"It's an unusual place, isn't it?" she said. "So much lightness and warmth. It's the children, they make it so joyful. I can tell you, I feel this way year-round. Even in late fall, when you know winter is imminent."

Rachel nodded, although she wasn't feeling light or joyful.

"I first came to this place in late fall," Madame Gare

continued as they approached the front step. "It has a special meaning for me, the fall. But spring, of course, is lovely, too. June is especially beautiful. I used to teach about the seasons. What's that expression? You can take the teacher out of the school, but you can't take the school out of the…"

She halted on the step and looked at Rachel. "You look like you have the weight of the world on your shoulders. Is there anything I can do?"

"No. I'm sorry. I'm fine," Rachel said.

"I have days like that," the woman said, ignoring her denial. "And when I'm feeling blue, I spend time with the children. Even just watching them in their classroom."

"Thank you, but I'm… I'm really okay. I'm just getting ready to go back home, taking a last look around. But I need to stay until Alain returns. I need to talk to him before I go."

"Come in for a little while," she said. "If there's nothing else pressing, that is. I saw how much you enjoyed playing with the children yesterday. Maybe you'd like to spend a little more time with them. They are learning about holidays this morning. We teach all the holidays. We want them to be citizens of the world. Today I believe they are learning about Chanukah. Come, let me bring you in. I think you'll enjoy it."

The woman led her through the house, then out the back door and to the classroom behind the main building. She opened the door and waved to the young teacher, then led Rachel to a small round table at the back. They both lowered themselves onto the child-sized chairs, Madame Gare proving herself quite limber. The children were sitting on the rug facing their teacher, who was pointing to a Chanukah menorah on a table beside her, the brightly colored candles lined up in their holders waiting to be lit. Rachel was grateful that Madame Gare took it upon herself to translate the teacher's words, softly so as not to disturb the lesson.

"Chanukah is a holiday about miracles," the teacher said,

according to Madame Gare. "It's a holiday about surviving even when things are at their worst. The story of Chanukah tells us about one specific miracle. A miracle of a lamp burning for eight days, even when there was enough oil to keep it lit for one night only. Now, you may wonder why I said oil. And the reason is that this was a long time ago. There was no electricity. No light switches. Oil was used to provide energy for light."

The children peppered her with questions, and Madame Gare continued to translate: What kind of oil? Where did the oil come from? How did the oil work? How did they know how long it would keep the light on? Couldn't they get more oil from the store?

Rachel watched the teacher patiently try to answer. It was heartening, how inquisitive the children were. They wanted so much to understand this story that took place so long ago and involved so many things that were outside of their experience. She sympathized with the teacher, who was trying her best to make the story understandable. Because it wasn't a story that corresponded with logic. And Christmas was the same way. Yes, you could think that everything in the stories really happened. But you didn't have to. You didn't need proof that it was accurate. You were allowed to simply believe. As a child, she remembered questioning things that didn't feel logical. Like why her father left his family when her friends' fathers didn't. And why her grandfather took care of her when other grandparents just visited for weekends or holidays or special events like school plays or soccer games. But she'd also had faith in things she wanted to believe in. The tooth fairy. Santa Claus. A little fish who could evade capture by swimming through the ocean and somehow stay alive and free even when the possibility of capture and destruction was so high.

She'd had faith in her grandfather, too. She'd believed in his goodness despite evidence showing that others didn't think he was good at all. She'd had faith that he was lovable. And worth caring about. And the sadder he was, the more she'd believed. He'd had faith that she could spot goodness when she saw it.

That was what she was wrestling with. Her faith had been misplaced. She'd been fooled. And she had no idea how to cope.

The teacher dismissed the children back to their tables, encouraging them to use the waiting art supplies to draw and cut out their own Chanukah menorahs. Madame Gare took her leave, but the teacher smiled and nodded at Rachel, inviting her to stay and participate. Rachel was glad to remain. She liked being in the classroom and didn't need to know French to enjoy the project. A few children joined her at her table and she engaged with them, opening tubes of glitter glue, coloring with markers, and helping to sprinkle confetti.

When the teacher called the children back to help mount their artwork on the bulletin board, though, she knew it was time to go. She didn't belong here; she was merely a visitor. She gave a wave and left the room, thinking she'd go back to her guest house to pack. She would stop by here again tomorrow to see if Alain had returned. Hopefully he'd be here, and she could tell him the truth and then head back home. And figure out what to do. How to deal with the rest of her life. Would she ever not feel guilty for the person her grandfather had been?

She was walking through the kitchen on her way out when she heard someone say her name. She looked up to see Madame Gare by the stove.

"You're still here," the woman said. "You stayed a while, did you?"

"The kids are so cute," she said. "You can almost forget all the things bothering you."

"So there is something bothering you."

Rachel shrugged.

"Maybe I can help," the woman said. "I know how it is to be

a stranger. I just brewed a fresh pot of tea. Won't you join me? I think there are some wonderful *petits fours* here, too."

Rachel paused, then nodded. She didn't want to be rude. And there was something lovely about this woman. She seemed wise and kind.

"Thank you. I'd love to," she said.

The woman brought to the table two cups and saucers, dessert plates, and a platter of pastries. Rachel was charmed. The woman did have an American accent, and yet she also seemed very European. She went about the kitchen looking for things. "Where did I put the good linen napkins? Where did I put the milk pitcher?"

Rachel smiled as she took a seat.

"What is it?" the woman said.

"It's just so nice listening to you," Rachel answered. "I love how everyone is like family here. You're talking about where you put the napkins. I don't know—back in New York, everyone in an office... well, I've had plenty of jobs, and I never felt as homey as you do here."

Madame Gare poured the tea and then sat down opposite her. "There's a history here. Which I can share with you. But I think you said you have something else on your mind. What did you come to speak to Alain about? Was it about the author you came here to investigate, the one who wrote the picture book? Alain told me you'd mentioned that."

Rachel looked down. She didn't know why, but she felt compelled to open up. She trusted this woman.

"Yes, C. Tailleur," she said. "You see, I came here to find out her relationship to my family. And I found out something I'd never wanted to know."

"Oh?"

"I've loved her book since I was a little girl. And my grandfather loved it, too. I know that the author was arrested by the Nazis and killed when she tried to save a Jewish baby.

At least that's what seems to be true. And I've learned that my grandfather knew her, the author, and that he might have even been in love with her. But what I found out yesterday was that..."

She took out the history book and opened it to the page with the picture of him among the other French officers. She pointed to the image. "This is my grandfather. Henry. There's no mistaking him.

"My grandfather... was responsible for what happened to C. Tailleur."

The woman looked at the picture. And then she looked up at Rachel and shook her head. "Oh, my dear. Is this what you're struggling with? No wonder you're so upset. Tell me. Is your grandfather still alive?"

She nodded. "And that's another thing. How do I even face him, knowing what I know? My grandfather turned in the author and maybe other Jews in hiding. He was a Nazi collaborator. How do I live with that?" She shook her head. "I don't know why I'm telling you this. It's my life, it's my problem. I just... I'm just shocked. And overwhelmed. And I don't know what I do now."

The woman paused a moment. "No, you were right to tell me," she said. "Because I believe I can help you. First of all, you should know that we haven't been completely honest with you. I don't just work here. I own this house. And Alain is my grandson."

"Your grandson?" Rachel said. "Why didn't he tell me that?"

"Because I'm a private person," she said. "Alain is protecting me. That's what grandchildren do. It's what you're about to do. If your grandfather believes what you just said, you're about to ease his mind a great deal."

"I don't understand."

"I know," she said. "But you're about to. You see, Rachel,

your grandfather couldn't have caused the death of Cece Tailleur. Or of the child Cece rescued."

"How do you know?"

"Because I am Cece Tailleur," she said. "And I'm the author of *The Little Lost Fish*. Your grandfather wasn't responsible for my death.

"In fact, he saved my life."

TWENTY-ONE
MARCH 1943

Celina gathered clothes and supplies for herself and the baby, while Rémy filled a sack with cloth bags and metal containers of cheese, bread, fruit, and water. At the last minute, Celina also packed the envelope with Emile's illustrations and her verses. She didn't want to part with them, because they meant so much to her. But more important, she realized it would be dangerous to leave them behind. If Red or any German officer arrived and searched the house while they were gone, the clues on the pages would reveal their escape route.

Then Celina penned a short note to Adele, telling her she had decided to make her way back home so Brielle could meet her grandparents in the States. Of course, Adele knew full well that Brielle was not Celina's daughter; but Celina was certain Adele would understand the purpose of the note, and would produce it if any stranger came by and demanded to know what had become of the American teacher.

When the preparations were complete, Celina picked Brielle up from her crib and carried the sleeping baby downstairs. Rémy had fashioned a rucksack out of some sturdy sheets in the linen closet, so he could carry Brielle on his back. Brielle rustled a bit when Celina put her in the contraption, but she remained asleep, her cheek resting softly on the back of Rémy's shoulder, her lips parted, and her breathing rhythmic and steady. Rémy left the house, and Celina watched him limp toward the front steps, knowing he was still in pain from his fall on the ice and the soldier's kicks. But he only smiled at her when he looked back.

Celina walked to the doorway and, before switching off the nearby table lamp, took one last look at the living room, her eyes burning with tears. This was the place where she had come alive after all the grief of the long months before. She remembered how she'd first felt when she arrived in Paillettes. Up until then she'd been going through the motions of living. After Emile was murdered, his friends worried that the Nazis would come after her next, so they helped her move from Paris to a small flat in Lyon. She'd tried to make a new life there, but even after a year had passed, she still found her grief too much to handle and decided she needed to go home. If Max hadn't crashed the car, if she hadn't found Brielle under the tree, she'd be in Maryland right now.

And that would be wrong. Not that her family was bad. They loved her and wanted the best for her. But they didn't know the Celina that Rémy did. The Celina that she now knew. Maryland was nice, but she was meant for something else. A life where she could make a difference for others. She wasn't cut out to wait for things to get better. She was cut out to *do*.

And it was here, in this house, that she'd regained her footing and found her purpose. By meeting the children in this remarkable place, by teaching them and watching them thrive. She had been working to teach them letters and numbers and colors and the rest, but they had taught her lessons much more important. They had taught her how to rebound and how to

THE SECRET ORPHANAGE 221

forward. She had learned that it's okay to laugh and to love, even when caught in a windstorm of danger and despair.

How she loved this beautiful home. How she loved her little classroom behind the main house, where she'd watch the children stack blocks or collect sticks or take crayon to paper. Where they'd written their first words: *le jardin,* the garden; *les arbres,* the trees; *les montagnes,* the mountains. And, of course, the most important words of all: *ma maison,* my home; *ma chambre,* my room; *mes amis,* my friends. How would things only have been different if she'd known what Rémy would ask her to do tonight? If she'd known that Adele would be teaching tomorrow's lessons, and that when she bid the children "*Faites de beaux rêves,*" it would be the last time in a very long while. That Adele would be wishing them sweet dreams now.

And soon she'd be saying *au revoir* to Brielle. Except it wouldn't be *au revoir* in the literal sense: until we meet again. It would be *adieu au toujours.* Farewell forever.

Her hand gripped the doorknob, refusing to loosen. She'd once read that people find a moment in time that connects with their deepest desires, and they spend the rest of their lives trying to reclaim it. Would these last five months be the moment she'd always want to reclaim? Or was there some other exceptional moment still to come? It was hard to imagine so.

She gave the living room one last look. The living room, with its worn furniture and Rémy's armchair, its heavy stone walls and tiny windows, was beautiful to her. The damp, cold place that she'd come to call home. What would happen now? Would the three of them make it to Switzerland? Would they reach Brielle's mother? Would she and Rémy live to see this place and these beautiful children again?

She picked up the bag she'd packed with clothes and supplies, softly closed the door, checked that it had locked behind her, and then walked quickly to catch up to Rémy and

Brielle. She yearned to explain to Rémy what she was feeling, and to find comfort in his smile. But this was no time to talk about feelings. It was no time to feel anything. She needed to stay focused. They'd heard that several Jewish people had run into the woods these last few weeks, now that the weather was growing a bit warmer. Nobody knew if they'd made it to Switzerland or not.

But now it was their turn. The woods were like the magical jungle in the storybook Rémy had once read to the children. The jungle, according to the story, looked fearsome, dangerous. The little girl standing at the edge was scared. But her brother had said, "Take my hand." And when she did, the jungle transformed into a beautiful garden. The message, of course, was to look to those you love when you are scared, because people united are stronger than people alone. She longed to take Rémy's hand now. But one of his hands was gripping a tall broken branch he was using as a walking stick, and the other was holding the strap of one of their bags of supplies. And so she walked alongside him, holding the other bag and occasionally patting Brielle, grateful for the moonlight to guide their way.

They approached a bridge near the spot where she and Max had veered off the road. The cliffs were in shadow, the chasm vast, the gorge below invisible although she could hear the water rushing over the rocks she knew were there. She had a sense of smallness—the smallness of their steps, the smallness of this rocky bridge, the smallness of their existence. But surprisingly, the feeling wasn't so much frightening as it was elevating. The land, the region, the universe was large and powerful and unending. It made her aware that the Nazis—however malevolent, however lacking in humanity—were small, too. No match for all that existed before and would exist again. No match for all the potential inherent in the little baby who slept now against Rémy's back, her head peaceful on his shoulder. Celina knew it was absurd and probably incredibly naïve, but as they walked she couldn't help but feel hopeful. Even if she didn't survive this journey, others had and others would. And the universe would continue on.

They reached the other side and started down a long slope that would guide them in the right direction. In the last few weeks, Rémy had apparently done his research, so he knew where to go. The warmer temperatures had caused the snow to melt, and now the ground was thick and slippery, and she watched Rémy dig his feet into the dark mud, stumbling and fighting the suction of the earth beneath him, using his stick for leverage. Looping the strap of her bag over her elbow, she held Brielle steady on his back with one hand and clutched his elbow to keep him from falling with the other. Filtered through the tall pines, the moonlight let her see Rémy's face in profile, how sweaty his forehead was, how he grimaced as he walked. She admired his bravery so much and could only hope that she would be as brave as he needed her to be.

Below, she could see an upcoming split in the ravine, one channel bearing right toward a rocky incline and the other continuing straight toward dense woods. Rémy looked over his shoulder at her and gestured with his chin that they would head toward the hill. He started to turn right.

And then, he froze.

She came up beside him, and he held out his arm like a gate. She thought he was reassessing which route to take, maybe trying to remember what he'd been told by the villagers who'd returned after guiding groups of Jewish adults along this first leg toward safety. But when she looked at his profile, she knew he wasn't merely thinking. His jaw was clenched and his eyes were locked straight ahead.

He had heard something.

"Rémy," she whispered, and he drew his hand back and put a finger to his lips. She could hear a sound like leaves rustling, which seemed to be coming from the grove of trees just before the ravine split. It didn't seem ominous. No doubt, early spring could be windy in the mountains. And there was plenty of dead brush and twigs on the ground, newly released as the snow melted these past few weeks.

"I think it's okay," she whispered. "I think it's just the wind—"

But before she could finish the sentence, a shadow appeared on the ground. The rustling grew louder, and a moment later, a figure emerged from among the trees. She didn't know what it was at first, human or animal. But then the figure straightened, and by the light of the moon, she could see a shock of hair the color of fire.

Red.

She gasped and put her hand to her mouth. She couldn't formulate any coherent thoughts to utter. The only words that came to mind were, it's over… it's over… it's over—the short consonants, vowels, and syllables repeating in her head until they had no meaning. This was where her life would end. The war would take her, just as it had taken Emile and so many others. She only wished that Brielle and Rémy would be safe. She would gladly lay down her life for them.

"Hey, Henri!" Rémy said. "Nice night, huh? Taking a little stroll?"

Celina admired his coolness, calling the officer by his first name, acting like they were old pals who just happened to encounter one another while out on a spring evening. This was how Rémy got along in the world, his "we're all friends here" approach. But Celina knew it wasn't going to work. Not this time. Red was a policeman reporting to the Nazis. He'd probably seen them leave the house. He'd probably driven ahead and then crossed a more southern bridge on foot so he could cut them off here.

"No," she said. "Please, Officier Dumont. The baby—"

"I know all about the baby," he said. "I know she's *cachée*. I saw the note before your brother crashed the car."

She looked at him, speechless. What was there to say? He'd known all along about Brielle. He'd known she wasn't Brielle's mother. Maybe he knew about all the children in the house. She wondered how he could be so cruel. Not only was he capturing them—he was doing it now, well after they had left town. Catching them at the moment they were starting to believe they would make it.

She saw him look around, first to his left and then right. She wondered why he was prolonging this. To torture them? Where were the Nazi soldiers, with their ugly salute and the pistols and rifles they carried? Where were the ugly German commands? She hoped Brielle would continue sleeping. It would be so hard to hear the baby crying. She would have to comfort her somehow. It was too awful to contemplate what Red might do to her if he found her wails too annoying or feared they would warn other Jewish escapees to steer clear.

"Henri," Rémy said. "She's just a baby…"

His words faded away as Red took a step closer. Celina held her breath.

Red lowered his chin. When he spoke, it was barely a whisper.

"Don't take the turnoff. They're waiting there. Keep following the channel straight to the end. Then you can turn and head east into the woods. You'll find her mother in Beerli. As I wrote on those pages."

Celina stood still, shocked to her core. What had he said? Could it be true? Red, the police officer they'd feared so much— *he'd* written the clues? She'd never dreamed he would want to help her bring Brielle home. How had she misjudged him? And yet, there was no way she could have done otherwise. He'd never given any indication that he was on her side. And now she realized how smart that was. Only by being so frightening, only by behaving as a loyalist to the Nazis, had he been able to keep himself safe—which is what allowed him to make this scheme work.

She opened her mouth to speak, but before she could thank him, he waved her off. Then he walked past them and started back in the direction of Paillettes.

When they could no longer hear his footsteps, she turned to Rémy. He looked at her and raised his palms. She knew what he was thinking—that he didn't know how to proceed. Should they follow Red's instructions? Or was this a trap?

"He's telling the truth," Celina said. She was sure of it. Because as frightening as Red was, she'd often seen discomfort, awkwardness, and maybe even regret in his eyes and his demeanor. She'd found him so unnerving to be around. But now she realized he was playing a part. He didn't have the innate cruelty the Nazis did. He was an ordinary man forced into a horrible assignment.

And when it mattered most, his humanity had prevailed. She was only sorry he hadn't let her say thank you.

"I know," Rémy said. And they began walking once again, bypassing the turnoff and continuing straight.

Celina didn't know how long they kept going. She had no sense of time. The fear she'd felt when they'd first seen Red was lodged deep in her bones. It was all she could do to keep moving forward, propelled by the consistent, rhythmic beat of their footsteps, which became a kind of lullaby. But eventually she felt the ground become harder beneath her feet. Eventually the channel narrowed. And then, looking ahead, she saw faint bands of pink, orange, and peach starting to stretch across the sky. Dawn was breaking.

She paused and placed a hand on Brielle's back, as the baby continued to sleep against Rémy's shoulder. She wanted to stare at the sky for just a moment longer. She needed to memorize the sight, so she could later put it into words. This would be what the little fish would see on the final page of her book. A new beginning with all the promise of color. The way the future would look. For the fish. For Brielle. For everyone they'd left behind.

For everyone.

TWENTY-TWO
MARCH 1943

Celina was still looking at the sky a moment later, when a yellow dome made its appearance at the horizon.

She'd never seen the sun rise before. Only once had she been up all night. It was soon after she'd arrived in Paris. She and Emile, then dating, had attended an extravagant party hosted by the magazine Emile worked for. There had been champagne in tall crystal flutes and women in sparkly gowns and all kinds of delicious foods and delicacies—caviar and éclairs and fondue and chocolates laced with liqueur. She and Emile had paid way too much for their outfits—he looked dashing in a tuxedo and she'd worn a silky black dress with a bead-encrusted bodice. She'd been so glad to be with Emile, to be falling in love, to be living in this magnificent city, to mingle with Paris's elite, who had come out to celebrate the magazine's talented writers and artists.

Yes, the signs had been there—Hitler's ascendancy, the German invasions of Poland, Norway, and Denmark, the signs that Europe was a tinderbox and other countries in Europe including France could fall. But nobody that night had wanted to recognize such a possibility. The swanky partygoers all laughed and kissed and clinked glasses through the haze of alcohol and gluttonous excess. She and Emile stumbled back to his flat shortly before dawn and fell asleep on the sofa, too tired and drunk to find their way to his bed or get out of their evening clothes. She'd been elated that night, so in love with her beautiful beau and her exciting life. So glad to have left home, so sure she'd made the right decision. She trusted that the future would hold only more of everything she wanted. More time with the man she believed would eventually be her husband. More delicious foods. More finding her creativity and inventiveness with Emile as inspiration. He had turned something on inside of her, something electrifying, and she never wanted it to stop.

Now she looked at the sky and, unobstructed by champagne and the foolishness of innocence, she had clarity. She knew that today, this day, was real, and that what she was doing had meaning. And no matter how it ended for her and for Rémy, it was worth everything.

As the sun rose higher, they came across a small clearing surrounded by dense trees, and Rémy suggested they stop for a bit. She took Brielle off his back. Rémy spread out the blanket she'd packed, and she took out from his sack the food he'd loaded inside. She gave the baby a bottle of milk and some bread and softened fruit, pears and apples. Rémy suggested they get some sleep, and while she worried it wasn't safe to pause for long, she knew he needed to rest. She rolled his jacket into a pillow for him, shaken that he seemed so weak and that the cut above his eye had reopened and looked like it could be infected. She hoped they would make it to Switzerland while his wounds were still treatable. As he slept, hidden beneath the trees, she took Brielle for a walk, letting her sit in the soft weeds and helping her collect twigs and wildflowers and leaves. When she couldn't keep her eyes open anymore, she went back to the blanket and curled up near Rémy, pulling the baby close to her. She stared at Rémy for a few moments. His face twitched, and she hoped he wasn't getting feverish.

When she woke, the sun was overhead, and Rémy was preparing a snack for them. They ate quickly and then rose to start to walk.

"Do you want me to hold her?" Celina asked as Rémy began setting up the backpack to slip the baby into. "You're in such pain. Do you need to stay put for a little while more?"

"I can make it," he said. "There are helpers ahead. We will get help tonight, if we can just keep going."

They continued on all afternoon, stopping every couple of hours to rest and let Brielle play and tire herself out. And then, as the sun was setting, they came upon the encampment Rémy had told her about. There was an abandoned cabin, and a group of three men and two women gathered outside. They'd been told by earlier refugees that more might be coming, so they were prepared. One of the women brought them hot tea and some roasted meat, explaining that they had a small cookstove inside. The other woman took care of Brielle so Celina and Rémy could go inside and rest.

Inside the house, Rémy sat on a cot, while Celina found some towels. She dampened them with cooled water from a pot on the cookstove and, sitting next to him, patted the area above his eye, trying to soften the crustiness.

"We are going to have to get this looked at," she said.

He nodded.

"Do you hurt? Is it your hip? Your ribs?"

"I don't know. Both."

He slid down onto his side and lowered his head onto the pillow. "So, this is what I promised you, isn't it?" he said. "That day you showed up."

"Well, you didn't quite promise this," she joked, gesturing toward the dark, dusty room.

"I never said it would be luxurious."

"And you were right."

He turned onto his back. "Look up," he said.

She sat down on the rug next to the bed and looked through the slats of the roof. With no light from any nearby village, the darkness was deep, and the stars and the moon were more brilliant than she'd ever seen before.

"It's magnificent," she said. "It's peaceful."

He nodded and turned on his side again, looking at her. She shifted on the rug so she was looking at him, too.

"Celina," he said. "Tell me about the night Emile died."

"I told you everything."

"I don't think you did."

She exhaled. Why not tell? There seemed no reason to hold back any longer.

"It's a story you've heard countless times about countless people already," she said. "He wanted to do his part." She told him about the underground newspaper and the meeting he'd gone to, the informant in the group, the fire that officials claimed was caused by a candle that had toppled. "Everyone at the meeting was killed," she said.

Rémy took her hand. "And?"

He knew there was more. She opened her mouth, starting to speak. But nothing came out. Nothing about later that night. Nothing about the bleeding. Nothing about her frantic knock on her landlady's door. Nothing about the hospital. Nothing about the months of grief, which finally caused her to contact her brother in Switzerland: *Come get me. I want to go home.*

She looked up again and saw the light from the moon and stars trickling through the slats, which seemed to be saying there was another morning ahead.

The next day, they were up at dawn. The others shared their breakfast, packed them some food, and drew them a map to show the route ahead and the additional safe houses where they could rest.

They continued on, spending the next two days and nights in the woods. On the third morning, the woods opened up on to a tiny village, even smaller than Paillettes. They stayed back, enveloped by the trees, waiting until dusk, when the streets would be empty and they could cross through without attracting any attention. That night, they arrived at a house that belonged to a couple with ties to the Maquis, a Resistance force in rural France. The couple urged them to stay for two nights, as there was word that Nazi soldiers had been stationed just outside of town, searching the rocky terrain for Resistance fighters known to be hiding out in the area. They put them up in the attic, with plenty of pillows and blankets to make them comfortable.

Celina was glad for the relative safety of the shelter, but she knew Rémy was anxious to move on. He was worried about the children left behind, and also about Adele, Robert, and Marie, and wanted to get back as soon as he could. He didn't know if they'd be able to withstand the pressure and keep their stories straight if the Nazis were to show up.

"They'll be okay," Celina said as she tried to teach Brielle to clap her hands, relying on the light of a small candle. "Don't forget about Red. He's on our side. He'll help them."

Rémy nodded. But she didn't think he believed her. She didn't completely believe what she was saying either. While she trusted everyone in the village, she knew that a Nazi soldier might have seen Red talking to them that night by the bridge. Red might have been arrested that night and dragged away to who knew where. For saving their lives, he might now be dead.

She looked at Rémy as he drifted off to sleep. The cut over his eye was still not healing, and there was a spot near the edge that looked faintly green. He was walking slower and limping more with each passing day. The couple in the house dressed his wound with ointment and a bandage, but he needed a doctor. There was nothing they could do now, she thought, except press on.

The next evening, rested and fed, they left the house and proceeded in the dark on the next leg of their trip. They slept for a short time beneath some tall shade trees, and when the sun rose, Celina gathered their supplies and then picked up Brielle to give Rémy a break from carrying the little girl on his back. As they started to walk, she saw Rémy freeze and then hold out his arm the same way he had that night Red had appeared. He pointed in the direction from which they'd come. She heard it too. Voices in the distance. Speaking German.

He motioned to her, and she stepped carefully, avoiding twigs that could snap. He led her to a group of thick bushes that reminded her of the place where she'd found Brielle last November. *S'il vous plaît, prenez soin de ma petite fille jusqu'à ce que nous puissions être à nouveau ensemble. Elle s'appelle Brielle Aimée.* The memory was so vivid, her desire to protect her baby so strong, her decision to stay in Paillettes so right. She felt tears come to her eyes as she thought of how much love she felt for the two beings with her right now. Would the Nazis find them, when they were so close to the finish line? Would this be her end?

Crouching alongside Rémy, she held her breath and pressed Brielle close to her coat. She hoped the baby also felt something familiar in these bushes, something comforting about once again being in a spot like this, cradled in Celina's arms. A minute passed—the longest minute Celina thought she'd ever lived. And then, slowly, the voices faded away. The men were moving in a different direction. Rémy looked at her and nodded, and she smiled in return. Once again, they had made it through.

Celina rose, Brielle still in her arms, and watched Rémy strain to push himself up to standing. "It can't be much further now," he said. "Can it?"

"One day at a time," she said.

They continued on. And after two more stops at safe houses and several more nights in the woods—Celina stopped counting how many—they finally reached the border.

They crossed into Switzerland without any obstacles, and a stranger showed them the way to the bus station. When they told the stationmaster they were heading to Beerli, he pointed to the bus they should take. With coins the Resistance fighters in the woods had given them, they paid the fare. A half-hour into the ride, the driver motioned that they'd reached their stop. They asked a few people in the town if they knew of a woman missing her baby, and one directed them down the road. They reached the place, a two-story house on a small farm. They walked up the steps and knocked on the door.

The woman who answered was in her twenties in a simple brown dress covered with an apron. She was slim with long, dark hair pinned back from her face. She stared at them and then put her hand to her mouth.

"Brielle," the woman whispered and reached out her arms. "Brielle…"

And all Celina could do was watch the reunion play out, her arms empty of the baby but now wrapped around Rémy's elbow. She remembered the moon and the stars twinkling through the slats of the little house last night, the way they'd promised a new day ahead.

And so it was, she thought, as she rested her head on Rémy's shoulder. A baby cradled in her mama's arms. What more did she need to believe that sometimes, sometimes, the world made sense?

"Welcome home, Brielle," she murmured. "Welcome home."

TWENTY-THREE
OCTOBER 2018

"Wait—you're Cece Tailleur?" Rachel said. "You wrote *The Little Lost Fish*?"

Cece nodded.

"You knew my grandfather?"

"I did. We called him Red—in case you don't know, he had fiery red hair when he was young. That spring he had to decide whether to follow orders or his conscience. And he did the right thing in the end. With no credit either. He's not a villain. He's a hero."

"But... how?" Rachel said.

Cece proceeded to recount her story, the way she'd come to Paillettes as a widow intending to sell the house and return to her family's home in Maryland. "Not only was my husband dead, but I had suffered a dreadful miscarriage," she said. "They told me I would never be able to have children. I had lost both my husband and my baby."

She continued that a bizarre car crash ultimately led her to find the baby Brielle and a new purpose in her life. And to find the next love of her life, too. "His name was Rémy," she said. "And he ran the whole operation here. The secret orphanage.

"And here's where the little fish comes in," she said. "I had been finishing a story I'd started with my husband. And something very strange happened—let me show you."

She went to a cabinet across from the table and returned with two large envelopes. One contained a stack of drawings—the original illustrations that her husband had painted for the book. The pages were old and weathered, but the drawings of the fish were detailed and colorful. Beneath the drawings were the verses of the book, and Rachel could see that the original pages had been altered. Cece went on to explain that the alterations were messages intended for her, revealing that the baby's mother was alive and in Switzerland.

"And then, a few years ago, I was cleaning out some closets and I found these." She handed Rachel the second envelope. "One of the children who lived here back then loved photography. He'd been given an old hand-me-down camera, and he was always snapping photos, often when we didn't even know it."

Rachel lifted the flap of the envelope and slid out the black-and-white photographs. "Oh my God," she said, examining the photos. "That's my grandfather."

"Yes, it is," Cece said. "And if you look closely, you'll see that he's writing on the pages. He's leaving the clues that would take us to Brielle's mother."

Rachel looked up at Cece. "And this is how he saved your life?" she asked.

"This, and something else, too," she said and described how Red had met them in the woods the night they fled and showed them the path to take. "That was when he told us he had written the messages," she said. "I still can't believe he did that. If he'd been found out... I can't even imagine what they would have put him through. *That's* how your grandfather saved me, Rachel."

Rachel shook her head. She felt terrible for all the thoughts she'd had about her grandfather. "And the baby?" she asked, her voice breaking.

"Because of your grandfather, we delivered her safely. She still lives in Switzerland. Brielle Aimée Catheday."

Rachel felt her eyes widen. "Brielle Aimée," she said. *"She's* who you dedicated the book to?"

Cece nodded, and Rachel looked down, embarrassed. "I thought it... I thought you might have dedicated it to my mother. There was even a part of me... well, that thought she could have been your daughter. Brielle Aimée—that's her name, too. Was, I mean."

"Was?" Cece asked.

"She died when I was a little girl," Rachel said. "I guess I know the truth now. My grandfather must have convinced my grandmother to name my mother after the other Brielle Aimée. The one he thought had died."

"But now you know that she didn't die," Cece said. "She grew up and has had a very happy life. We've stayed in touch all these years. I wish your mother could have known what your grandfather did. Brielle has seven children and eighteen grandchildren. All those children would never have been born if not for your grandfather."

"If not for my grandfather," Rachel repeated, her voice a murmur. It was astonishing to know this. She felt a swell of pride rise in her chest. He had been brave and he had done the right thing all those years ago. And she was his granddaughter.

She looked up at Cece, realizing something else. "If not for you, too," she said. "You made it to Switzerland with the baby. What did you do then?"

Cece explained that after delivering Brielle to her mother, she decided to return to her family.

"But here's the surprise," she added. "You see, I didn't go alone. It turned out the doctors were wrong.

"Soon after I arrived back home, I found out I was pregnant."

TWENTY-FOUR
APRIL 1943

Two hours later, Celina and Rémy were seated at a round wooden table in a sun-filled kitchen. It had been a long time since Celina had been in a bustling town not bordered by mountains and gorges and forests. She was charmed by the tightly furnished house, with blue curtains on the windows and cheerful, red and yellow braided rugs on the floor. Brielle's mother—whose name, they found out, was Maritza—had brought them in and invited them to clean up. Celina was happy to be in a real bathroom with running water and soap after three days in the woods. Maritza had given her a long-sleeved top and blue cotton pants to wear. When she came downstairs, she saw that Rémy had cleaned up, too, and was wearing gray slacks and a red flannel shirt that Maritza had borrowed from neighbors.

They were greeted in the kitchen by what seemed a feast to her, with boiled eggs and fresh bread and jam, pastries, and an array of fruit including plums, cherries, and berries. Celina's stomach was unsettled after all that had happened, but soon the inviting smells won her over. It had been a long time since she'd been at a table with food so plentiful. There was a square, wooden playpen in the corner under the window where Brielle was sitting, happily chattering and playing with rattles and blocks. A middle-aged woman was slicing bread, and Maritza introduced her as her friend Canna. The table was set for four, which felt to Celina both normal and startling. She'd gotten used to meals with the table set for four or five adults and six children still learning their table manners.

Maritza picked up Brielle, and with the baby on her lap, she told them her story. She'd been living in northern France with her husband, mother, brother, and two younger sisters, after the family fled from Germany in early 1940. They planned eventually to leave for America. When she found out that she was pregnant, she and her husband decided to delay their escape, sending the other family members on ahead. They were able to acquire false papers, which they thought would keep them safe. But they were wrong. Brielle was only ten weeks old when the police showed up to arrest them. Maritza left the baby in a box in the closet just before they were forced to leave their apartment. There was a neighbor next door who had always been kind. She'd hoped the neighbor would find her.

Maritza and her husband spent a few weeks in a work camp in France and then were put on a train that they knew was headed for Poland. "During one of the stops, my husband and some other prisoners had the idea to sneak off," she said. "I don't know how we managed it, but we were able to escape from the train. We ran into the fields and the soldiers started shooting. I kept running and when we finally stopped, my husband was no longer with us."

Celina put down her fork and listened as the woman calmly recounted the events. It was hard to believe that she was here, serving this meal in this pleasant kitchen in this lovely little house. She felt terrible for all Maritza had gone through, and she felt a kinship with her, too. They'd both lost their husbands at the hands of the Nazis. She couldn't help but notice that the woman's appearance had changed in the short time they'd been together. She looked taller and sturdier than she had when she'd answered the door. Celina was certain it had to do with having her baby back.

And now, more than ever, she missed the house in Paillettes. There was something so life-affirming about being with children.

"We finally made it across the border into Switzerland," Maritza continued. "And we found our way to the Jewish refugee center in the next town. I stayed there for a few weeks. Canna"—she pointed to her friend—"was a volunteer there, and we found out we had a lot in common. She brought me here to stay and to help with the small farm out back. To wait out the war and then go back and try to find my baby.

"And here she is," she added. She kissed her forehead and then pointed to the tiniest of indentations on the baby's cheek. "See this dimple?" she said. "Her father had a dimple just like this. She is her papa, my baby."

Celina couldn't take her eyes off the two of them. Brielle had settled right into her mother's arms, as if they'd never been apart. Celina had tried to be Brielle's mama. And if she'd never known about Maritza, if those clues in her drawings had never shown up, if Maritza hadn't been alive, then Celina would have kept her and loved her and raised her as her own. But of course, this was the best outcome: the reunion of this beautiful little baby with her mother, who had made a heartrending sacrifice, leaving her child behind to try to keep her safe.

"Where did you find her?" Maritza asked.

Celina pressed the back of her hand to her mouth, taking a moment to steady her shaky breath before answering. "Believe it or not, under a bush," she said with a smile, and went on to describe how she and Max crashed after driving into the mountains and how she learned of what had become of the house she'd inherited.

"But how did she get to the mountains?" Maritza asked.

"Some good Samaritan must have brought her," Rémy said.

"And how did you find Maritza?" Canna asked.

Celina shook her head. "I don't even know how to explain it," she said. "I'm... well, it starts with a children's book I was writing with my husband."

Maritza pointed to Rémy, raising her eyebrows.

"No, no," Celina said and explained about Emile. "I was working on it, and I started to find clues about your whereabouts in the verses. It turned out that someone we never expected knew where you were and wanted to help us bring Brielle back to you."

"We had a lot of help," Rémy added. "A lot of people who took such risks to get us through to the border." Celina knew he was talking about the people who'd fed them and given them shelter in the safe houses. And also Red, who not only wrote the clues but showed up to guide them that first night by the gorge.

"I'll spend the rest of my life trying to come up with a way to say thank you to all of you," Maritza said. "I promise my baby will know who saved her. And one day when she's old enough to understand, I'll make sure she meets the people who brought her back to me."

Brielle made a sighing noise and then some clucking noises with her tongue, and everyone smiled. Celina paused and inhaled deeply before lifting her fork. It was hard to eat again. Her work here was nearly done. It was almost time to say goodbye.

Celina and Rémy spent the next two days at the little farmhouse. Maritza and Canna insisted that they do so, to build up their strength for what would come next. Canna, a nurse, was able to treat and bandage the cut above Rémy's eye, and she assured them that in time it would heal completely. Celina enjoyed the fresh air and helping out on the dairy farm. She had never worked on a farm before, milking cows and collecting newly laid eggs, and she delighted in the physical effort. They all came together in the afternoons and had picnics on the lawn, enjoying the unusually warm spring. At night, Canna would play classical music on the piano in the living room. It was a quiet, idyllic life, and there were times Celina wished it would never have to end.

Especially when Rémy took her hand or put his arm around her shoulder and squeezed her close, days when they found there was much to laugh about, the puppies in the garden or the chickens making the most silly noises or even Brielle chattering and giggling and drooling a river as she started to cut her first tooth. Rémy was looking stronger and healthier, the color returning to his face. Sometimes Celina wondered what it would be like if they stayed here—if they forgot what had come before and what was yet to be. If they could make a life here as Maritza had.

But she knew it wouldn't be that way. She was no longer the girl who had fallen in love with Emile, and with Paris, and with art and a life full of creativity and passion. That would have been a wonderful life, too. But not everything wonderful was possible. There was no choice but to believe in something different and yet equally wonderful ahead. That was the nature of hope.

Sometimes she wished she had known Rémy as a boy. And sometimes, when he lifted Brielle in the air and spun her around, or examined a blossom or a leaf on a tree, she could see the boy he once was. The boy who'd been beaten by his father and sacrificed by a mother who was too weak to do anything. The little boy who'd protected his older sister, who never stopped wanting to save others. He had found a way to put his awful past to good purpose.

And sometimes Celina thought about her home. Though

she had resisted it for so long, she now knew she couldn't go back to Paillettes. Rémy had been right that evening of their fight when he said it would look suspicious if she returned home without Brielle, her alleged daughter. Even though they now knew they could trust Red, the raid that had resulted in Rémy's injuries made it clear that their little village had caught the attention of the Nazis. She had to go back to Maryland. There was nowhere else for her. She didn't belong here in this little town and she didn't belong in Paris. The place she belonged, Paillettes, was a place she could no longer be. It was the right decision, to move on. Often the hardest decision was the right one.

A few nights before they were to part, she sat on the patio swing with Rémy. The days were getting warmer, little by little. Summer would come next, and then fall. She had taught the seasons to the children in her classroom behind the house. It had given them comfort, she believed, to know what to expect. To know what a person can always count on.

"Canna will help you plan your trip," Rémy told her. They'd all decided it was best if she didn't return to France but headed for Portugal instead. "Once you get to Lisbon, you'll be able to board a ship home."

She nodded.

"And you'll get in touch with your parents?" he asked.

"They'll wire me whatever money I need. They'll be glad to have me back." She looked down. "Will I ever see you again?" she asked softly. "Will I be able to come back?"

He took her hand. "Of course you will. When the war is over, I'll send for you. And we'll start a new life together." He chuckled. "Unless your parents have too much for you to do. Too many parties, too much excitement, and you forget all about me."

"That will never happen," she said.

He nodded. "I know."

She looked down. "I'm worried for you."

"There's no need to be."

"How can you make that trip through the woods again?"

"I'm fine," he said. "If I can make it with a baby on my back, I can certainly make it alone. I bet it will take me half the time, without the two of you to slow me down. I'm sure there will be help, as there was before. And maybe I can bring another child or two to safety. Maybe I can cross again. Maybe Adele and I are bring all the kids here."

He smiled. "And then you can finally sell your house."

She blinked away tears. "I couldn't ever think of selling it now," she said.

He put his arm around her shoulders. "We'll be okay," he told her. "The hard part is over."

That night, Celina tiptoed downstairs to the room where Jerry was sleeping. There were only hours left for them to be together. And that's what she wanted. To be alone with him and feel they were the only two in the whole universe. The only two that mattered. The world could take care of itself for one evening, the horrible world where children and parents were torn apart and the killing and torture were endless.

For now, she didn't need to think about that. The horrors of the world would still be there tomorrow. They could pretend they were gone for tonight.

She knelt by his bed. His eyes opened and he sat up, raising her to him.

"My love," he said as he took her face in his hands. "My beautiful Celina. We can't. What if..."

She put her fingers to his mouth. "This was the part I didn't tell you. It can't happen. It's okay..."

And as he put his warm mouth over hers, she felt the world melt away. Even though it wasn't forever. It was for now. And that would be enough.

It had to be.

TWENTY-FIVE
OCTOBER 2018

"Your baby—it was Rémy's child?" Rachel asked. "So he went back to Maryland with you?"

Cece pressed her lips together and shook her head. "I'm afraid not. We agreed that he had to come back to Paillettes for the sake of the children still here. We thought we'd eventually be together after the war ended. But it never happened. He never even made it back here. The Nazis arrested him as he was returning to France. He died in Auschwitz."

"Oh no," Rachel said. "I'm so sorry."

"My heart was broken when the war was over and I finally heard from his sister," she said. "But I'm grateful, too, that in a way, he's always been with me. Our son is a grown man now, a grandpa even, and lives in Maryland with his wife. They have four children. Alain is their youngest. And Rémy is his grandfather."

She went on to explain that in Maryland, she finished writing the book and went on to find a publisher. "I was delighted that people loved it. But I never wanted readers to know who I was. The proceeds from the book have always gone to charities fighting hatred. I don't want fame, I simply want the world to be better. Even here, people don't know I'm Cece. They know only that I'm the old lady who helps out at the school. You'll have to forgive Alain. He lied to you only because he knows how I wanted things to be."

She added that she never forgot Paillettes and returned to the house after her son was grown to turn it into a school. Its charter, she noted, included the proviso that it would always house at least one preschool class and provide free tuition to any family in need. "But I'm not a young woman anymore," she said. "It became harder and harder for me to manage things. So you can imagine my delight when Alain decided to come here and run the operation. He feels a great tie to the history of this place. And one day it will all be his. I see so much of his grandfather in him."

She blinked a few times, and Rachel gave her a moment. It was eye-opening, hearing about Alain. She'd already developed a great affection for him. But she'd had no idea of how much good there was inside of him.

Cece dabbed at the corner of one eye with her finger. "Oh, these memories," she said. "They are so deep in my bones. And I do regret that I never was able to tell your grandfather how our story together ended. I never got to say thank you. I didn't know how to find him. My goodness, he made his way to New York and I was in Maryland. All those years, we were just a few states apart."

"I can only imagine how much it would have meant to him to see you again," Rachel said. "It would have changed everything. He had a very sad life. He never let anyone get close to him, except me. I think he felt so guilty. And up until now, I never knew why."

"I would give anything to go see him," Cece said. "But I'm far too old to make such a trip. So it's up to you, Rachel. Now that you know what happened, you must tell him for me. You must carry my story to him."

Rachel nodded, rising. It was no longer important that she wait to talk to Alain. Cece could explain everything to him. What mattered was telling her grandfather what she'd learned while there was still a chance the story would reach him. She wasn't sure he'd understand, but she had to try.

"My bags are packed," she said. "I can catch the soonest train to Lyon. I guess I'll have to wait until I get there to check the flights—"

"No, no, you can do it on your way," Cece said. "Didn't you hear? It must have happened when you were in the classroom. The phones are restored. We are back online."

Less than an hour later, Rachel was at the station in Paillettes waiting for the train to Lyon. She was sorry she hadn't said goodbye to any of the people she'd come to like in this little town—not to Claude, not to the owner of the restaurant where she'd eaten on her first night in town or the singer that Claude was in love with; not to the kind librarian who'd lent her the history book, and worst of all, not to Alain. But all that mattered was that her grandfather would finally know how he'd saved Cece and the baby.

Standing on the platform, she was able to use her phone to book a flight home that evening. It was remarkable, really, how strong the cell service was, now that it was working. She calculated that if the train was on time and she could move through the city and to the airport without too much traffic, she'd easily be at the airport well before boarding. By tomorrow morning she'd be back in South Cove. And face to face with her grandfather.

Hang on, Papy, she thought. *Don't drift away yet. Hang on just a little bit more.*

The train arrived, and as she settled in for the trip down the mountain, she opened her phone and went through the dozens of emails and texts she hadn't been able to access over the last two days. There were notes from Nancy and Nick asking how she was; emails from Kate assuring her that her grandfather was calm and eating well; and emails from Nick about upcoming meetings and events at work.

And then there were the texts from Griffin:

Hey, bummer about the internet and cell service. They said it wouldn't last too long. Hope you get this message before you lose touch with the outside world. Sorry I couldn't stay, but we got this great scoop about the missing pilot. I joked with the guy at the guest house that you stood me up, LOL. Left Paillettes this morning. Will let you know where I land.

I know you may not see this for a few days, but I'm in Arles. Gorgeous old city. They think our missing pilot may have stopped here. The magazine is connecting me with a local photographer. This could be my break!

Hey, aren't you reachable yet? I can't believe you may not even be seeing my texts. The thing is, I'm leaving France. Heading further south. I think we're on to something here. Will update you when I'm settled. How's it going? Did you see the stuff about your author? Hope you're having fun. Don't forget to try all the great food there!

Boy, this outage is lasting a while, isn't it? If I were less secure, I might think you were ghosting me. But, hey, I know we both want to meet. How do you feel about Spain? More soon.

So it looks like our pilot may have spent some time in Majorca. I'm hoping this is the stop that seals the deal for my career. I have back-to-back interviews next week, but nothing to do this weekend. Assuming you'll see this in time, why don't you hop over? We can finally have our face-to-face on this gorgeous island. Food, wine, beach... Text me when you have your flight scheduled, I'll meet you at the airport.

Rachel looked at the date of his last text. It had been sent this morning. He was hoping communications would be back up today—as they were. He was hoping she would make her way to Spain. No, not just hoping. He really thought she'd do it.

She chuckled to herself. Griffin wasn't a bad guy. He was earnest and energetic and ambitious and clever. He'd been that way ever since she'd first connected with him. He'd never been deceptive—a little restless, perhaps, but not deceptive. He'd been consistent. He'd never changed.

But she had. In these last few days, she'd changed. She didn't quite know how. She couldn't label or define it. A little smarter, perhaps. With a better handle on life.

She closed her phone. She'd explain it all to Griffin another time. She wished him success. She hoped that one day, she'd see him on TV.

She hoped that one day, it would be Alain she'd see in person.

She settled back and looked outside at the mountains and the cliffs and the gorge below. And at some point she fell asleep. Suddenly the conductor was announcing that they were approaching the station at Lyon. She couldn't believe how soundly she'd slept. But then again, she hadn't slept much at all last night. It was amazing how peaceful a settled conscience could make you.

That was what she needed to deliver to her grandfather. A settled conscience.

When the train arrived, she pulled her suitcase off the luggage rack and stepped onto the platform. She couldn't help but remember the last time she'd done that. It was the evening had arrived in Paillettes. She'd been expecting Griffin to be here, as he'd promised he'd be. But he wasn't.

She stood on the platform for a moment as commuters and travelers rushed by her. She was alone again. She realized that she'd been hoping someone would be here waiting for her. She desired his wide smile and his way of looking at her as if she were the only person who mattered.

And then... there he was.

She walked toward him and he met her halfway and took her suitcase.

"I don't understand," she said. "Why are you here?"

"With the phones finally working, my grandmother called me," he said. "She told me that she told you every story she had. She told you my grandfather's story. She told you your grandfather's story. She told you the story of the house. She told you her own."

"That's true," Rachel said.

"But she said the one story she didn't tell you... was what happens next with us," he said. "Because it's not even written yet. But she thinks there could be a story here."

"Well, your grandmother is the author of the most beautiful book in the world," Rachel said with a sideways look.

"I agree," Alain said. "And if she thinks there's a story... who are we to argue?"

EPILOGUE
JUNE 2023

"Rachel Eggerton. Doctor of Philosophy, Comparative Literature."

With a deep inhale, Rachel started across the stage, feeling the weight of her royal blue commencement gown enveloping her shoulders and draping down to her calves. It wasn't so much that the gown was heavy; the feeling of weight came from deep inside, a mixture of pride, triumph, and solemn anticipation of the future. She could never forget the long, important road still ahead. Her degree was a stepping stone, not a destination.

She continued on, handing her hood—lined in blue and gold—to her favorite professor before turning around to allow him to slip it over her head and adjust it across her shoulders. Then she turned back, as all the candidates had been instructed to do, to pose for a photo. She smiled widely, looking out into the darkness of the filled auditorium. Though she couldn't see him, she knew Alain was out there somewhere applauding for her. Sitting next to him would be their three-year-old son, Rémy. Their second child was currently beneath the small bump that her commencement gown was covering. Another boy, they'd found out last week. They'd decided to name him Henry.

Diploma in hand, Rachel continued to the edge of the stage, down the steps, and back to her seat among all the other newly minted doctoral graduates. It had been a long road to get here. There had been hurdles to jump before she was readmitted to the Ph.D. program, combined with a wedding, a son, and now another pregnancy underway. But it was nothing she wouldn't have done again in exactly the same way if given the chance. She was happier than she'd ever expected to be. She now had her Ph.D.—but her future was in Paillettes. Where a new school for children from war-torn countries was finally about to open. It was to be called *L'aquarium*—The Aquarium, in honor of Cece's book. And she and Alain were co-directors.

Her only moment of sadness today was when she thought about how much her grandfather would have wanted to be here seeing her graduate. And how much she wished he were. But she was grateful for what they had had together in those last days of his life. When she'd arrived back on Long Island, she'd gone straight to the nursing home. It was a lovely fall day, and she found her grandfather sitting on the back patio, his face turned up to the sun. Kate touched her elbow and confided that in the last day, he'd stopped talking and was hardly eating. "I'm so glad you made it back," she said.

She'd gone to the patio and sat next to him and taken his hand. "Papy, it's me," she said. "And please listen. I have something you need to know." She'd gone on to tell him what Cece had shared. "She's alive. You saved her. You saved the baby Brielle, too. Look, Papy," she said, showing him the photograph of Cece she'd snapped on her phone before leaving Paillettes. "Cece is a mother and a grandmother. And so is Brielle. All the people Cece loves now—they're alive because of the clues you wrote on the drawings.

"You were brave, Papy," she said. "You were a hero."

And in that moment, she saw a change in him. His hand trembled. His eyebrows rose. And his lips spread into a smile. He had heard her. And he had understood.

Two mornings later, Kate called to tell her that her grandfather had died peacefully in his sleep. "I think he was waiting for you," she said. "I think he was hanging on so he could say goodbye."

No, Rachel thought. *He was waiting for absolution.*

She was so glad she could finally give that to him.

Alain was by her side at the funeral. And he was by her side, both here in New York and back at Paillettes, ever since. Rachel had seen in him the qualities that Cece would often list in describing Alain's grandfather—wisdom and charm, kindness and generosity. He was grounded and purposeful. He had a vision for his future, a drive to make life better for those in need. He was an activist but also a philosopher. He was everything she'd ever wanted, even before she realized she wanted those things.

When the last graduate had been hooded, everyone made their way to the champagne reception on the other side of the building. Rachel entered the large terrace and soon spotted Alain and Rémy, who was munching on a cupcake, his mouth covered in chocolate.

"Mama!" Rémy cried from Alain's arms when he saw her, and he reached out his arms. Alain kissed her cheek and murmured, "Congratulations, my love," as he handed Rémy over and tried to wipe his mouth with a napkin. "You're going to get chocolate all over Mama's gown," he warned.

"I don't even care," Rachel said as she nuzzled Rémy's cheek. It was what she'd always wanted—a loving family, with chocolate stains to prove it.

"How are you feeling?" Alain asked.

"Very happy. Very tired."

"Hungry? Thirsty? Sorry you can't have any champagne, but can I get you some juice? Club soda?"

"All I want is to get back home and climb into bed," Rachel said. "And maybe we can order in a pizza? I'm in the mood for pizza."

"What a surprise," Alain said and Rachel laughed. She was always in the mood for pizza when she was pregnant.

Rachel took a few moments to walk around the room, saying congratulations to some of her fellow graduates and thanks to her professors, as well as Nancy and Nick, who'd come for the ceremony. Then she made her way back to her family and they left the building to find their car and head home. They'd be eating on paper plates tonight because everything was packed. They would be on their way back to France tomorrow morning. For good. With her grandfather gone, it was time for her to leave South Cove. Rachel was glad she was departing this way—with a direction, and an exciting future, and a family she loved. She remembered how desperate she'd been for Griffin to save her five years ago. How she'd imagined that he was her Prince Charming. She'd mistakenly believed that she was powerless to change her life, and that she needed someone like Griffin to swoop in and carry her away to wherever he wanted to go.

Which was why she was so grateful that she'd run into Cece in the kitchen that morning just as the phone service was restored. Grateful, too, that Cece opened up to her despite having kept her identity secret for so long. So much so that even Claude, whom Cece had known as Daniel, hadn't recognized who she was. Although, he'd later confessed, there were times when he suspected it.

Still, things had changed for Cece, too, after that kitchen encounter. She'd finally decided to quietly let the community know that she was the author they all had immortalized. It had had a big effect on many in the town, including Claude, who had at last proposed to the jazz singer Rachel had listened to on her first evening in town. And Cece had found that being open felt better than she'd expected. Not good enough for her to reveal her story to the world. She hadn't wanted to appear in Rachel's thesis. Fortunately, the original Brielle Aimée in Switzerland had been open about telling her story. Rachel had been able to complete her thesis including those aspects.

Still, after a frightening bout with Covid, Cece had decided that her story should ultimately be out in the world. She'd told Alain and Rachel that she wanted them to be the ones to tell it. She'd given them permission to share everything, in whatever format they chose, after she had passed.

Although Cece was closing in on her hundredth birthday, Rachel still hoped that wouldn't happen for a long, long time.

She tucked Rémy into his car seat and took a last look at the campus. She was proud that she'd earned her degree. Her studies had been a big part of her life story. And now they were a chapter that had closed.

She rubbed Alain's arm as he backed out of the parking space and headed to their home for the last time. This was one of many goodbyes in her life, and it was one she could live with.

There was so much more of her story yet to write.

A LETTER FROM BARBARA

I want to say a huge thank you for choosing to read *The Secret Orphanage*. If you did enjoy it, and want to keep up to date with my latest releases, just sign up at the following link. Your email address will never be shared and you can unsubscribe at any time.

www.bookouture.com/barbara-josselsohn

In spring of 2024, I embarked on a wonderful trip through southern France—a trip that truly changed my life and filled me with unforgettable images and memories to last a lifetime. Among the many adventures we took, we boarded the Tournon town train one morning for a picturesque trip through the Ardèche region. The views of gorges, mountains, and wilderness would have been spectacular enough—but along the way, our guide told us an amazing story about a town in that region, Le Chambon-sur-Lignon, which—along with some surrounding villages—saved more than three thousand Jewish people, mostly children, during the Nazi occupation of France. Some estimates put the number as high as 5,000.

I was fascinated to learn more about these courageous people who risked their lives to join with their neighbors to do what was right. I wanted to learn about the leaders who spurred them to answer this call, about the lengths to which they went and the legacy they left behind. And, of course, the novelist in me turned to the burning question of "What if?" What if someone behaved cowardly? What if someone didn't want to go along with the plan? What if someone couldn't be trusted?

And then our guide added a compelling tidbit. She told us that many decades after the war, a German officer who'd been stationed in Le Chambon was interviewed, and asked how this huge effort could have gone on behind his back. How could he not have known? His reply to the question: "Oh, I knew."

I couldn't help but wonder about that response. Was he telling the truth? Or reinventing history to hide his shame about what he'd done during the war? And if he was telling the truth, what made him decide to turn a blind eye?

So many questions, so much to explore! That trip on the steam train started me on the uncharted path to creating the story you've just read. My wish is that it inspires you, too, to think about life, courage, and love in a new way.

I hope you loved *The Secret Orphanage* and if you did, I would be very grateful if you could write a review. I'd love to hear what you think, and it makes such a difference helping new readers to discover one of my books for the first time.

I love hearing from my readers—you can get in touch through social media or my website.

Thanks,

Barbara

www.BarbaraJosselsohn.com

facebook.com/BarbaraJosselsohnAuthor
x.com/BarbaraJoss
instagram.com/Barbara_Josselsohn_Author
tiktok.com/@barbarajosselsohnbooks

REFERENCES

Below are books I highly recommend if you're interested in reading more about southern France and the Resistance during World War Two.

The Plateau by Maggie Paxson (Riverhead Books, 2019)

Lest Innocent Blood be Shed: The Story of the Village of Le Chambon and How Goodness Happened There by Philip Hallie (Harper & Row, 1979)

The Resistance: The French Fight Against the Nazis by Matthew Cobb (Pocket Books, 2010)

ACKNOWLEDGMENTS

It was deeply moving and important to me to travel in my mind to southern France to write this novel. I couldn't have told the stories of Rachel, Alain, Celina, and Rémy without the help of many wonderful people, and I appreciate the opportunity to thank them here.

As always, I extend my most heartfelt thanks to my agent, Cynthia Manson, who continues to be my advocate, advisor, rock, and cherished friend. Astonishingly, with each book I discover to an even greater extent how talented and wise she is, and how strong her passion for what she does. And with each book, too, I realize anew how much I rely on her judgment and advice. What a gift it has been for me to work with her for more than a decade!

My most profound thanks also go to my extraordinary editor, Jennifer Hunt. I can't even describe how remarkable it is to work with an editor who not only understands my ideas but sees where they can go and what they can become. I'm truly in awe of her creativity, generosity, and amazing insight into what connects readers to a story. Ours has been such a meaningful and productive partnership, and my gratitude is immeasurable.

Thanks to all the publishing, editorial, marketing, rights, and sales professionals at Bookouture—a fabulous team! I'm so grateful for your expertise and commitment. And a special shout-out to Kim Nash, Author Community Director, and Sarah Hardy, publicist extraordinaire! I don't know how you all find the time to do everything that you do for us Bookouture authors. And speaking of Bookouture authors, let me just add that you are all such talented writers. I love reading your books and I'm delighted to be part of the community!

I am so lucky to have a wonderful circle of close friends who mean so much to me and teach me every day the lessons of friendship steeped in this book: Margie, Barbara, Stephanie, Helene, Ronnie, Lisa, and all the Susans! Thanks again for inspiring me, Nancy Clarson Kruse, my teacher from fourth grade and now my friend. Meeting you again after so very many years taught me anew that we reinvent ourselves every day by the people who serendipitously show up in our lives! I'm inspired, too, by the amazing group of writer friends and mentors I've acquired over the years: Thanks to Jimin Han, Patricia Dunn, Marcia Bradley, Jennifer Manocherian, Diane Cohen Schneider, Ines Rodrigues, Linda Avellar, Gosia Nealon, Ellie Midwood, Fredric Price and Diana Asher.

Thanks, too, to Christine Peckett and Amanda de Vaulx, who helped me with the French in this book, and to the lovely Dr. Andrea Thompson, who lent her expertise about library sciences, library positions, and a career in academia.

I'm deeply appreciative once again to Kerry Schafer, who continues to be an Author Genie—what better name for her business? Kerry is a great person, and I love working with her (and reading her novels—check out her books at allthingskerry.com). Thanks, too, to Jessica Sorentino, a talented branding professional who helped me so much in connecting with readers. What fun working with you!

Thanks to Westchester Reform Temple in Scarsdale, N.Y., and to the entire clergy team, led by the always inspiring Rabbi Jonathan Blake. I am moved by your words and elevated by your teachings.

To all the wonderful writers affiliated with the Women's Fiction Writers Association, the Writing Institute at Sarah Lawrence, the Scarsdale Library and its Writers Center, and

Westport Writers Workshop, and all those students who have trusted me with their work: thank you for sharing your stories, your inspirations, and your love of writing with me. I learn from you all every day. Thanks, too, to Mark Fowler and Jessica Kaplan, owners of Bronx River Books in Scarsdale, N.Y., my hometown bookstore. What a special place and a special couple!

As I've mentioned, *The Secret Orphanage* was inspired by stories shared during a river cruise that my husband and I took through southern France with my sister and brother-in-law, Janice and Ed. Thanks, guys, for the adventures and laughs, and for being such amazing travel companions. Thanks, too, to the local guides we encountered who shared the most wonderful anecdotes about the places we visited. I wish I knew your names, but since I don't, I'll simply say that the visitors you have yet to lead are very lucky indeed!

A special thanks to all the online bloggers and reviewers I've come to know over the last several years, including Lisa, Bea, Elaine, Annie, Reena, Lori, Jennifer, Denise, Dorothy, Dawnny, and many, many more. I am lucky to call you my friends!

And finally, I am beyond grateful for my beautiful family: my husband, Bennett; our three children, David, Rachel, and Alyssa; and my writing partner, our mini-schnauzer named Albie. My exploration of family in this book has been enhanced and enriched in the most wonderful of ways this past year, as our family has grown with the addition of a daughter-in-law, Brittany, and a soon-to-be son-in-law, Ben. And what's more, all of their relatives have become family to us, too! You all teach me every day what truly matters in life—a lesson that's embedded in this book and will always be a part of the stories that I write.

PUBLISHING TEAM

Turning a manuscript into a book requires the efforts of many people. The publishing team at Bookouture would like to acknowledge everyone who contributed to this publication.

Commercial
Lauren Morrissette
Hannah Richmond
Imogen Allport

Cover design
Debbie Clement

Data and analysis
Mark Alder
Mohamed Bussuri

Editorial
Jennifer Hunt
Charlotte Hegley

Copyeditor
Jenny Page

Proofreader
Anne O'Brien

Marketing
Alex Crow
Melanie Price
Occy Carr
Cíara Rosney
Martyna Młynarska

Operations and distribution
Marina Valles
Stephanie Straub
Joe Morris

Production
Hannah Snetsinger
Mandy Kullar
Nadia Michael
Ria Clare

Publicity
Kim Nash
Noelle Holten
Jess Readett
Sarah Hardy

Rights and contracts
Peta Nightingale
Richard King
Saidah Graham

RAISING READERS
Books Build Bright Futures

Dear Reader,

We'd love your attention for one more page to tell you about the crisis in children's reading, and what we can all do.

Studies have shown that reading for fun is the **single biggest predictor of a child's future life chances** – more than family circumstance, parents' educational background or income. It improves academic results, mental health, wealth, communication skills, ambition and happiness.

The number of children reading for fun is in rapid decline. Young people have a lot of competition for their time, and a worryingly high number do not have a single book at home.

Hachette works extensively with schools, libraries and literacy charities, but here are some ways we can all raise more readers:

- Reading to children for just 10 minutes a day makes a difference
- Don't give up if children aren't regular readers – there will be books for them!

- Visit bookshops and libraries to get recommendations
- Encourage them to listen to audiobooks
- Support school libraries
- Give books as gifts

There's a lot more information about how to encourage children to read on our websites: **www.RaisingReaders.co.uk** and **www.JoinRaisingReaders.com**.

Thank you for reading.

Printed in Dunstable, United Kingdom